CALL FOR THE
SAINT

LESLIE CHARTERIS
THE SAINT BOOKS

These are the titles in order of sequence
(the original titles are shown in brackets)

CONTENTS

I

THE KING OF THE BEGGARS

1

"Sins of commission," said Simon Templar darkly, "are very bad for the victim. But sins of omission are usually worse for the criminal."

The only perceptible response was a faint ping as a BB shot ricochetted from an imitation Sèvres vase which had been thoughtfully placed in a corner. Hoppy Uniatz shrugged shoulders that would not have disgraced a gorilla, popped another BB in his mouth, and expelled it in the wake of its predecessor, with better aim. This time the ping was followed by a faint rattle.

"Bull's-eye," he announced proudly. "I'm gettin' better."

"That," said the Saint, "depends on what field of endeavour you're talking about."

Mr. Uniatz felt no offence. His speed and accuracy on the draw might be highly regarded in some circles, but he had never claimed to compete in tournaments of subtlety. Anything the Saint said was okay with him.

He had not yet even wondered why they had stayed in Chicago for three days without any disclosed objective. In the dim abyss of what must perfunctorily be called Hoppy's mind was some vague idea that they were hiding out, though he could not quite understand why. Murder, arson, and burglary had not figured in the Saint's recent activities, which in itself was an unusual circumstance.

However, Mr. Uniatz had spent some time in Chicago before, and he still found it difficult to walk along State Street without instinctively ducking whenever he saw brass buttons. If Simon Templar chose to remain in this hotel suite, there were probably reasons. Hoppy's only objection was that he would have liked to kill time at the burlesque show three blocks south; but since this didn't seem to be in the cards, he had bought himself a bagful of BB shot and was taking a simple childlike pleasure in practising oral marksmanship.

Meanwhile the Saint sat by the window with a pair of high-powered binoculars in his hand, staring from time to time through the lenses at the street below. Mr. Uniatz did not understand this either, but he had no wish to seem unco-operative on that account.

"Boss," he said, "maybe I should take a toin wit' de peepers."

Simon lowered the glasses again.

"And just what would you look for?" he inquired interestedly.

"I dunno, boss," confessed Mr. Uniatz. "But I could look."

"You're such a help to me," said the Saint.

Strange emotions chased themselves across Hoppy's unprepossessing face, not unlike those of a man who has been butted in the midriff by an invisible goat. His mouth hung open, and his small eyes had a stricken expression.

The Saint had a momentary qualm of conscience. Perhaps his sarcasm had been unduly harsh. He hastened to soften the affront to an unprecedented sensitivity.

"No kidding," he said. "I'm going to have plenty for you to do, soon enough."

"Boss," Mr. Uniatz said anxiously, "I think I swallered a BB."

Simon sighed.

"I don't think it'll hurt you. Anyone who's eaten as much canned heat as you have shouldn't worry about the ingestion of a tiny globule of lead."

"Yeah," Hoppy said blankly. "Well, watch me make another bull's-eye."

Reassured, he popped another BB in his mouth and expelled it at the vase.

Simon picked up the binoculars again. Outside, the traffic hummed past dimly, ten stories below. From the distance came the muted roar of the Elevated. For several seconds he focused the street intently.

Then he said: "You might as well keep up with the play. We were talking about sins of omission, and have you noticed that woman across the street, near the alley?"

"De witch? Chees, what a bag," Mr. Uniatz said. "Sure I seen her. I drop a coin in her cup every time I go by." He grimaced. "When I get dat old, I hope I drop dead foist."

"So she's a professional beggar. But she's only been there two days. There was a blind man on that corner before. What do you think happened to him?"

"Maybe he ain't so blind, at dat. He gets a load of her and beats it."

The Saint shook his head.

"She's been committing sins, Hoppy."

"At her age?"

"Sins of omission. She's never on her corner at night. And she wasn't there Saturday afternoon."

"Okay. Maybe she gets tired."

"Beggars don't get tired at the most profitable hours," Simon said. "It's the theatre crowds that pay off. I'm wondering why she's never around when she'd have a chance to get some real moola."

Hoppy had a flash of perspicacity.

"Is dat why we been hanging around her?"

"I've been waiting for something. I don't know what, but . . . I think this is it!"

The Saint was suddenly standing up, dropping the binoculars into the chair which seemed to have ejected him with a spontaneous convulsion of its springs. He was out of the apartment before Hoppy could decide what to do with the BB in his mouth.

This problem proved far too difficult for snap judgment. Hoppy was still rolling the shot on his tongue when he joined the Saint at the elevator.

"This is the first time I've regretted being ten stories up," Simon said, leaning heavily on the button. His eyes were no longer lazy; they were blue flames. "Hoppy, I'm going to walk down. You take the elevator. If you win the race, find out why that beggar woman just went up the alley with a man who looked exactly as. if he had a gun in her back."

"But——" Mr. Uniatz began, and closed his mouth as the Saint whipped out of sight through a door marked STAIRWAY. He made sure that his Betsy was with him, in

Betsy's comfortable leather nest under his coat. But he still kept the last BB on his tongue. A guy never knew when he might need ammunition.

II

Simon Templar turned into the alley and was instantly alone in improbable isolation. Two blocks away, on Michigan Boulevard, sleek cars were tooling along their traffic lanes, and people were strolling on the sidewalks, safe and secure, because dozens of casual eyes were flicking past them. But as he turned the corner that world dropped into another dimension, forcing remembrance of itself only by the roar of traffic coming in from behind him and before him, yet at the same time made even more remote by the knowledge that the sound of a shot would probably go unheard in Chicago's noisy morning song. And in the backwater where he had landed there was nothing but the old woman, the gunman, and himself.

The man was backed up against a wall, rubbing his eyes furiously with his left hand, while his right waved a heavy automatic jerkily before him. The beggar woman was holding a gun, too; but her finger was not on the trigger. She seemed to be trying to get close enough to grab the automatic from the man's grip. Her rags flapped grotesquely as she jigged about with surprising agility for a woman who had previously seemed to be crippled by a combination of rheumatism, arthritis, and senility.

A whiff of something sharp and acrid stung the Saint's nostrils. He recognised ammonia, and instantly realised why the gunman was scrubbing so frantically at his eyes. But the advantage of an ammonia gun is to disarm the enemy through surprise. The cursing gentleman with the automatic was not yet disarmed, and at any moment he was just as likely to start shooting at random.

The Saint stopped running, side-stepped silently, and came on again on his toes. He took two quick steps forward and brought the edge of his hand down sharply on the gunman's wrist, and the automatic clattered to the ground. The Saint's swooping movement was almost continuous, and when he straightened he had the butt of the automatic cuddled into his palm. He listened for a moment.

"What language!" he remarked reprovingly. "You're liable to bite your tongue, Junior."

He batted the gunman lightly on the chin with his automatic, and the resultant inarticulate mouthings seemed to prove that the Saint's warning had been justified.

The beggar woman looked like a puppet whose strings had stopped moving. Her dirt-rimmed eyes glared at the Saint in indecision, and her puffy features twisted unpleasantly. And yet as the Saint gazed at her he felt the stirring of a preposterous intuition.

"What's eatin' de old witch?" Mr. Uniatz demanded from somewhere in the background. "No ya don't!" He deftly intercepted the woman as she made a dart for safety. "Not wit'out ya broomstick ya don't make no getaway. Gimme dat rod."

The Saint finished frisking the gunman. Then he stepped back a pace and regarded the beggar woman again, with a small crinkle forming between his brows.

Hoppy said: "Hey, what kind of a heater is dis?"

"It squirts ammonia," Simon said. "Junior here got a whiff of it in his eyes. I wonder——" He glanced along the alley. "Perhaps at this point we should adjourn. This alley would be perfect for a quiet murder, but it isn't private enough for a confessional, and I want Junior to open his heart to me."

Junior profanely denied any intention of making Simon Templar his confidant. The Saint rapped him across the head again and said: "Quiet. We'll be bosom pals before you know it." He turned his clear blue gaze on the beggar woman, who had subsided into sullen quiet. "My hotel's across the street," he said. "Shall we have an audition there?"

For an instant her eyes flashed across his, startlingly bright and alert. The thing Simon had already sensed—the incongruous vitality under those shapeless rags and puffy features—was unmistakable for that fleeting moment before the mask dropped again.

"I dunno what this is all about, mister. I don't know nothing. I got my own troubles——"

Simon said : "You'll be back in time for the perform-ance."

Her eyes searched his face. When she spoke, her voice had changed. It was deeper, more resonant.

"All right," she said. "I'll take a chance."

"The service elevator is indicated, I think. Hoppy, if you'll escort the lady, I'll follow with Junior."

"Okay, boss."

Simon Templar captured the gunman's arm and bent it deftly upward.

"You're going to be a good boy and come quietly, aren't you?"

"Like hell," Junior said.

Simon applied a little more torque.

"I'm not an unreasonable man," he remarked. "I'll give you a choice. Either stop wriggling and keep your mouth shut, or let me break your arm and give you something to yell about. I should warn you that I have a weakness for compound fractures. But don't feel that I'm trying to influence you. You're perfectly free to take your pick."

III

Junior, by request, sat cross-legged in the middle of the carpet, his unclean hands in his lap.

"Should we tie him up?" Hoppy asked.

The Saint had a better idea. He wound a piece of wire several times around Junior's thumbs and twisted the ends tight.

"There," he said, stepping back and beaming down at Junior. "He's safe as houses. Besides, we may need the rope later to hang him."

The captive remained silent, his thin, pinched face sulkily intent on the carpet. Aside from the fact that he rather strikingly resembled a rat, he had few distinguish-ing characteristics.

"All right," the Saint said. "Keep an eye on him, Hoppy. Kick his protruding teeth in if he tries to get up."

He moved to a side table and did things lovingly with ice and bourbon. But his eyes kept returning to the beggar woman.

She had come alive. There was no other word for it. Even under the patched and threadbare dress her body had shed thirty years. And her eyes were no longer dull.

She said : "You're the Saint, aren't you?"

Simon said : "You're one up on me. I don't know your name . . . yet."

"I recognised you. That's why I came along."

"What will you have?"

She nodded at the glass he was holding and Simon moved across the room and gave her the drink. Then he knew that he had been right. His fingers touched hers, and what he felt was proof enough. Her hand was firm and yet soft, the skin like satin.

She had done a beautiful job of make-up. The Saint could appreciate it. Quite frankly, he stared. And through the muddy blotched surface and cunningly drawn wrinkles her real face began to come into view, the clear, clean sculpture that even disfiguring rolls of wax padding in mouth and nostrils could not entirely hide.

She looked away.

The Saint did not. Presently he murmured :

> *"Small is the worth*
> *Of beauty from the light retired;*
> *Bid her come forth——"*

She opened her mouth to speak, but Simon Templar's low voice went on :

> *"Suffer herself to be desired.*
> *And not blush so to be admired."*

Hoppy said : "Huh?"

It was a young woman's laughter that sounded then. And it was not the cracked voice of the beggar woman that said : "Mr. Templar, I'm beginning to understand the reasons for your reputation. How did you know I was an actress? You didn't recognise me?"

The Saint replaced his drink, gave Hoppy a bottle to himself, and sat down, stretching his long legs.

"I just realised why you were never at your corner dur

ing theatre hours. A real beggar would have been. That's
when the money flows fastest. Saturday afternoon you
weren't there either—a matinée, I suppose? But I didn't
recognise you, no."

She said : "I'm Monica Varing."

The Saint raised his brows. Varing was one of the great
names, as well known in theatrical circles as he was himself in his own peculiar field. Drew, Barrymore, Terry,
Varing—they were all names that had blazed across the
marquees of the world's capitals. For ten years Monica
Varing had been that rare thing, an actress—not merely a
star, but a follower of the tradition that has come down
through the London Globe from the Greek amphitheatres.
More than that, if he remembered other pictures of her,
she was the most unchanged beauty of the modern stage.
She nodded towards the man squatting on the rug and
said : "I don't know whether I should say any more in
front of him."

"In case he gets away—or talks, you mean?" Simon suggested, his blue eyes faintly amused. "You needn't worry
about that. Junior's not going to talk indiscriminately
from now on. We can manage that, can't we, Hoppy?"

Hoppy said broodingly : "I never hoid nobody talk after
dey was dropped in de lake wit' deir feet in a sack of
cement."

"Listen !" Junior yelped. "You can't do this to me !"

"Why not?" the Saint asked, and in the face of that
logical query Junior was silent.

Monica Varing said : "I never thought this would happen. I set a trap, with myself as the bait——"

"Start at the beginning," Simon interrupted. "With
your predecessor, say. What happened to him?"

Monica said : "John Irvine. He was blind. He was a
stage manager in vaudeville—where a lot of us started. He
was blinded ten years ago, and got a begging permit.
Whenever I played Chicago, I'd look him up and put
something in his cup. It was a—well, a libation, in the
classic sense. But it wasn't only that. No matter how long it
would be between runs, John would always recognise my
footsteps. He'd say hello and wish me luck. On opening
night I always gave him a hundred dollars. I wasn't the

only one, either. Plenty of other troupers were big enough to remember."

"Last Wednesday," Simon went on for her, "a bum named John Irvine was found shot to death in that alley where we met. He'd been beaten up first. . . . He left a widow and children, didn't he?"

"Three children," Monica said.

The Saint looked at Junior, and his face was not friendly.

"Quite a few beggars have been beaten up in Chicago in the last few weeks. The ones who were able to talk said the same thing. Something about a mysterious character called the King of the Beggars."

"The beggars have to pay off a percentage of their earnings to His Majesty," Monica said bitterly. "Or else they're beaten up. The gang made an example of Irvine. To frighten the others. It just happened to be him; it might have been any beggar. The police—well, why should they make a big thing of it?"

"Why should you?" Simon asked.

She met his impersonal gaze no less directly.

"You may think I'm crazy, but it meant something to me. I knew the cops should have taken care of it, but I knew just as well they wouldn't. There weren't any headlines in it, and no civic committees were going to raise hell if they let it drop. . . . I'm a damned good actress, and I know make-up—the kind that'll even get by in daylight. I thought I might get a lead on something. I'd rather catch that King of the Beggars than star in another hit on Broadway."

"Me too," said the Saint. "Not that anyone ever offered me Broadway."

But there it was—the Robin Hood touch that would undoubtedly be the death of him some day . . . but literally. The whisper of a new racket which couldn't help reaching his hypersensitive ears, tuned as they were to every fresh stirring in the endless ferment of ungodliness. Something big and ugly, but preying on small and helpless people . . . A penny-ante racket, until there were enough pennies . . . *So you wanna be a beggar, pal? Okay, but you gotta pay off, pal. You gotta have protection, pal. We can make sure*

*you don't have no competition on your beat, see? But you
gotta join the Protective Association, pal. You gotta kick
in your dues. Otherwise you dunno what might happen.
You might get run off the streets; you might even get hurt
bad, pal. We're all for you, but you gotta play ball. . . .*
And somewhere at the top, as always, some smooth and
bloated spider grew fat on the leachings from the little
unco-ordinated jerks who paid their tax to Fear.

The Saint said : "That's why I've been sitting in this
joint for days. That's why I watched you, until Junior
hustled you into the alley. I'm just trying to move a step
up the ladder."

Monica Varing said : "I'm going to find out——"

"You've got courage," Simon told her. "We know that.
But this job needs more than that. Let's say—a certain
skill in unusual fields. For example, the trick of getting
people to confide in you." He turned to his silent guest.
"Who's the King, Junior?"

Junior said rude things.

"You see?" said the Saint. "The atmosphere isn't right.
But just wait till I have a heart-to-heart talk with him.
I'll even bribe him, if necessary. I'll introduce him to a
good dentist. I know he can't enjoy being mistaken for a
rat every time he passes an exterminator service. Besides,
I'm sure he can't chew his food properly. Bad digestion
probably soured his temper in youth and led him into a life
of crime. We can fix that. We take him to a dentist, and
just ask him whether he'll have it with or without novo-
cain. Now if you call me to-morrow——"

Monica Varing, to her astonishment, found that she
was at the door.

"Wait a minute !" she protested. "I started this——"

"And a nice job you did," said the Saint sincerely. "But
Junior's vocabulary may shock you when we really go to
work on him. And I promised you wouldn't be late for
your curtain. But I'll report progress—do you get up for
lunch?"

He closed the door after her, and came back to stand
thoughtfully over Junior.

"Chees," said Hoppy, giving voice to a profound conclusion. "Who'd ever tink dat old sack was an actress?"

"She may surprise you next time you see her," said the Saint, "even if she doesn't use fans in her act. . . . She's given me an idea, too. Hoppy, I feel Thespian urges."

Mr. Uniatz appeared shocked. Luckily, before he could speak, Simon set his mind at ease.

"I'm going to be an actor. I'm going to play the rôle of a beggar. After all, I can be bait just as well as Monica Varing. . . . First, though, we'd better put Junior on ice."

"Dat's gonna be tough, boss," Hoppy said dubiously. "Won't de cement stores be shut?"

"Then we'll have to try something else," said the Saint cheerfully. "Do you know where we can park Junior till they open? A warm, cosy oubliette?"

Hoppy considered.

"Lemme see. I useta know a guy called Sammy de Leg."

"Then by all means pick up the phone and call Samuel. Ask him if he'd like to have a house guest."

"Listen!" the latter burst out. "I don't know nothing about this beggar racket! That dame chased me up the alley ——"

"With your gun in her back," Simon agreed. "I saw it. You need protection. If beggar women keep chasing you up alleys, you won't be safe till you're locked up where they can't get at you. Hoppy and I feel we must take care of you."

He finished his drink contentedly while Mr. Uniatz completed a cryptic conversation.

"It's all set, boss," Hoppy announced finally. "We can go dere right now."

"I ain't goin' nowhere!" Junior cried desperately.

"How you do talk," said the Saint.

IV

Two miles north of Wheaton, Simon Templar turned his car, at Hoppy's direction, into a driveway bordered by high hedges.

Even the Saint's fortitude was slightly shaken by the rambling lunatic monstrosity of a house that squatted like Tom o' Bedlam in the midst of well-kept lawns. Simon was no great authority on architecture, but he felt that the man who had designed this excrescence should have been shot, preferably in the cradle. It had once been a mansion; there was a carriage house, converted into a garage, and servants' quarters hung precariously on the structure's grey scaling back, like a laggard extra hump on a camel. Gambrels, cupolas, balconies, railings, warts, wens, and minor scrofulous scraps were all over the house. It was a fine example of the corniest period in unfunctional design.

"Dis is it," Hoppy said proudly. "De classiest jernt in de county, when Capone has it."

Simon brought the car to a halt, and smiled encouragingly upon the troubled passenger beside him.

"Don't let the rococo touch scare you, Junior," he said. "I've seen mortuaries that looked like night clubs, too. . . . Unpack him, Hoppy."

Mr. Uniatz, the other half of the sandwich whose ham was Junior, had already emerged. He jerked the rug from Junior's knees and deftly unbuckled the strap that had immobilised the gunman's ankles.

"C'mon," he said. "I seen lotsa better guys dan you walk in here, even if dey was carried out."

The rickety front porch creaked under them. Hoppy rang the bell, and almost instantly something resembling a beer barrel covered with a thick pelt of black fur rolled out and began beating Hoppy violently about the ears. Simon watched in amazement. Yells, curses, and jovial threats curdled the air. Mr. Uniatz, a horrible grin splitting his anthropoid face, locked in a death struggle with his opponent, and in this manner they revolved across the threshold and vanished into the house. A muffled bellowing leaked out behind them.

"Don't leave us," the Saint said, reaching out to collar Junior. "You wouldn't get anywhere."

He lugged his burden through the doorway, where he found that the brawl had broken up, and Hoppy and the beer barrel were lumbering around each other, cursing furiously.

"Is this Queensberry rules, or would anyone like a knife?" Simon asked interestedly.

A voice boomed from the beer barrel.

"I be Gah-damned," it said. "So you're this here Saint

character? What kinds mob you runnin' round with now, Uniatz? Hey, mitt me, bud. Any friend o' Hoppy's a pal o' mine, chum."

"Meet Sammy de Leg," Hoppy said unnecessarily.

"What a grip," Sammy yelled, extricating his paw from Simon's palm and shaking it vigorously. "Come on in. Have a beer."

With shouts and cries he fell upon Mr. Uniatz and bore him beyond a beaded portière. The Saint followed at a discreet distance, propelling his Junior ahead of him.

There was a huge white refrigerator set up in one corner of an old-fashioned living-room, and Sammy the Leg was already extracting bottles and handing them around. He paused before Junior.

"This the guy you want put away?" he asked. "Well, he don't get none. Siddown an' shaddup."

He thrust Junior violently into the depths of a chair and made faces at him.

The Saint relaxed and drank beer. Its cold, catnip flavour tingled pleasantly at the back of his throat. He felt agreeably at home. Simon Templar had a feeling that he was going to like Sammy the Leg very much indeed. The man had a certain directness that was refreshing, once you decided to sidetrack Emily Post.

"For a pal," Sammy said, waving his bottle, "anything in the whole wide world, as far south as Indianapolis. You don't need to say a word. When I bought this here place, I'm my own boss. Nobody bothers me. I can keep a guy under wraps here, but indefinitely."

The Saint leaned back more comfortably. He nodded towards his prisoner.

"Ever seen Junior before?"

Sammy's small eyes dug tiny holes in the specimen.

"Uh-uh. He's imported. Not one of the Chi boys. Though I could be wrong, at that, I guess. Where'd you blow from, bub?"

"You go to hell," Junior said unoriginally; but his voice cracked.

Sammy the Leg bellowed with laughter.

"Tells me to go to hell! What a joker. Ja hear him?"

"A character," the Saint said. "I've an idea he's working for another character. Somebody called the King of the Beggars."

"Look, pal," Sammy said cautiously, "I don't know from nothin'. I just rent rooms. Now I'm gonna take a walk. When you want me, ring that bell over there by you, Saint. Then I'll put your chum under wraps for you. There's more beer in the icebox."

He grinned, and waddled out.

Simon listened to the tinkling of the beaded portière as it fell back into place. It jingled again as Sammy the Leg thrust his face back through it.

"Get that there electric broiler down from that shelf an' stick his feet in it," he advised. "It works well."

He vanished; and the Saint gazed speculatively at the indicated shelf.

"Not a bad idea," he drawled. "Hoppy, what goes with Sammy?"

"Huh?" Hoppy said. "He went out."

"Yes, I noticed. What I want to know is whether you're sure Sammy the Leg is levelling with us."

"Lissen," Hoppy said, almost indignantly, "Sammy an' me was in Joliet togedder."

He made this statement more devastatingly than any Harvard graduate identifying a brother alumnus, and in the face of such credentials Simon relaxed.

"In that case," he said, "go ahead and plug in the broiler."

Junior jumped out of his chair. The Saint did not rise. His foot shot forward, and Junior sat down again abruptly.

"My God," Junior gasped. "You wouldn't d-do——"

Simon's eyebrows were an angelic arch.

"Why not? Prosthetic devices are being improved all the time. You should be able to get along beautifully with an artificial leg. Maybe you'll only need a foot, though. It'll depend on how soon you start talking."

Junior said frantically: "I'm talking right now. Keep that damn thing away from me. I'm talking, see? For God's sake ask me some questions."

"Hold it, Hoppy," the Saint said. "You might leave the broiler plugged in, though. Our friend can look at it to cover awkward lulls in the conversation. There's only one question you need to answer, though, Junior. Who's the King?"

"Believe me," Junior said earnestly, "I wish to God I knew. I'd spill it. After that I'd start travelling. For my health. But I never seen the King."

He was telling the truth. Simon knew that; he was a connoisseur in such matters. Junior was obviously afraid of the King's power, but he was more afraid of the Saint. After all, Simon Templar was only a few feet from him, and the King of the Beggars was not—at the moment.

Simon said : "I'd have been surprised if you'd said anything different, this early in the story. Still, there must be a few precious pearls of information nestling in your head. I'd love to hear them. Start where you first heard of the King."

Junior was talking before the Saint had finished. He was, it seemed, a native of San Francisco. Travelling for his health a few months ago, he had landed in Chicago and naturally gravitated to the lower depths. There he had been approached by one of the King's ambassadors, who had been intrigued by Junior's obviously criminal appearance.

"But I never seen the King," Junior repeated. "Frankie's my contact."

"Frankie who?"

"Frankie Weiss. I'm just a collector, that's all. I make the rounds and collect the percentage off the beggars. I hand the dough over to Frankie an' he pays me off. That's all I got to do with it."

"A beautiful, literate, well-motivated story," the Saint said. "Except one point. You forget to say why you took Miss Varing up an alley."

"She was a new one. She hadn't joined our . . . She told me to go to hell. People what don't want to kick in, we sorta convince 'em." Junior's voice trailed off weakly.

"A beating usually does the trick, I imagine," Simon said very lightly. "Did you by any chance help to convince a beggar named John Irvine?"

"I didn't have nothing to do with that. Honest to God!"

"Then who did?"

Junior swallowed.

"It could have been Frankie."

There was an almost inaudible *ping*, and Junior clapped a hand to his cheek with a startled expression, as if he had been sharply stung by some unsuspected insect.

"It should have been in de eye," Hoppy Uniatz said enigmatically. "Ya lousy stool-pigeon."

"Don't discourage him yet," said the Saint. "Tell me, Junior, what happens when a beggar does agree to kick in?"

"Well, then he joins the Society."

"Society?"

"The Metropolitan Benevolent Society. . . . Then I take him to Frankie. But that's all I got to do with it. Frankie's waiting somewhere in his car and drives off with the guy. It ain't my business after that. I don't ask questions."

"Where do you meet Frankie?"

"It's different all the time. I was to see him next Wednesday night, at eight o'clock—corner of State and Adams."

"I hope he won't be too disappointed when you don't show up," said the Saint gently.

Junior gulped.

"Now lissen," he pleaded. "I told you everything. I run off at the mouth——"

"You certainly do," Simon conceded. "What worries me is that it may be a habit with you. And I certainly don't want you going to the King, or Frankie Weiss, and running off some more about this little *tête-à-tête* of ours. So while we decide whether we're going to kill you, we'll just have to keep you out of circulation. . . . Can you get Samuel back, Hoppy?"

Mr. Uniatz solved this problem by exposing his tonsils in a stentorian bellow which made the chandelier vibrate. In a few seconds Sammy the Leg came in, beaming hospitably.

"All through?" he shouted softly. "Oh—I forgot. This is Fingers Schultz. You remember Fingers, Hoppy?"

"Sure," Hoppy said. "Where is he?"

Sammy stepped aside, revealing a small, colourless man who blinked blankly at the Saint. Hoppy said: "Hi, Fingers."

Mr. Schultz nodded and kept on blinking.

Sammy the Leg said : "Can't run a joint like this alone. Fingers gives me a hand." He looked startled. "Hey. I made a joke. Fingers—hand. It ain't bad."

Nobody laughed. Simon said : "Will you keep Junior on ice for a few days?"

"It'll be a pleasure," Sammy said. "At twenty-five a day, that'll be one seventy-five. I always get a week in advance." He kept his palm extended. "Board and room," he explained. "Cut rate to you, though."

Simon opened his wallet and laid several bills on the waiting paw.

"Thanks," Sammy said. "If you want to stop keeping him, lemme know, an' maybe we can take care of that, too."

"I'll let you know," Simon assured him gravely. "Come along, Hoppy."

He had a last glimpse of Junior's white, staring face as they went out.

v

He met her for lunch at the Pump Room, and almost failed to recognise her as the head-waiter ushered her to his booth. Half-remembered pictures of her were too posed and static, and the last time he had seen her across the footlights was a year or more ago, in a costume piece with powdered wig and baroque skirt.

In the flesh, and modern dress, she was not less beautiful but different. And certainly a thousand times different again from the character part in which he had first met her.

She crossed the room towards him with splendid assurance in every motion. Someone had spent a great deal of loving thought upon the cut of her Scotch tweed suit, which managed deftly to emphasise breath-taking lines beneath the tweed. The Saint permitted himself to dwell admiringly upon the exquisite long curve that swept from waist to knee with every long, sure step, and on other unmasculine curves beneath the tailored jacket. The time-honoured banalities of greeting seemed more than ordinarily empty as he rose to let her slide into the seat beside him.

He ordered cocktails for them both; and then there was a little silence while Monica Varing looked at him, and Simon leaned back and allowed himself the ordinarily quite expensive pleasure of gazing his fill upon Monica Varing. That wonderful mutable face was never twice quite the same, and the warm vitality that radiated from it gave her a transcendent vividness which critics had hymned and artists tried in vain to capture. Three generations of actresses named Varing had carried that inner illumination, the Saint thought; it must have come down from mother to daughter like a burning flame handed along the unbroken line.

She looked world-weary to-day—and eager as a schoolgirl beneath the weariness. She was exciting to look at and exciting to inhale; the perfume that floated across the table was just elusive enough to tempt Simon to edge closer and closer to identify it.

"Well, Mr. Templar," she said at last, her voice pitched so low that it ran a velvety finger along Simon's nerves and made them tingle, "do you always stare like that?"

"Always, when there's anything like you to stare at," he said shamelessly.

She made a face that still didn't reject the obvious compliment entirely.

"Give me a cigarette," she said, "and tell me what I really want to hear."

As he offered his pack and a light he thought it all out again.

He knew quite well that the cold, wise course would have been to avoid Monica Varing entirely. Monica was used to a starring rôle. She had been the centre of her own stage long enough to feel the limelight was hers by right, and her essay at detection in beggar garb proved her resourceful and determined, if not strictly sensible. She was unlikely to sit quiet and let the Saint take over her part without wanting to share in the fun—and the King played for keeps. There would be no coming out for smiling bows after the curtain fell on a performance before the King of the Beggars.

The Saint's logic told him all this. But the impatience to see her again, and without disguise, had been stronger than any logic. And now that she was here, and all her real loveliness within inches of him, logic became almost meaningless.

"There really isn't much to tell," he tried to hedge.

"What happened last night?" Monica demanded, leaning forward distractingly and clasping long coral-tipped fingers on the table. "Remember, this was my party before you crashed it."

"I had an impression it was open to the public," he said. "I just asked myself in to help an old woman. I was watching before that, and I'm going to have to watch some more. I want to see what men are on the board. The King's got himself protected very thoroughly. Getting close to him is liable to be dangerous."

"You can't leave me out. I want to *do* something, Saint. I had a reason for getting into this business, if you haven't forgotten."

"You'll have your chance. I don't know yet where I'm going to need you most."

He quirked an eyebrow at her and his eyes brightened with an interestingly irrelevant tangent to that idea; but Monica was not to be diverted.

"Keep that wicked look out of your eyes," she said, "and stick to the subject. What did you find out from Junior?"

"Not very much, I'm afraid."

He told her just what he had learned, holding back nothing but Sammy the Leg's address. There was nothing much else to withhold.

"I think Junior came clean—as clean as he could," he concluded. "The King wouldn't last long if any little jerk like Junior could put the finger on him. The only thing Junior may have weaselled on is how much he really had to do with the Irvine killing. We might burn that out of him, but it wouldn't stand up in court. So maybe we'll have to kill him anyway, just to make sure."

His tone was casually serious enough to make her shiver.

"Then we might get further if I went out and played beggar again," she said; but the Saint shook his head.

"I hate to criticise your performance, but I think the

part is going to have to be played another way. And that's a way I wouldn't let you risk."

It took three days. For Frankie Weiss did not appear at his rendezvous with Junior on Wednesday night; and, after the Saint had waited for an hour, he began to feel a familiar tingling sensation at the roots of his hair. The move had been taken away from him. The best he could hope was that Junior's disappearance from his usual haunts had been reported without making Frankie suspect anything more than that Junior had skipped town—with some of the take.

But there had to be other agents than Junior, and they would still be operating; and that was what Simon's plan was based on.

In the evenings he became a beggar. It took an elaborate make-up to disguise the fact that Monica Varing would have needed to beg for anything; but for him it was easier. A few skilful lines to put ten years on his face, a slack vacancy expression, a pair of dark glasses, and he was half dressed for the part. An old suit, picked up at a Halstead Street pawnshop, a white cane, a battered hat, a tin cup and a sheaf of pencils, and a few smears of grime artfully applied to his face—for a blind man cannot use a mirror—and he was ready to pass any scrutiny. Hoppy lounged by at intervals to check with him, and continued his practice in the art of spitting BBs. He found it more satisfactory now to work with living targets, as he strolled along the streets, and his aim was improving prodigiously.

And then there were lunches with Monica Varing, and superbly wasted afternoons, and late suppers after the theatre; and quite naturally and in no time at all it became accepted that it must be lunch again to-morrow and supper again that night, and the same again the day after to-morrow and the day after that.

So three days went by much faster than they sound, too fast, it seemed, sometimes; and while they talked a lot about the King of Beggars, a very different community of interest began to supersede him as the principal link between them.

It was Mrs. Laura Wingate who brought the Saint luck. Or perhaps it was Stephen Elliott, though the grey-haired philanthropist was not the one who dropped a coin in Simon's cup.

"You poor dear man," a treacly voice said sympathetically. "I always feel *so* sorry for the blind. Here."

She was a woman out of a Mary Petty drawing, protruding fore and aft, with several powdered chins and a look of determined charity. The man was a nonentity beside her, spare and white-haired and silent, his gaze fixed abstractedly on the far distances and his fingers fumbling with the watch chain stretched across his vest.

"Thank you," the Saint mumbled. "God bless you, ma'am."

"Oh, you're welcome," the treacly voice said, and, startlingly, giggled. "I always feel I *must* give to the poor unfortunates."

"What?" The man let go of his watch chain. "Laura, we'll be late."

"Oh, dear. Of course——"

She went on, her ridiculously high heels clicking busily and helping to exaggerate the undulant protrusion of her behind.

Hoppy Uniatz, coming by on one of his visits just then, leaned against the wall by the Saint and craned to peer into the cup.

"A lousy dime," he observed disgustedly. "An' I could get ten grand right around de corner for dem rocks she's wearin'."

"It's the spirit that counts," said the Saint. "Didn't you recognise her?"

"She ain't anudder of dem actresses, is she?"

"No. But she doesn't do all her charity with dimes. That's Mrs. Laura Wingate. I've seen her in the papers lately. She's been backing Stephen Elliott—the abstracted gentleman you just saw."

"What's his racket?"

"Founding missions and homes for the poor. Philanthropy. . . . Take a walk, Hoppy," the Saint said abruptly, in the same low tone, and Mr. Uniatz's eyelids flickered. But he did not look around. With a grunt he reached for a coin, dropped it into the tin cup, and moved away.

"God bless you," the Saint said, more loudly now.

Another man stood in front of him. He was tall, bitter-faced, sharply dressed. Pale blond hair showed under an expensive hat. A hairline moustache accentuated the thin lines of the down-curved mouth.

Simon intoned : "Help a poor blind man. . . . Buy a pencil?"

The man said : " I want to talk to you."

"Yes, sir ?"

"You're new here, aren't you?"

Simon nodded.

"Yes, sir. A friend told me this was a good corner—and the man who had it died just lately——"

"That's right," the clipped, harsh voice said. "He died, sure enough. Know why he died?"

"No, sir."

"He wasn't smart. That's why he died. Maybe you're smarter. Think so?"

"I . . . don't quite understand."

"I'm telling you. Ever hear of the Metropolitan Benevolent Society?"

Simon moved his head slowly, with the helpless searching motion of the blind.

"I'm new in town," he whined. "Nobody told——"

"The head guy is the King of the Beggars."

It sounded unreal in the mechanical hubbub of the Chicago street. It belonged in the time of François Villon, or in the lands of the Arabian Nights. Yet the fantastic title came easily from the thin, twisted lips of the blond man, but without even the superficial glamour of those periods. In terms of to-day it was as coldly sinister as a levelled gun-barrel. Simon had a moment's fastidious, cat-like withdrawal from that momentary evil, but it was purely an inward motion. To all appearances he was still the same—a blind beggar, a little frightened now, and very unsure of himself.

Even his voice was high-pitched and hesitant.

"I've . . . heard of him. Yes, sir. I've heard of him."

The blond man said : "Well, the King sent me especially to invite you to join the Society."

"But suppose I don't——"

"Suit yourself. The guy who had this corner before you didn't want to join, either. So?"

The Saint said nothing. Presently, very slowly, he nodded.

"Smart boy," the blond man said. "I'll pick you up at ten to-night, right here."

"Yes, sir," Simon Templar whispered.

The blond man went away.

VI

"Dat was Frankie," Mr. Uniatz announced a few minutes later. "He ain't changed much."

"Frankie himself, eh?" Simon smiled. "Well, we're moving at last. Frankie is going to initiate me into the Metropolitan Benevolent Society, and it's just possible that I might get an introduction to the King."

"An' den we give him de woiks, huh?"

"You know, Hoppy, I've never committed regicide." For a brief second the blind-beggar face showed the same lawless grin that had heralded the end of more than one particularly obnoxious career. "It might be a new sensation. . . . But it's not going to be so easy."

"If I get next to him wit' my Betsy——"

"The trouble is, you weren't invited. And it might look strange if I showed up with an escort. This time, anyway, your job is going to be to Lurk."

He gave more detailed instructions.

By ten o'clock the Saint's profit for the day amounted to thirty dollars, twenty-seven cents, and a Los Angeles street-car token, which he evaluated at six and a quarter cents. Since he expected to be searched, he carried no lethal weapon, not even the ivory-hilted throwing knife which in his hands was as fast and deadly as any gun. This trip would be an advanced reconnaissance, and nothing would have been more foolish than to count on turning it extemporaneously into a frontal assault.

At ten o'clock he carefully ignored the unobtrusive dark sedan that rolled silently to a stop at the kerb a few feet away. The driver's features were in shadow under a low-pulled hat, but the hands that lay on the steering wheel

were not those of a King. The nails, Simon decided, were
too septic to belong to royalty, even a racket royalty.
Besides, when did royalty ever drive its own cars, except
such rare cases as ex-King Alfonso. And look what happened to him, the Saint told himself as he stared at nothing
through his dark glasses and apparently did not see
Frankie Weiss get out of the car and move towards him.

The blond man looked no more sunny and warm-
hearted than he had before dinner. His shark's mouth had
presumably just grabbed for a tasty mackerel and got hold
of an old boot instead. Working this organ slightly, Mr.
Weiss paused before the Saint and stared down.

Simon jingled his cup.

"Help a blind man, sir?"

"Lay off the act," Frankie said. "You remember me."

The Saint hesitated.

"Oh. Oh, yes. You're the man who . . . I know your
voice. But I'm blind——"

"Maybe," Frankie said sceptically. "Let's get going."

"Why . . . yes, sir. But I'd like to know a little more
about this . . . this business."

Frankie grasped the Saint's arm with bony fingers that
dug deliberately into the flesh.

"Come on," he said, and the Saint had only time to
assure himself that Hoppy Uniatz was at his post half a
block away before he was in the back of the sedan, the
clash of the closing door committing him irrevocably to
this chapter of the adventure.

The chauffeur's unkempt neckline confirmed his opinion
that the man was a subordinate. Simon had little chance
to study his subject, for as the car slid smoothly into gear
Frankie lifted the dark-lensed glasses from the Saint's nose,
dropped them casually into Simon's lap, and replaced them
with a totally opaque elastic bandage. Simon slipped the
spectacles into a pocket and put up a mildly protesting
hand.

"What's that? I don't need a blindfold."

The driver laughed shortly. But Frankie's tone held
no amusement as he said: "Maybe. And maybe not."

"But——"

"Forget it," Frankie said. "Save it for the cops. What

the hell do you think we care whether you're blind or not? A guy's got a right to make a living." Unpleasant mockery sounded in his voice now. "That's where we don't hold with the authorities. We don't make any stink about handing out begging licences. If you're sharp enough to get away with anything, that's fine—as long as you don't try it with us."

Simon was silent. Frankie slapped the Saint's knee.

"That's none of our business. There's only one question we ask. How much?"

"Yeah," the driver said, laughing again. "This guy's gonna be a smart apple, though, ain't he, Frankie?"

"Shut up," Frankie said without rancour. "Sure he is. But nobody's asking you."

His hands worked over the Saint, efficiently exploring every inch from head to foot where a weapon could have been concealed.

Simon said pleadingly: "I don't understand this. Where are we going?"

"It's like a lodge, see?" Frankie told him. "You gotta be introduced and sworn in, see?"

Simon tried to keep up with their route by ear, but even a man born and bred in Chicago would have been finally baffled by the turns and back-tracks the car took. He could only hope that they would not be confusing enough to shake off Hoppy in spite of the trained bloodhound talents which, like his celerity on the draw, were among the few useful legacies of his vocation during the Volstead Era.

A little more than half an hour later, as near as the Saint could judge, the car stopped and the door clicked open. Simon put up a hand to his blindfold, but Frankie slapped it down. The same cruelly probing fingers gripped his arm again and guided him out of the sedan and across a paved area where the wind blew mildly against his face. There was very little noise of traffic now, and the air had the cleaner smell of a residential district.

A door opened and shut. Simon could hear his footsteps echoed, and presently another latch clicked, and he was guided down a steep flight of steps.

"Okay, turn on the lights," Frankie said. The guiding hand let go. Frankie said: "Stay where you are."

The Saint stood still, and in the hushed pause that
followed he was aware of tiny scuffs and rustles of movement, such as would come from a small group of people
waiting in conscious silence.

Then the blindfold was lifted from his eyes, and a painful intensity of light blazed directly into his face.

He did not wince, though the glare was brutal. The
new blindness which it induced made little difference—he
knew that it would have been impossible to see past
those spotlights at any time. This was the police line-up,
with a difference. He stood motionless, knowing that eyes
were studying him from behind the lights, but that these
were not the eyes of guardians of the law and peace. They
belonged to brothers-in-arms of Junior, alert to recognise
him if he were a spy for any opposition gang, or memoris-
ing his features in readiness for future shakedowns.

A voice began to speak, artificially through a crude
public-address system.

"We welcome you to the Metropolitan Benevolent
Society," it said unctuously—"an organisation designed
for the aid and protection we can give will be at your
service. . . ."

It was a formalised little speech, which might have been
a phonograph recording for all Simon could tell; he
guessed that it had been used often before and was a part
of the regular routine. Again that flash of monstrous
incongruity struck through him at the situation—ruthless
killers making a Rotary Club speech, the Arabian Nights
in Chicago. But his face showed nothing but a slightly
vacuous listening intentness.

The speaker went on to observe that begging was one of
the most ancient and honourable professions, that ancient
monks had practised it respectably, as the Salvation Army
did to-day, but that in these time the individual practi-
tioner was in danger of all kinds of arbitrary persecution.
And just as exploited Labour had been forced to band
together to safeguard the rights which no lone individual
could defend, so the professional mendicants had been
obliged to band together and declare a closed shop for
their fraternity—this same fraternity, of course, being the
Metropolitan Benevolent Society.

It sounded good, the Saint admitted to himself. He was beginning to be able to see a little now, through the swimming spots and dazzles of his maltreated retinas; but there was not a great deal to see—only part of a bare cement-walled room with one door in it, and a portable loud-speaker on the floor to one side, with wires trailing from it and disappearing behind the lights.

The voice went on smoothly :

"In return for your protection," it said paternally, "you will turn in one-half of your daily take to Big Hazel Green, manager of the Elliott Hotel, where you will be given lodgings at a nominal price. She will be your contact with headquarters, and will supply you with all information and assign you your territory. One thing more. . . ." The voice became more greasily friendly than ever. "Don't try any chiselling. You will be watched constantly, and any violation of our rules will be severely punished. If you have any questions now, Frankie will answer them."

The Saint had many questions, but he knew that this was no time to ask them. He realised that he had not under-estimated the cautiousness of the King. Even if the King was actually there at all, which Simon now doubted more than ever, His Majesty or any of his privy council could have potted him like a sitting rabbit before he even got through the shield of lights.

There was going to be no quick checkmate. This was not even the time to give check.

"No, sir," he said weakly. "No questions now."

"Let's go," Frankie said.

He replaced the elastic bandage and gripped the Saint's arm. Again the latch clicked, and they went up the stairs. Again there was a cool wind and concrete underfoot.

Something chinked in the Saint's pocket and rattled on the pavement. Simon stopped and bent over, groping hesitantly, but Frankie's hand jerked him upright again. Suspicion rasped in the man's voice.

"Hey, what's the idea?"

Then the chauffeur : "It's only half a buck the guy dropped. Here it is."

"I'm sorry," Simon stammered. "I guess I'm . . . kind of nervous."

That carried conviction, and both men laughed briefly.

"You won't get rich that way," the chauffeur said, and put the coin in the Saint's hand. "Come on. We're taking another little ride."

"Where to?"

"Around," Frankie said. "Just around. And back where we picked you up. Just so you won't come back without being invited. The King don't like visitors."

VII

Simon had cocktails already ordered when Monica Varing came into the Buttery at noon the next day. She was the most punctual woman he had ever met. He had discovered that you could set a clock by her; and it amused him to have the drinks arriving, freshly chilled, at the very moment when she walked in.

"Well," he said as she sat down while their hands still held, "I am fraternally yours as of last night."

Her beautifully drawn eyebrows rose.

"What have I done?"

"A figure of speech," he explained hastily. "I don't feel at all fraternal. But I am now an accredited member of your fraternity of beggars. I even had an audience with the King."

"Tell me everything."

The Saint told her.

"When I dropped the coin," he concluded, "it was the signal to Hoppy that everything was under control and that was the joint he had to get the address of. He got it all right—they hadn't shaken him off with their zig-zagging around the town—and we went back there later and did a small job of housebreaking. Unfortunately it didn't pay off. It's a vacant house. The electricity's turned on, and there was that loud-speaker and a mike in the basement room, but nothing else except the spot-lights."

"Who owns the house?" Monica asked, and the Saint shrugged.

"I'm trying to find out. Meanwhile, we have another lead. There's this Big Hazel Green, manageress of the

Elliott Hotel. And you know who that joint belongs to? Stephen Elliott."

"Stephen Elliott? The philanthropist?"

"It says here. At any rate, the Elliott Hotel is more or less a charity, according to the inquiries I've made. The point is, does Elliott know that his manageress is a liaison officer for the King of the Beggars?"

"Or," she said slowly, "could Elliott be the King?"

The Saint nodded.

"Just like a detective story. But such things have happened. . . . I should like to have a talk with Brother Elliott in an official sort of way."

Monica wrinkled her brow.

"Could I help?"

"I read in a society column this morning that Mrs. Laura Wingate is giving a cocktail party for him to-day. Do you happen to know her?"

"No, but I'm sure to know somebody who does. Let me make a few phone calls."

Simon called a waiter, and lighted a cigarette for her while a telephone was brought and plugged in. Then he went to a phone booth outside and made a call for himself.

"Hoppy?" he said. "Did you get a report from that real-estate company yet?"

"No, boss." Mr. Uniatz's voice, which had never been distinguished by any flutelike purity of tone, had a perturbed croak in it which registered on the Saint's sensitive ear just a second before he blurted out its cause and explanation. "I got a cop here, boss. I dunno what goes on, but he wants to talk to ya. Only he ain't got no warrant."

"No warrant is required for that," Simon said. "If he longs to hear my dulcet tones, we can accommodate him. Put him on. It's all right, Hoppy."

"I hope so," Mr. Uniatz muttered dubiously.

Then a cool, deep-pitched voice sounded in the Saint's ear.

"Mr. Templar?"

"Yes."

"This is Detective Lieutenant Alvin Kearney. I'd like to see you about a matter."

Simon drew a slow, careful breath.

"Are you selling subscriptions to the police fund?" he inquired genially. "If so, you can count on me. This business of taking out old policemen and shooting them has always struck me as unnecessarily cruel."

"What?" Kearney said. "Look, Mr. Templar. I want to see you."

"So you said," the Saint agreed. "About a Matter. But just at the moment I'm already seeing someone about a Matter. Perhaps if you told me the nature of this Matter of yours I'd be more co-operative. How do I know it's important?"

"We've got a body down at the morgue, and we'd like you to look at it. That's all."

"Ah," said the Saint, and was briefly silent while he lighted a thoughtful cigarette. "I'd love to, Lieutenant. I've always said that Chicago is one of the most hospitable cities in the world. But I've already seen the Art Institute and Marshall Field's and the Natural History Museum, and I don't think I need a corpse to increase my liking for your city. Unless it's got two heads. Has it got two heads?"

Kearney said doggedly : "It's only got one head and we want you to look at it. I'm being polite, Mr. Templar. But I don't have to be, you know."

Simon knew it. He had heard that tone of voice before. And he was very definitely curious.

"I know," he murmured. "It's just your better nature. Well, I'd do almost anything to make you happy. When and where do you want me to ogle this cadaver?"

"If you could come on down to the morgue right now, I could meet you there. It would help."

"Fine," Simon said. "In about twenty minutes?"

"That'll suit me. Thanks, Mr. Templar."

"Not at all," said the Saint, and went more soberly back to the table.

Monica had finished her calls. The dark richness of her hair tossed like a wave of night as she looked up at him.

"It's all set," she said cheerfully. "We're going with the Kennedys. I didn't tell them about you. You'll be a surprise."

Simon said, "I hope I can make it. Somehow the police

seldom see things my way." He sat down. "There's been a corpse found, and it seems they want me to identify it. Why anyone should think I might supply the clue is something else again. It isn't my corpse or yours or Hoppy's— we know that."

Her face was only a shade paler—or that might have been a change of lighting on her camellia skin.

"Then—who could it be?"

"As a betting proposition," said the Saint, "I'll take three guesses. And Stephen Elliott is not one of them."

VIII

The last time Simon Templar had seen the man who lay on the morgue slab was in the parlour of Sammy the Leg. Junior's rat face was as unattractive in death as in life —less so, in view of the small blue-rimmed hole that marred his forehead. As the Saint looked at it, he was conscious of a curious urgency to dematerialise himself, drift like smoke towards the house near Wheaton, and ask Sammy questions.

Lieutenant Alvin Kearney was a very tall, very thin man with protruding brown eyes and a bobbing Adam's apple. He seemed to be mainly fascinated by the body, in a sort of dull, desperate way.

"Know him?" he asked.

"What makes you think I would?" Simon countered cautiously.

"Ever seen him before?" Kearney insisted.

The Saint said plaintively : "I very seldom meet people with bullet-holes in their foreheads. They're so taciturn they bore me."

Kearney closed his mouth and juggled his Adam's apple. His cheeks darkened a trifle.

"You're funny as a crutch," he said. "I want a straight answer."

Simon's innocent blue gaze met Kearney's squarely.

"I'm sorry," he said. "I can't help you. I can't even tell you the man's name. Who is he?"

"Dunno," Kearney said. "Unidentified so far."

"Oh. Did he have a note in his hand directing that his remains be sent to me?"

"Not quite," Kearney said. "There was a sort of tie-up, though. We found him in a house just north of Wheaton. Ever been there?"

The Saint took out a cigarette and turned it between his fingers, correcting minute flaws in its roundness. His face wore no more reaction than a slight, thoughtful frown; but a prescient vacuum had suddenly created itself just below his ribs. It had always been obvious that Kearney hadn't called him out of sheer civic hospitality. Now the showing of cards, led up to with almost Oriental obliquity, was starting to uncork a Sunday punch. But it was starting from such a fantastic direction that the Saint's footwork felt stiff and stumbling.

He said: "Wait a minute, Lieutenant. You found this man *in* the house, you say?"

"Not me personally. But he was in a basement room there, yes."

"Does the local patrolman's beat include the *inside* of houses?"

Kearney said: "I get it. No, there was a phone call. An anonymous tip. The usual thing. We gave it a routine check-up, and there was this house with this guy in it."

"No clues?" Simon said.

"Clues!" Kearney chewed the word. "Well—maybe one. We checked up to see who the house belongs to."

He was staring at the Saint. Simon merely nodded and looked brightly interested.

Kearney said: "It belonged to a gonsel called Sammy the Leg, up to yesterday. Then a deed of gift was filed. Now it belongs to Mr. Simon Templar."

So that was it. . . . The hollow space under the Saint's wishbone filled up abruptly with fast-setting cement.

It was nightmarish, absurd, impossible; it was something that not only shouldn't but happily couldn't happen to a dog. He could only theoretically sympathise with the emotions of this hypothetical hound upon watching some rival pooch dig up a treasured bone miles away from its established burial-ground—and upon discerning that the bone had also been booby-trapped in transit.

Somehow he managed to strike a match and set it to his cigarette without a quiver.

"Somebody should have told me," he murmured. "I always wanted to be a real-estate tycoon."

"You didn't know about it, huh?" Kearney said. "I kind of thought you didn't. You ever meet Sammy the Leg?"

The Saint shook his head.

"Of course not. I didn't sign any deed of gift either."

"Uh-huh. We're checking. We got plenty of records on Sammy." Kearney produced a pad and pen. "Mind signing this? I want to compare a few signatures."

Simon obligingly scribbled his name.

"If you'd show the deed to me, I could tell you right away if it was a forgery. In fact, I can tell you that now."

"Can't take your word for it," Kearney said flatly. "I admit it looks like a frame, and a lousy one. On the other hand, we've got to be sure. You got a certain reputation, Saint."

"So they tell me," Simon said. "I'm surprised you don't lock me up."

Kearney suddenly grinned.

"We thought of it. But the Commissioner said no. You must have done him a favour some time."

Which happened to be true. But Simon didn't answer the implied question. He was staring thoughtfully at Junior's corpse.

"That house at Wheaton—isn't anyone living there?"

"Nobody's shown up there since we got the call."

"With this housing shortage, too," Simon drawled. "You'd think they'd have been around it like ants as soon as a dead body was taken out. . . . Well, it seems as if someone's adopted me for an heir. I'm only sorry I can't help you. If I do run across anything, I'll let you know, though. All right?"

Kearney said : "Sure, that's all right. Of course, if this is a frame, it might mean you're mixed up in something. It might mean somebody's gunning for you. You wouldn't know about that, would you?"

Simon's attitude changed. He leaned forward confidentially.

"Well," he said, "if you'll consider this just between ourselves, and not for publication, I can tell you that I *am* engaged in a small crusade just at present."

Kearney's eyes opened.

"Yeah?"

"Yeah," Simon said, and brought his mouth close to the detective's ear. "Don't breathe a word of it, but I've decided to kill everyone in Chicago."

He went back to the hotel and told Hoppy the story; and Mr. Uniatz's jaw sagged lower and lower as it proceeded.

"I don't get it," Mr. Uniatz said finally, making a great confession.

"Neither do I, to put it mildly," said the Saint. "And fortunately, neither does Kearney. But he's no fool. I didn't want him to start asking me the wrong questions. He was on the right track, you know."

"Yeah?" Hoppy said.

"He knows I'm mixed up in something. And I can't let the police in on this yet. If I did, the King would simply go underground. As long as I keep His Majesty thinking there's only one man on his track, he won't be frightened into a strategic retreat. Ever try to scrape a sea anemone off a rock?"

"What would I wanna do a t'ing like dat for?" Hoppy inquired aggrievedly.

The Saint considered the question solemnly.

"Let's say the anemone had murdered a great-aunt of yours, if you must have a motive. The aunt's name was Abigail. She used to eke out a precarious living by blackmailing anemones. Got that straight?"

"Sure," said Hoppy, satisfied.

"If you scoop fast, you can scrape up the anemone. But if you aren't quite fast enough, it'll retract and fold up into such a tight knot that you can't pry it loose. I don't want the King to retract."

Hoppy said : "Sure."

"The King doesn't know I'm the blind beggar—I hope. That's something. And I don't think his murder frame has a chance to stick." Simon frowned. "Or . . . perhaps he's smarter than I thought. We'll have to wait and see. At worst, you can get an anemone to reopen by feeding it."

"Hey," Hoppy said suddenly. "What's an anemone?"

Simon decided it would be more discreet to leave this alone.

"What we want to know," he said grimly, "is how this all happened. Who did what to who? Did Junior dig through a wall and escape? Then who bumped him off and called the cops? Is something wrong about that stooge —what was his name? Fingers Schultz? Who talked too much to who—and brought my name into it? And how much too much has been said? Most important of all, what made Sammy run?"

"It couldn't of been Sammy," Hoppy said miserably. "I'd trust Sammy wit' my right eye. If he signs a receipt, dat is."

"We didn't get a receipt," Simon pointed out.

IX

The Saint had expected Mrs. Laura Wingate's penthouse on Lake Shore Drive to be fairly palatial, but he was not quite prepared for the rococo perspectives that opened before him as he followed Monica Varing out of the elevator and the cocktail party exploded around them like a startled barn-yard.

"My God," he said in a dazed undertone, as he fought their way through the seething throngs. "Monica, are you sure this is the right place?"

"I think so. We could have crashed the gate without any trouble. Everybody's here."

This seemed fairly correct. Across the broad acres of terrace, tables were set up, beach umbrellas made gay patterns, and trays of cocktails were levitated towards thirsty throats. The Saint seized two passing Martinis and shared his loot with Monica.

"Let's cruise around," he suggested. "I don't know exactly what we're looking for, but there's one way to find out. If you stumble on a clue, such as a rigid body with a knife-hilt protruding from its back, whistle three times."

"I wouldn't be too hopeful," she said. "The servants must be too well trained to leave rubbish cluttering up the lawn. Still, there may be some rigid bodies around here before the day's over," Monica pondered, watching a sleek young socialite tossing off drink after drink with the desperation of a fire-breathing dragon trying to put itself out.

They drifted through the yammer of high-pitched voices, conveniently allowing an eddy among the other guests to cut them off from their sponsors, the Kennedys. The Saint's casually roving eyes inventoried the crowd without finding in it anything to give direction to his unformed questions. It seemed to be composed of fairly standard ingredients—playboys old and young, business men, and politicians, blended with their wives, mistresses, and prospectives. He sought and failed exasperatingly to find a single sinister aroma in the brew.

Then through a gap in the crowd he glimpsed a white head that looked like Stephen Elliott, and started to steer Monica towards it. Before they had made much progress the throng parted in another quarter, spilling away like a bow wave before the onrush of a monumental figure that bore down upon them like an ocean liner. Simon had only a moment to hope that it could stop in time before it rammed them with its monstrous bosom.

"I thought I recognised you," Mrs. Wingate cried, ignoring Simon to concentrate on his companion. "It must be Monica Varing. Imagine!"

Monica smiled and said: "I'm afraid I wasn't invited, Mrs. Wingate, but I was with the Kennedys this afternoon, and they insisted I come along with them. I do hope you won't mind."

She played the gracious lady with such perfect restraint and charm that even Simon was impressed, while Mrs. Wingate almost swooned.

"I'm so glad. How could I possibly mind? I've admired your art for so long, my dear Miss Varing—oh! A cocktail?"

She beckoned urgently, and a servant came with his tray. He offered it to Simon last, and Mrs. Wingate's attention was directed to Monica's escort.

"Oh, dear—I should know you, too," she gushed—and giggled helplessly. "I'm sure I should. I have such a dreadful memory for names."

"There's no reason why you should know mine," said

the Saint amiably. "I'm uninvited, too. I came with Miss
Varing. My name is Templar. Simon Templar."

"Simon Templar," Mrs. Wingate echoed, looking at him
along her nose, over a battery of chins. "It's familiar, somehow. Oh, I know. The Senator from——"

Behind the Saint a deep, mild, slightly treacly voice
said : "Not quite, Laura. Not quite."

Stephen Elliott moved into the group with a sort of
apologetic benevolence that reminded the Saint of an
undertaker associating with the bereaved.

Seen without interference by the dark glasses through
which Simon had observed him first, there was a fresh pink
tint to his long, aristocratic features rather similar in con-
tour to those of a well-bred horse, which suggested that he
had arrived fresh from a facial. His skin strengthened the
impression with a smooth softness which implied the same
attention daily. Whatever his other philanthropies may
have been, it was evident that he must have been a benison
to his barber.

Simon admitted him to their circle with an easy geniality
that contained no hint of recognition.

"I'm not in the public eye just now," he said. "Though
there was a time when I was, rather painfully."

Mrs. Wingate fixed him with a sharp stare.

"I can't remember names, but I have a wonderful
memory for faces. I—oh, no. Of course not."

But her eyes were puzzled.

Stephen Elliott's deprecating smile and unnaturally
soothing voice implied that all was for the best as he said :
"Mr. Templar is the Saint, Laura. Surely you've heard of
the Saint?"

"Oh, heavens," Mrs. Wingate said, losing her poise and
clutching at a sapphire pendant sitting like a mahout on
the elephantine bulge of her bosom.

"My dear Mrs. Wingate," Simon said lightly, "even if I
were still actively pursuing my profession, I could never
bring myself to swipe sapphires from such a charming
throat."

Mrs. Wingate giggled; but she relinquished her grip on
the pendant rather reluctantly.

"Surely you're not—I mean——"

She glanced around apprehensively. Simon smiled at her.

"Even Jack the Ripper must have had his social hours," he said. "Please consider me on my best behaviour. You need have no fears for your sapphires, your silver, or your honour, though the latter . . ." He beamed at Mrs. Wingate, who snickered again, unaware that the sentence might have been finished in many more ways than one, and at least half of them unflattering.

Elliott introduced himself. "—since Laura is too flustered, I gather," he said gravely. "Miss Varing? How do you do? Meeting two such notable figures is rather an event. I'll celebrate it by joining you in a drink."

He beckoned to a passing tray.

"To crime," the Saint suggested, and they drank, though Mrs. Wingate had a moment's startled pause first.

"To crime," Elliott repeated. "I'm surprised to hear that from you, Mr. Templar. I thought the Saint changed sides a while ago."

"There was a war on at the time," Simon said casually, "and some of it seemed sort of important. But now I'm back to stirring up my own trouble. You might call it my private reconversion problem. . . . As a matter of fact, I'm working on a case now, and I find I haven't lost much of my knack."

"A case?" Elliott asked.

"Yes. It should interest you, in view of the work you've been doing among Chicago's poor. Have you ever heard of someone called the King of the Beggars?"

Simon threw out the phrase with perfect carelessless, and just as airily made no point of watching for a reaction.

It would have made little difference if he had. Stephen Eliott's Santa Claus eyebrows merely drew together in a vaguely worried way; while Mrs. Wingate bridled as if her position in the Social Register had been questioned, and then said : "It's fantastic. Utterly fantastic. I've heard rumours, of course, but—Mr. Templar, you *must* realise that such things are—are——"

"Fantastic?" the Saint prompted.

"Not too much so, in my opinion," Stephen Elliott answered him. "There certainly is some sort of criminal organisation victimising the poor in Chicago. I'm not blind, Mr. Templar. But just how widespread is it?"

Simon shrugged.

Elliott's distinguished equine face worked uncomfortably.

"I know," he said at last. "It's a pernicious racket, no matter how small. It should be stamped out. And you say you're going after it?"

The Saint flipped a mental coin, and decided to hold his course.

"Yes. I haven't been able to find out much yet. I wonder if you could help me?"

Elliott pursed his lips.

"I'm afraid they don't talk to me. Not about that. It's hard to break down the wall of reticence a socially unfortunate man has had to build up. I can inquire, if that will help."

"You haven't been interested enough so far to ask questions?" Monica put in.

"It's a police matter. I feel that I can do more good in my own way. . . . Of course, if I could be of any use——"

Mrs. Wingate said abruptly: "Why, you're the blind beggar!"

This time the Saint was naturally watching Elliott. He saw blank startled astonishment leap into the man's eyes. He held his own reflexes frozen under an unmoving mask of bronze and waited, while Mrs. Laura Wingate babbled on.

"I don't understand. I'm *sure* I can't be mistaken. But —but—I *never* forget a face, Mr. Templar. What in the world——"

Elliott's hand moved towards the watch-chain stretched across his vest.

"What do you mean, Laura?"

"I'm sure I must be making a fool of myself. But, Stephen, you *know* I've got a photographic memory. I think you were with me, too. . . . Yesterday! Mr. Templar——"

The coin had come down and bedded itself flatly in hot solder. There wasn't even a theoretical chance any more of it landing on its edge. Its verdict had been delivered with more finality even than the Saint had played for. But he had always been a sucker for the fast showdown, the cards on the table and the hell with complicated strata-gems. . . .

He relaxed with an infinitude of relaxation, and smiled at Laura Wingate with a complete happiness that could only stem from that.

"She's perfectly right," he said. "I often travel incognito. As a matter of fact, I was trying to get some information about the King's organisation. To do that I had to pose as a beggar. I hope you'll keep it confidential."

"Oh, goodness," Mrs. Wingate said breathlessly. "How romantic!"

Stephen Elliott maintained his mildly worried expression.

"Since we've stumbled on something that's apparently secret," he said temperately, "I suspect we'd better not ask any more questions. If Mr. Templar really has taken up the chase, and if his quarry should learn about it, it might be extremely dangerous for him. Perhaps even"—he shot the Saint a deliberate measuring glance—"fatal."

"I wouldn't *dream* of telling a soul," Mrs. Wingate protested. "I just wish I weren't so curious!"

Elliott's attention remained on the Saint.

"In fact," he said, "I'm not at all sure that it's wise for you to go on with this project, even now. From what little I have heard, the King of the Beggars protects his abso-lute sovereignty as ruthlessly as any despot. I have a great admiration for your exploits, and I should hate to see anything happen to you."

"Thank you," Simon said. "I've a great admiration for yours."

Elliott hesitated, staring.

"Scarcely in the same category——"

"I mean your charities. The Elliott Hotel, for example."

The philanthropist nodded.

"I am trying to follow a plan," he said, a slightly fanati-cal glaze coming into his eyes. "I'll admit that the several rooming-houses I own in Chicago aren't in the same class as the Palmer House, but I think all told, I have more guests in my various establishments than any single Chicago hotel. The greatest good for the greatest number of the needy automatically means that one must supply bread, not éclairs."

"Also," said the Saint, holding his gaze directly, "the dispenser of bread can hardly stand by while some racketeer taxes the needy for the privilege of receiving it."

"I can only work within my limitations and in my own way——"

Mrs. Wingate was off on a tangent, figuratively clutching Elliott's coat-tails and riding along.

"There must be roses, too," she remarked, and everyone looked at her blankly.

Finally Simon said: "*Chacun à son goût*" in such a significant manner that Mrs. Wingate nodded several times with intense solemnity, as if she had heard the Pope affirm a historic dogma.

"Man does not live by bread alone," she said. "Stephen is concerned with the bodies of the poor. My interest is in their souls. The unfortunates do have souls, you know. I try to bring something more than bread into their dark, narrow lives. You should see. . . . Stephen! Do you think——"

"What, Laura?"

"I'm sure you'd be willing to help us, Mr. Templar. You're notorious for your charities——"

Elliott said: "Notorious is perhaps the wrong word, Laura. And, if I may say so, the Saint's charities are not exactly in line with what we're trying to do."

Mrs. Wingate plunged on excitedly, as if she had not even heard him.

"And you, Miss Varing—of course. You see, we try to make the unfortunates realise something of the higher things. It gives them incentive. We arrange to put on little entertainments for them sometimes. Now to-morrow night there's one at the Elliott Hotel——"

"In the boiler-room," Elliott said with dry humour. "You mustn't give the impression that it's like the Drake."

"But it's an *enormous* room," Mrs. Wingate went on, no whit dashed. "There'll be songs and coffee and—and —speeches, and it would be simply wonderful if you both could drop in for just a few moments. If you could do a

reading, Miss Varing, and Mr. Templar, if you, could
—ah——"

"Now, just what could I do?" Simon asked thoughtfully.
"A lecture on safe-cracking would hardly be quite the
thing."

"A speech, perhaps, showing that crime does not pay?"
Elliott seemed in earnest, but the Saint could not be sure.

Mrs. Wingate clasped her hands in front of her bust.

"At eight-thirty? We would *so* appreciate it!"

"I'm afraid eight-thirty is my curtain time," Monica
said, with an excellent air of regret. "Otherwise I'd have
loved it."

Mrs. Wingate blinked.

"Oh, of course. I'd forgotten. I'm so sorry. Thank you,
my dear." She forgot Monica completely as she turned
back to the Saint. "But you'll be able to make it, won't
you, Mr. Templar?"

Simon only hesitated a moment.

"I'd be delighted," he said. "I don't think I can get
much heart into the speech till I work myself into the right
mood, but I'll do my best. You see," he added, beaming at
Elliott, "it's been my experience that crime pays very well
indeed. But, as I said before——"

"*Chacun à son goût?*" Elliott suggested unsmilingly.

"How true," Mrs. Wingate said vagely. "Another cocktail, perhaps?"

X

Simon left Monica at the theatre and went back to his
hotel to receive a purely negative report from a discour-
aged Hoppy Uniatz. Hoppy had spent the afternoon cir-
culating among various pool halls and saloons where he
had old acquaintances, and where Sammy the Leg was also
known. That his peregrinations had done little to satisfy
his chronic thirst for bourbon was understandable : the dis-
tilling industry had been trying in vain to cope with that
prodigious appetite for years. But that his thirst for information had been unslaked by as much as one drop of news
was a more baffling phenomenon.

Sammy the Leg had been seen in none of his usual
haunts, and none of his dearest cronies had heard either

of or from him. Nor had rumour any theories to advance.
He had not been reported dead, sick, drunk, in love, in
hiding, or departed from town. He had simply dropped
out of the local scene, without a word or a hint to anyone.

"I don't get it, boss," Mr. Uniatz summed up, confirm-
ing his earlier conclusion.

Simon rescued the bottle from which Hoppy was en-
deavouring to fill some of the vacua which had defied the
best efforts of Chicago's bar-tenders, and poured himself
a modest portion.

"We now have," he said, "a certain problem."

"Dat's right, boss," Hoppy agreed.

He waited hopefully for the solution, experience having
taught him that it was no use trying to compete with the
Saint in such flights of speculation. A man without
intellectual vanity, he was content to leave such scin-
tillations to nimbler minds. Also this saved overloading
his own brain, a sensitive organ under its osseous over-
coat.

"The question is, who knows how much about what?"
said the Saint. "If anyone at that cocktail party is connected with the King of the Beggars, I might as well walk
barefooted into a den of rattlesnakes as show up to claim
my reservation at the Elliott Hotel. But by the same token,
if I don't show up, I'm announcing that I have reasons
not to—which may be premature."

"Yeah," Hoppy concurred, with the first symptoms of
headache grooving his brow.

"On the other hand," Simon answered himself, "if the
ungodly are expecting me to-morrow, they won't be expecting me to-night, and this might be a chance to keep
them off balance while I case the joint."

"I give up," said Mr. Uniatz sympathetically.

The Saint paced the room with long, restless strides. He
was at a cross-roads before which far more subtle strate-
gists than Mr. Uniatz might well have been bewildered,
with the signpost spinning over them like a windmill.
Simon even felt his own cool judgment growing dizzy with
its own contortions. He was in a labyrinth of ifs and buts to
which there seemed to be no key. . . .

Mr. Uniatz pinged BBs monotonously through his teeth

at the electric light, drawing from it the clear, sharp notes of repeated bull's-eyes.

"I get better at dis all de time, boss," he remarked, as if in consolation. "Dis afternoon I stop in a boilicue an' get in de toid row. Dey is a stripper on who is but lousy—she shoulda stood home wit' her grandchildren. Well, I start practisin' on her wit' my BBs. I keep hittin' her just where I'm aimin', an' she can't figure where dey come from. It breaks up de act——"

The Saint halted in the middle of a step and swung around.

"Hoppy," he said, "I never expected to see you cut Gordian knots, but I think you've done it."

"Chees, boss, dat's great," said Mr. Uniatz. "What did I do?"

"You've given me an idea," said the Saint. "In your own words—if the ungodly can't figure where it's coming from, it might break up the act."

"Sure," Hoppy agreed sagely. "But who is dis guy Gordian?"

Simon Templar had always lived by inspiration, even by hunches; but his recklessness had no relation to any unconsciousness of danger. On the contrary, he was never more watchful and calculating than in his rashest moves. He diced with fate like a seasoned gambler, taking mathematical risks with every shade of odds coldly tabulated in his head. It was simply that once his bet was down he gave himself up to the unalloyed delight of seeing how it would turn out. The anxiety was over for him once the dice began to roll. After that there was only the excitement of riding with them, and the taut invigoration of waiting poised like a fencer to respond to the next flick of steel.

"Which is a nice trick if you can do it," he mused, blinking through his dark glasses as he tapped his way along the sidewalk towards the Elliott Hotel a couple of hours later.

He looked interestedly at the huge ramshackle structure, which, despite its new coat of brown paint, could scarcely have brought much inspiration to the souls of the poor unfortunates who inhabited it. The building had been constructed after the Chicago fire, but not much later; and

THE KING OF THE BEGGARS 51

it had an air of rather desperately sterile cheer, like an asthmatic alderman wheezing out Christmas carols.

The front door yawned, more rudely than invitingly, Simon decided. He made pleading gestures at a passing pedestrian.

"Excuse me, sir. I'm looking for the Elliott Hotel. Can you tell me——"

"Right here," said the florid man Simon had accosted. "Want to go in?" He took the Saint's arm and guided him up the steps to the door. "Okay now?"

"Thank you, sir. God bless you," Simon said, and the florid man, who does not hereafter appear in this record, vanished into the Chicago evening.

The Saint stood in a broad, high-ceilinged hall. There were doors and a drab carpet and merciless light bulbs overhead. Fresh paint could not disguise the essential squalor of the place. A few framed mottoes told any interested unfortunates it might concern that there was no place like home, that it was more blessed to give than to receive, that every cloud had a silver lining, and that a fixed and rigid smile was, for some unexplained reason, an antidote to all ills. The effect of these bromides was to create a settled feeling of moroseness in the beholder, and Simon had no difficulty in maintaining his patiently resigned expression beneath the dark glasses.

Through an open door at the Saint's left a radio was playing. At the back of the hall were closed doors, and facing Simon was the desk clerk's cubbyhole, occupied now by an inordinately fat woman who belonged in a freak show, though not for her obesity. The Saint greatly admired the woman's beard. It was not so black as a skunk's nor so long as Monty Woolley's; but 'twas enough, 'twould serve.

The woman said : "Well?"

Simon said tremulously : "I'm looking for Miss Green. Miss Hazel Green."

"Big Hazel Green?"

"Yes—yes, that's right."

"You're talking to her," the woman said, placing enormous forearms on the counter and leaning forward to stare at the Saint. "What is it?"

"I was advised to come here. A Mr. Weiss . . ." Simon let his voice die away.

Big Hazel Green rubbed her furry chin. "Yeah," she said slowly. "Mr. Weiss, huh? I guess you want to move in here. Is that it?"

Simon nodded.

Big Hazel said: "Shouldn't you have been here before?"

"I don't know," Simon said feebly. "Mr. Weiss did say something about . . . But I had my rent paid in advance at —at the place where I was staying. I couldn't afford to waste it. I—I hope I haven't done anything wrong."

He could feel her eyes boring into him like gimlets.

"That isn't for me to say. I just take reservations and see who checks in."

The woman rang a bell. A thin meek little man came from somewhere and blinked inquiringly.

Big Hazel said: "Take over. Be back pretty soon." She forced her bulk out of the cubbyhole and took Simon's arm in strong fingers. "I'll show you your room. Right up here."

The Saint let her guide him toward the back of the hall, through a door, and up winding stairs. Behind the glasses, his blue eyes were busy—charting, noting, remembering. Like many old Chicago structures, this one was a warren. There was more than one staircase, he saw, which might prove useful later.

"How much higher is it?" he asked plaintively.

"Up top," Big Hazel told him, wheezingly. "We're crowded. But you've got a room all to yourself."

It was not a large room, as the Saint found when Big Hazel conducted him into it. The single window overlooked a sheer drop into darkness. The furniture was clean but depressingly plain.

Big Hazel said: "Find your way around. I'll register you later."

She went out, closing the door softly. Simon stood motionless, listening, and heard the lock snap.

The shadow of a smile touched his lips. In his pocket was a small instrument that would cope with any ordinary lock. The lock didn't bother him—only the reason why it had been used. The vital point was whether it was merely a house custom, or a special courtesy. . . .

He felt his way methodically around the room. Literally felt it. There were such things as peepholes; there were creaking boards, and floors not soundproofed against footsteps. He was infinitely careful to make no movement that a blind man might not have made. He tapped and groped and fumbled from one landmark to another, performing all the laborious orientations of a blind man. And in fact those explorations told him almost as much as his eyes.

There was an iron bedstead, a chair, a lavatory basin, a battered bureau—all confined within a space of about seventy square feet. The walls were dun-painted plaster, relieved only by a framed printing of Kipling's *If*. There was the one little window, of the sash variety, which he was able to open about six inches. He stood in front of it, as if sniffing the grimy air, and noted that the glass panes had wire mesh fused into them.

After a while he took off some of his clothes and lay down on the bed. He did not switch off the one dim light that Big Hazel had left him. He might have been unaware of its existence.

He dozed. That was also literally true. The Saint had an animal capacity for rest and self-refreshment. But not for an instant was he any more stupefied than a prize watchdog; and he heard Big Hazel's cautious steps outside long before she unlatched the door.

He didn't know how much time had gone by, but it must have been about three hours.

He was wide awake, instantly, and alert as a strung bow, but without the least movement.

"Who is it?" he mumbled grumpily; and even then he could see her clearly in the doorway.

"It's Hazel Green. I didn't mean to disturb you. Some people came in late and held me up."

"That's all right," he said, and sat up.

She came in and shut the door behind her, and stood looking down at him.

"Everything all right?"

"Yes, thank you, ma'am."

"What's your name?"

He remembered that she had never asked him before.

"Smith," he said. "Tom Smith."

"Like all the rest of 'em," she observed, without rancour. "You been in town long?"

"No, not long."

"How's it going?"

"Not bad."

"You're not a bad-looking guy to end up in a dump like this."

"That's how it goes." He took a chance, keeping his eyes averted. "You've got a nice voice, to be running a dump like this."

"It's a job."

"I suppose so." He ventured another lead, making himself querulous again. "Why did you lock me in? I wanted to go to the bathroom——"

"There's a thing under the bed. We lock everybody in. It isn't only men who come here. You have to keep a place like this respectable. Women stop here too."

For no good reason, an electric tingle squirmed up the Saint's spine. There was nothing he could directly trace it to, and yet it was unmistakable, a fleeting draught from the flutter of psychic wings. Without time to analyse it, without knowing why, he deadened every response except that of his mind, exactly as he had controlled his awakening when she walked in, and turned the instinctive quiver into a bitter chuckle.

"You wouldn't expect them to give people like me any trouble, would you?"

"You never can tell." Big Hazel moved closer, her hands dropping into the pockets of her voluminous skirt. Her voice was still brisk and businesslike as she went on : "I'll make out your registration to-morrow, and you can put a cross on it or whatever you do."

"Thank you, ma'am."

"Would you like a drink?"

The Saint stirred a little on the bedside, as if in mild embarrassment, as the same reflex prickle retraced its voyage over his ganglions. But he still kept his face expressionless behind the blank windows of his smoked glasses.

"Thank you, ma'am, but I don't drink anything. Not

being able to see, it sort of makes me a bit dizzy."

"You won't mind if I do?"

Without encouraging an answer, she pulled a pint bottle of a cheap blend out of the folds of her skirt and attacked the screw cap. She held the bottle and the cap in pleats of her clothing for a better purchase, but even her massive paws seemed to make no impression on their union.

The Saint paid only incidental attention to her heavy breathing until she said : "The damn thing's stuck. Can you open it?"

He found the bottle in his hands, and unscrewed the cap with a brief effort of steel fingers.

"Thanks, Mr. Smith."

She took a quick gulp from the bottle, and guided his groping hand to replace the cap.

"Well, have a good night," she said.

She went out, and the door closed behind her. And once again he heard the lock click.

Simon lay back on the hard bed, remembering vividly that she had never touched the bottle except through the cloth of her skirt pocket. He rested all night in the same vigilant twilight between sleep and waking, revolving a hundred speculations and surmises; but nothing else disturbed him except his own goading thoughts.

XI

It was surprisingly easy to get out—almost too easy. In the early morning feet crept past the door again, and the lock clicked stealthily. When he tried the door, after a while, it opened without obstruction. He tapped his way downstairs, and the thin meek man at the desk scarcely looked up as he went by. Big Hazel was nowhere to be seen.

In the rôle of a blind man it would have been difficult to shake off any possible shadowers, but that seemed an unnecessary precaution. If he was suspected at all, everything would be known about him anyway; if not, he would not be shadowed. But he thought he knew which it was.

He showered and shaved at his own hotel; and he was finishing a man-sized breakfast of bacon and eggs when the telephone rang.

"Listen, Mr. Templar," Lieutenant Kearney said. "You're not figuring on leaving town, are you?"

"My plans are nearly completed," Simon informed him. "At the stroke of midnight a small blimp, camouflaged as a certain well-known Congressman, will drop a flexible steel ladder to the roof of this hotel. I shall mount it like a squirrel and flee southward, while the sun sinks behind beautiful Lake Michigan. It all depends on the sun," he added reflectively. "If I can only induce it to put off sinking until midnight, and do it in the east for a change, the plan will go off without a hitch."

"Listen——" Kearney said, and sighed. "Oh, well. So you know the Commissioner. So I've got to give you a break. Just the same——" His tone changed. "I've been getting some information around Chicago."

"Fine," Simon approved. "If you run across a good floating crap game, by all means tell me. I need a stake before I make my getaway."

Kearney went on doggedly: "This stiff we got in the morgue—we found out who he was. His name's Cleve Friend. He's a grifter from Frisco."

"You ought to make a song out of that," Simon told him.

"Yeah. Well, anyhow, what was the idea saying you didn't know him?"

"Did I say that?" Simon asked blandly.

"You implied it," Kearney snapped. "And that don't check with what I've been hearing."

Simon paused.

"Just what have you been hearing?" he asked.

"Things from people. People around town. Not in your social circle, of course." Kearney's voice was heavy with sarcasm. "Bums, pool-room touts, beggars."

"Beggars?"

"We ran Friend's picture in the paper to-day," Kearney said. "The photographer retouched it a little—that hole in his head, you know. And some people came in to look at him. They recognised him. He's a grifter, or I mean he was, and quite a few people have seen him around Chicago the last month or so. Some of them saw you, too. Some of them even saw you both together."

"Those chatter-boxes knew me by name, of course?"

"Listen," Kearney said, "don't kid yourself. The Saint's picture has been in the papers too, a lot of times. What was it you were seeing Friend about lately."

"I can't tell you," Simon said.

"You won't?"

"I can't. I'm too shy."

"God damn it," Kearney roared. "Maybe you can tell me why the autopsy on Friend showed he'd been shot full of scopolamin, then!"

Simon's eyes changed. "Scopolamin? That wasn't what killed him?"

"You know damn well what killed him. You saw the bullet hole. I'm not doing any more talking to you. Not yet. I will later. I don't care if you know the Commissioner or the Mayor or the President of the United States! Just don't leave town, understand?"

"Yes," Simon said. "I get it. All right, Alvin. I'll string along. In fact——" He hesitated. "I'll even tell you why I was seeing Cleve Friend."

Kearney said suspiciously: "Yeah? Another gag?"

"No. You might as well know, I suppose. I can't keep it quiet for ever."

"Okay," Kearney snapped. "Spill it." He could not quite keep the eagerness out of his voice.

The Saint said mildly: "We were plotting his murder. Good-bye, Alvin."

He hung up, leaving the detective gibbering inarticulately, and poured himself another cup of coffee.

"This is what is known as a cumulative frame," he remarked to Hoppy, who was starting his morning target practice. "I wonder how thorough it's going to be."

Mr. Uniatz bounded a BB accurately off the coffee-pot.

"I don't get it, boss," he said automatically.

"It works backwards," Simon explained. "First an un-identified body is found, and the only connection between it and me was a deed of gift. Now some people have recognised the body and say that I've been seen fore-gathering with Junior, hereinafter referred to as the un-lamented Mr. Cleve Friend, a grifter from Frisco. It's significant that some of these witnesses are beggars. Later, perhaps, a witness to the murder will pop up. By sheer accident, he happened to be passing when I bumped off Friend."

"But ya didn't bump him off," Hoppy said. "Did ya?"

"No, Hoppy, I didn't."

"Den it's okay, ain't it?"

The Saint lighted a cigarette and leaned back.

"I wish I could be sure of that." He blew a procession of three reflective smoke rings towards the ceiling. "Do you happen to know anything about scopolamin?"

"I never hoid of him. Is he in de same mob wit' dat Gordian?"

"It's a drug, Hoppy. It makes people tell the truth. And it seems that somebody gave it to Friend before he was bumped off. They wanted to know how much he'd spilled, and he must have told them. We can also be sure that they asked him all he knew about us. . . . So we can take it that the blind-beggar act is dead and has been for some time."

A scowl of dutiful concentration formed like a sluggish cloud below Mr. Uniatz's hairline as he worked this out and tried to reconcile its components. His mental travail appeared to deepen through successive minutes to a painful degree, and at last he brought forth the root of it.

"Den why," he asked, "don't dey give ya de woiks last night?"

"That's what I'm trying to figure out," said the Saint slowly. "Unless they're taking their time to cook up a much bigger and better frame. . . . Big Hazel has a whisky bottle with my fingerprints on it now, and there wasn't a thing I could do to stop her getting away with it. She really had me off balance—I was so busy turning down a drink that I was sure would be a knockout that the other angle just went by under my nose."

He blew another smoke ring very deliberately, devoting everything to the perfection of its rich full roundness, while he tried to make his inward thoughts match the calm of his outward movement.

"Also," he said, and he was really talking to himself, "it seemed to me that there was just the slightest sinister emphasis—just the merest trace of it—in the way Big Hazel talked about having women in the hotel. I wonder. . . ."

He picked up the telephone and called Monica Varing's hotel, but her room didn't answer.

They had parted on a tentative agreement to lunch again, and it was not likely that anyone so punctual as she was would be careless about an engagement. Probably, he told himself, she had gone shopping.

He called again every half-hour until one-thirty, and stayed in his own room for fear of missing her if she called him.

It was not an afternoon to remember with any pleasure or any pride. He must have walked several miles, pacing the room steadily like a caged lion and taking months of normal wear out of the carpet. He tried to tell himself that his imagination was running away with him, that he was giving himself jitters over nothing. He told himself that he should have kept Monica entirely out of it, that he should never have let her learn anything, that he would only have himself to blame if she tried to steal the play from him. He saw her all the time in his mind's eye, a composite of all her tantalising facets—sultry, impish, arrogant, venturesome, languorous, defiant, tender. He felt angry and foolish and frightened in turn.

Mr. Uniatz worked on his BB marksmanship with untroubled single-mindedness. He could learn nothing from the Saint's face, and to him the operations of the Saint's mind would always be a mystery. It was enough for him that there was a mind there, and that it worked. All he had to do was carry out its orders when they were issued. It was a panacea for all the problems of life which over the years had never failed to pay off, and which had saved untold wear and tear on the rudimentary convolutions of his brain.

At five o'clock Simon remembered that Monica might have a matinée, and verified it from the newspaper. He walked to the Martin Beck Theatre and went in the stage door.

"Miss Varing ain't on this afternoon," said the doorman. "She's sick."

With lead settling in his heart, Simon sought out the stage manager.

"That's right," said the man, who remembered him. "She called me this morning and said she wouldn't be able to go on. She said if I hadn't heard from her by this time she wouldn't be doing the evening performance either."

"She isn't sick," said the Saint. "She hasn't been in her hotel all day."

The stage manager looked only slightly perturbed. He said nothing about artistic temperament; but his discretion itself implied that he could think of plausibly mundane explanations.

Simon took a taxi to the Ambassador and finally corralled an assistant manager whom he could charm into co-operation. A check through various departments established that room service had delivered breakfast to Monica Varing's apartment at nine, that she had been gone when the maid came in at eleven. But her key had not been left at the desk, and no one had seen her go out.

"No one knows they saw her," Simon corrected, and asked his last questions of the doorman.

Already he knew what the answer would be, and wondered what forlorn hope kept him trying to prove himself wrong.

"An old ragged woman, looked like she might be a beggar? . . . Yes, sir, I did see her come out. Matter of fact, I wondered how she got in. Must have been while I was calling someone a cab."

"On the contrary," said the Saint, with surprising gentleness, "you opened the door for her yourself."

He left the man gaping, and went back into the hotel to call Lieutenant Kearney.

XII

The boiler-room in the basement of the Elliott Hotel was not quite as bleak as the description implies. This was only because the description does not mention several rows of hard wooden benches, the bodies of several dozen apathetic occupants of them, a few paper decorations left over from some previous Christmas, and the platform at one end where Stephen Elliott was filling in with some merry ad-libs as the Saint found his way in.

"And—ah—as the stove said to the kettle, I hope you're having a hot time." Nobody laughed, and Elliott went on : "We want you to enjoy yourselves, friends, and the next item on to-night's programme is a song by Mrs. Laura Wingate."

He handed Mrs. Wingate up to the platform, and the connection between his two statements became somewhat obscure as the piano began to tinkle out an uncertain accompaniment, and Mrs. Wingate cut loose with an incredibly piercing and off-key soprano.

> "*My heart is like a singing bird*
>   *Whose nest is in a watershoot,*
> *My heart is like an apple tree*
>   *Whose boughs are bent with thick-set fruit——*"

Stephen Elliott was taking Mrs. Wingate's place beside a tall, thin man to whom she had been talking when she was called. As Simon edged up behind them he recognised the tall, thin shape as Lieutenant Alvin Kearney.

"I'm sure I don't know what it's about," the detective was saying, in a voice that had no need to drop its level to avoid interfering with the ear-splitting stridencies that were welling from Mrs. Wingate's throat. "For all I know, it may be just another of his funny gags. But I'd look plenty silly if anything happened and I wasn't here."

Elliott took out a handkerchief and patted his temples, while Mrs. Wingate continued to liken her heart to various other improbable objects.

"I don't know anything about it," he said mildly. "But if he's working on a case——"

"Oh, is he?" Kearney snapped that up with the avidity of a starving shark. "What case?"

Elliott hesitated.

"I really can't say," he replied at last. "Why don't you ask him?"

"Yes, why not?" Simon agreed, and they both turned.

Kearney's lip thinned over his teeth as he met the Saint's affable smile. There was no thoroughly defensible reason for his reaction, yet it was a basic reflex which in its time had produced fundamentally identical effects upon such widely separated personalities as Chief Inspector Teal of Scotland Yard, Inspector Fernack of New York City, Lieutenant Ed Connor of Los Angeles, Sheriff Newt Haskins of Miami, and many others who will be remembered by the unremitting followers of this saga. It was perhaps something that sprang from the primal schism of law and disorder, an aboriginal cleavage between policeman and outlaw whose roots were lost in the dank dawns of sociology.

Lieutenant Alvin Kearney of Chicago liked the Saint, admired him, respected him, envied him, and hated him with an inordinate bitterness that loaded stygian tints into his scowl as he rasped : "All right, wise guy, you tell me. What was the idea phoning me to meet you here to-night because there might be a riot?"

"I guess it was a form of stage fright," said the Saint, with an aplomb which made Kearney feel as if he had two days' growth of beard and a dirty neck. "I'm not very used to these personal appearances, and I felt nervous. You can't tell what an audience like this might do, so I thought I should have some protection."

What the detective thought would have been inaudible even in the volume of voice which his congested face portended, for at that moment Mrs. Wingate's vocal analysis of her heart attained a screeching fortissimo that almost scraped the paint off the walls.

*"My heart is gladder than all these,
    Because—my lo-o-ove—has come to me!"*

As silence finally settled upon tortured eardrums, there was some perfunctory applause. It was rather nicely adjusted to show grateful appreciation without encouraging an encore. Since apparently the coffee and doughnuts would not be served until after the entertainment, the audience could not walk out, but it did not have to be hysterical.

Mrs. Wingate panted and bowed twitteringly to the very last handclap, which naturally came from Stephen Elliott.

"Thank you, thank you, my dear friends. . . . And now I see that our special guest of the evening has arrived, and I'm going to ask him to come up here and say a few words to you. It is a great privilege to be able to introduce— Mr. Simon Templar."

Simon stepped up on the platform to the resigned acclamation of the coffee-and-doughnuts claque. He raised Mrs. Wingate's pudgy hand to his lips and ushered her off in giggling confusion. Then he made a sign of dismissal to the piano player.

"I'm not going to sing," he said.

While the accompanist withdrew, he waved cheerily to the gaping Lieutenant Kearney, and ran friendly blue eyes over the faces of the rest of the audience. A few of them looked like the respectable struggling poor, some were ordinary shiftless down-and-outs; these would be bone fide beggars, helpless victims of the King's racket; and undoubtedly there were others who worked directly for the King. Big Hazel Green was nowhere in evidence, but he saw Frankie Weiss sitting a few rows back from the dais.

"Ladies, gentlemen, and others," Simon began. "Some of you may have heard of me. Some of you may not. I'm sometimes known as the Saint."

He waited till the low, resultant buzz died down, and little dancing devils of mischief showed in his eyes.

"I won't make a long speech," he said. "I know you're probably anxious to get at the refreshments. Anyway, I'm no good at speeches. I'd rather show you a few tricks which might come in useful; since it's been brought to my attention that some of you have been victimised by unscrupulous extortionists, which is a polite name for some dirty racketeering rats."

He ignored the dead silence that suddenly brimmed the room, and went blandly on :

"Now I'm sure it wouldn't need Detective Lieutenant Kearney, who is also here with us to-night, to remind you that carrying concealed weapons is illegal. But it's quite possible for a man to protect himself without carrying firearms. One good judo hold is often worth as much as a gun. So for the benefit of some of you who might want to defend yourselves one day, I thought I'd demonstrate a few for you. If I'm to show them properly, of course, I'll need a volunteer to work with."

There was no rush to volunteer. Mrs. Wingate chirped brightly: "Come on, somebody!"

Stephen Elliott stood up and beamed around with vaguely schoolmasterish encouragement.

Simon pointed a finger.

"You. No, not you—I mean the gentleman with the moustache. You look able to defend yourself. How about giving me a hand?"

Frankie Weiss huddled deeper in his chair and shook his head.

"Oh, come now," Simon insisted. "You never know when a little judo might come in handy. How do you know you won't meet some goon with a gun one of these days? Here!"

He bounced down from the stage and hurried up the aisle. Frankie tried to ignore everything, but the Saint was as irresistible as a radio interviewer. His hand appeared to stroke lightly over Frankie's arm and pause there. Only those in the immediate vicinity heard Frankie's yelp of pain, immediately smothered by the Saint's laughter.

"The man's got muscle!" he announced jovially. "You'll give me a fight, won't you, my friend? Come on, don't disappoint the audience."

He practically yanked Frankie out of his chair and caught him in a hold that left the man completely helpless, his legs in the air and his neck imprisoned under the Saint's arm.

"Just like that," Simon proclaimed. "Let's go up on the stage where the audience can enjoy it. We'll try it again more slowly."

He retraced his steps as resiliently as though he were not burdened with a tight-lipped, glaring assistant.

Lieutenant Kearney moved to get a better view. His face was a study in perplexed suspicion. Common sense told him that there was more in this than met the eye, but he couldn't guess what it was; and Simon hoped the detective's mind would continue, for a little while, to move slowly. He had his hands full with Frankie Weiss, who was struggling like a bear cat and growling unprintable inarticulacies which were fortunately smothered in the Saint's coat.

Laura Wingate gazed up in a glow of girlish eagerness, twisting her hands together in her overflowing lap. Stephen Elliott clung to a benign if somewhat nervous smile. The rest of the audience was divided between those who merely sensed a welcome variation in the schedule of innocent entertainment, those who derived personal gratification from the choice of the victim, and a smaller group of hard-featured hombres who seemed to be sweating out a purely private anguish of frustrated indecision.

"Let's do it again," Simon lectured, releasing his victim. "More slowly now. Watch!"

Frankie showed his teeth. He ducked away from the Saint, felt a long arm snake around his waist, and, turning swiftly, drove a vicious punch at Simon's groin. The Saint evaded it easily.

"Fine!" he exclaimed. "That's right. Fight me—make it look realistic. Now I'll do it slowly."

He did it slowly, and Frankie presently found himself involved in another excruciating posture from some manual of satanic yogi.

His mouth nearly touching Frankie's ear, Simon breathed: "Where's Monica Varing?"

"Let go of me! You goddam——"

"Sh-h! Lieutenant Kearney's out in front, Frankie. Don't give him any ideas."

The Saint wrenched slightly, eliciting a howl of pain from Frankie, and brought him back to his feet with dislocating solicitude.

"Everyone get that?" he asked. "Now let's try another one. This is harder."

He collared Frankie and tied him in an even more complex knot.

"*What about Monica?*"

"You son of a——"

"If you think I won't break your arm," the Saint whispered icily, "you're crazy. I can say it was an accident. I can even break your neck."

He proved this by applied pressure, with one hand gagging Frankie, though the audience could not see that.

It took three more holds, each a little more agonising

than the last, with Frankie trying desperately to escape, while none of his putative allies dared lift a finger to help him because Kearney was watching.

"So we've got her. Let go!"

"Where?"

"Second floor. Room by the stairs—*uh*!"

"Front or back?"

"Back——"

"Thank you, Frankie," Simon said, and his hands moved swiftly.

He jumped up. Frankie did not.

"He's fainted," the Saint gasped in well-simulated alarm. "It may be his heart. . . . Get a doctor!"

He leaped down from the platform and hurried towards the nearest exit; but Kearney caught him before he had gone more than a few steps.

"Just a minute," Kearney snarled. "What did you do to that guy?"

"I just gave him a mild chiropractic treatment," said the Saint wintrily. "I know it wasn't as good as you could have done at headquarters, but I thought a rubber hose might have been rather conspicuous. He'll wake up in about ten minutes and be as good as new."

The detective kept hold of his arm.

"What's the idea, anyway? And where do you think you're going?"

"I think I'm going to search this hotel, without bothering about a warrant," Simon answered in a flat voice. "Because my idea is that Monica Varing is being kept a prisoner here."

"The actress? Are you crazy?"

"I don't think so. In fact, just before Frankie passed out he told me she was upstairs."

Those of the audience who had moved were crowding towards the stage to obstruct the efforts of the first eager beavers who had moved to offer Frankie Weiss first aid. The others cast glances at the Saint but did not try to get near him, being probably kept at a distance by the presence of Kearney as much as anything else; so that the two of them might almost have been alone in the crowded room. At least until Mrs. Wingate bore down upon them, with

Stephen Elliott bobbing like a towed dinghy in her wake.

"Whatever is the matter?" she squeaked frantically. "This is terrible——"

"You tell them, Alvin," Simon suggested; and with a side-step as swift and light as a ballet dancer he made way for Mrs. Wingate to plough into a berth between them, and vanished through the door he had originally been heading for before the detective had the remotest chance of circumnavigating Mrs. Wingate's bulk to intercept him.

Simon raced up the stairs to the ground floor and from there to the second without interference. There were four doors back of the stairs, and he flung each of them open in turn. None of them was locked. Two of the rooms were six-bed dormitories, empty, but smelling rancidly of habitation. In the third room a very old man with a pock-marked face looked up with an idiotic grin from a game of solitaire.

The fourth room was empty—not only empty, but so cleaned out that it had the same prison bareness that he had found in the room he himself had occupied the night before. There were rumples in the bed that didn't follow the same contours as careless bedmaking; and he knew this must have been the room, even before he saw that the opaque window glass contained the same fused-in netting as his own window had had, even before his nostrils detected it the mustiness of the air, a clear fragrance that could only be Monica. . . .

Kearney caught up with him there a moment later and stuck a gun into his ribs.

"All right, Mr. Saint," he grated. "Don't try anything else, or I'll blast you."

"You blathering nitwit," said the Saint, with icy calm. "Why couldn't you stay downstairs and make sure they wouldn't smuggle her out?"

"From where?" Kearney jeered.

"From here. Frankie told me the truth. She was in this room. Don't you smell anything?"

The detective sniffed.

"It smells lousy to me."

Simon's eye caught a gleam on the floor. He ignored Kearney's revolver entirely to step forward and pick it up.

"Look."

"A tooth out of a comb," Kearney said scornfully. "So what?"

"A spring tooth," Simon said, "from the kind of comb women wear in their hair. And dark red-brown—the colour she'd use."

XIII

Mrs. Wingate and Stephen Elliott caught both of them up at that point. The philanthropist was quivering with a kind of pale-lipped restraint.

"This is the most outrageous suggestion I've ever heard, Mr. Templar," he said. "Lieutenant Kearney tells me——"

"Oh, I do hope you're mistaken!" babbled Laura Wingate. "She's such a *sweet* person, I'd *die* if anything happened to her.

"If anything happened to her, it would not be here," Elliott stated frostily. "Lieutenant, I think you'd better take Mr. Templar and his accusations to the proper authority."

Kearney nodded.

"It'll be a pleasure, Mr. Elliott."

"In spite of the comb?" Simon persisted.

"We have quite a number of lady guests," Elliott said stiffly. "If that is any grounds for this kind of behaviour——"

"It isn't," Kearney said. "And I'm going to enjoy booking the Saint on charges of disturbing the peace, just to keep him quiet for a while." He prodded Simon again with his gun. "Come along, you."

"I *loved* your show," Mrs. Wingate trilled, apparently feeling that some expression was due from her. "You must do it for us again one day."

Simon and Kearney went downstairs, passing a barrage of eyes that had seeped up from the basement.

"By the way," Simon said, "Frankie is wearing a gun."

"He has a permit," Kearney said. "I know the judge who issued it. Keep going."

They went out to the sidewalk, and there was a brief but awkward pause while the total cablessness of the street established itself.

"Why don't we take my car?" suggested the Saint accommodatingly. "It's right here."

"Okay," Kearney said belligerently. "I'll let you drive it—and just don't try anything."

He opened the door and followed Simon in. While the Saint was still fitting the key in the lock he reached over and snapped one loop of a pair of handcuffs over Simon's left wrist. The other cuff he secured to the steering wheel.

"All right," he said grimly. "Let's go."

Simon started the engine and nursed the car north for a few blocks. Kearney held the revolver in his lap and glowered with rather strenuously sustained triumph.

"How about your big case against me?" Simon asked after a while. "Aside from my breaches of the peace, I mean. Is that coming along?"

Kearney flexed his jaw muscles.

"We got a letter this afternoon. It was addressed to the Chief, and it was signed by Cleve Friend. It said he was mixed up in some deal with you and he was trying to get out of it because he'd got cold feet. And he was afraid you wouldn't let him get out. You'd threatened to kill him unless he played along. The letter said he was leaving it with a friend, to be mailed if he—died."

The Saint kept his eyes straight ahead.

"Did you check the signature?"

"It was Friend's signature all right. A little shaky, but it compared."

"Shaky?" Simon pondered. "And I bet the letter itself was typewritten."

"It was."

"It would be. Either Friend signed under the influence of scopolamin—which is a hypnotic—or else he was tortured into signing it."

"You can explain anything, can't you?" Kearney gibed. "Somebody's trying to frame you, of course."

"Of course," Simon agreed coolly. "That should be obvious, even to a policeman."

"Yeah? And how did they make this Varing dame disappear?"

"Probably through a secret passage. . . ."

His voice trailed away as the thought hit him like a splash of cold water between the eyes.

"My God," he said softly. "Secret passages. Of course. What a feeble-minded flop I am!"

"Hey!" Kearney squawked suddenly. "Where d'you think you're going? This ain't the way to Headquarters."

"It's the way I'm taking," said the Saint. "Come in, Hoppy."

Mr. Uniatz rose from behind the front seat and applied the muzzle of his Betsy to the nape of Kearney's neck.

"Okay, copper," he said. "Take it easy."

The detective's face went white, then red.

"You can't get away with this," he said desperately.

"We can try," said the Saint. "I've just had an inspiration, and I'm going to be much too busy to horse around with any footling rap about disturbing the peace."

He sped the car west on Roosevelt, and presently turned up Central Avenue to Columbus Park, where he stopped.

"Okay, Hoppy," he said.

"De woiks, boss?"

"Just let him take a nap," Simon said hastily.

Mr. Uniatz raised his gun and brought it down with professional precision; and the detective napped. . . .

Simon found Kearney's keys, unlocked the handcuffs, and transferred them to the detective's wrists. He took Kearney's badge and identification, figuring that a handcuffed man without credentials would be more than ordinarily delayed in starting a hue and cry. Then they took Kearney out of the car and laid him under a tree with his hat over his face, and drove quickly away.

The Saint's brain flogged itself pitilessly under the impassive mask of his face.

"Secret passages," he repeated, as he opened up the headlights on the road to Wheaton. "Hoppy, I ought to have my head examined."

"What for, boss?"

"Maggots. What the hell's the first thing you'd expect to find in a hide-out that used to belong to Al Capone? And don't you remember Sammy said he had a safe place to hide Junior?"

"Sure."

"Well, it was safe. So safe that Kearney couldn't find it. But we'll find it this time, if we have to blast for it. And then we'll know whether Sammy and his friend Fingers double-crossed us, or if the King caught up with them."

He reconnoitred the house carefully, but there were no signs of a police guard, and a ground-floor window succumbed in short order to the Saint's expert manipulation. It was after that that the problems began to multiply, and it took two hours of methodical labour to work them out.

They finally found the "safe place" by tortuously tracing a ventilating pipe that seemed to have an outlet but no inlet. Even then the field was merely narrowed down to the cellar, and it took an inch-by-inch investigation to settle on the probable entrance. Hoppy's reminiscences of bootlegging days were helpful and diverting, if sometimes gruesome; but in the end they had to use crowbars to break down the brick wall. There was a steel plate beneath that; but once its locking mechanism was revealed it surrendered to a piece of bailing wire.

It let them into a small, comfortably furnished room with a ventilating plate in the ceiling, where Sammy the Leg, trussed like an unsinged chicken, lay philosophically on a cot, and looked at them.

"Chees, pal," Hoppy said, as he worked on Sammy's ropes with a jack-knife. "We t'ought ya'd been bumped or sump'n."

"Not me," Sammy grunted. He tested his limbs experimentally. "Thanks, Saint. I figured I was gonna cash in for sure. Those lousy swine just meant me to lie here and starve."

"Didn't you hear us?" Simon asked. "You could have saved us some time if you'd yelled."

"It wouldn't have done no good. This room's sound-proofed. I heard you just now, sure, but you couldn't of heard me. Besides, how did I know who it was? I could tell somebody was busting in, so I let 'em bust. Not that I could of stopped you." Sammy walked stiffly back and forth like a shaggy bear, pausing at the door. "Had to break in, didn't you? It'll cost dough to fix that." He grimaced. "Hell. C'mon upstairs. I'm starving."

But the first thing Sammy the Leg did was to extract a beer bottle from his refrigerator, uncap it, and guzzle the contents. He wiped his mouth with a hairy hand, sighed, and eyed the Saint malevolently.

"Lousy double-crosser," he said. "Nope, not you. I mean Fingers. Go on, sit down. Have a beer. Wait a sec."

He went back to the refrigerator and brought out a plate of pig's knuckles.

"How did it happen?" Simon asked.

"Fingers Schultz," Sammy said, gnawing a knuckle. "Just goes to show. Never trust nobody. That little snake's been with me for three years. Thought I could depend on him. Sure I could—till he started figuring I was a has-been and somebody else could pay off better, and protect him."

"Like the King of the Beggars?" Simon prompted.

"I wouldn't know about that. Fingers brought Frankie Weiss here. They stuck me up. Fingers knew about that room downstairs and how to get into it. They took that guy you left here away with them, and left me like you found me. Funny—he didn't seem so happy about them finding him, like you'd expect."

"Junior's hunches were working fine," Simon told him cold-bloodedly. "They asked him all the questions they had to, and then rubbed him out."

Sammy reflectively chewed a knucklebone, his small eyes studying the Saint. Finally he sighed

"That's too bad. I guess he had it coming, but that don't do you no good." A pig's knuckle cracked disconcertingly in Sammy's huge grip. He got up, found another bottle, and lifted it to his mouth. "Who's gonna pay for messing up my cellar?" he demanded abruptly. "All it takes to open it is to stick a wire in the right place between the bricks. You didn't have to wreck it like that."

"How much will the repairs cost?" Simon asked.

"Say two hundred."

The Saint smiled.

"That's a coincidence. My charge for rescuing people who are tied up and left to die is exactly two hundred fish. Shall we call it square?"

Sammy said without rancour : "I didn't figure it would work on you, but there was no harm trying. Fingers is the guy who ought to pay for it. But when I catch up with Fingers he won't be in no shape to sign cheques."

Simon lighted a cigarette.

"You're right about Junior's rubbing-out doing me no good," he said. "As a matter of fact, they're working pretty hard at trying to frame me for it. You'll be interested to know that part of the frame was a deed of gift on this house from you to me. Now we know more about it, it wasn't such a bad set-up at all. You'd never show up to contest the title; and if anyone ever did find your body, it'd have been in my house and looked just as if I'd bumped you and forged the deed. . . . The King is quite a sweet little schemer, it turns out."

Sammy the Leg was staring at him with a mixture of grief and consternation that made him look as if he was going to cry.

"You mean . . . they gave you my house?"

His eyes actually grew moist as they stole lingeringly around the appalling interior.

"Don't worry—I'll give it back to you," said the Saint generously. "All I want from you is just as much as you can tell me. For instance : when Frankie and Fingers were talking, did they let anything drop that would give you any idea where the King of the Beggars has his main hide-away? Of where they might have kept Junior, if they'd wanted to keep him?"

Sammy chewed thoughtfully for a while, and made a decision.

"I ain't no squealer," he said, "but after what those two rats done to me . . . They didn't say much, either. But Fingers said, 'Why not work him over here?' and Frankie said, 'They're waiting for us at Elliott's, and we got a better trick there.' "

Mr. Uniatz came out of a prolonged silence during which he had been refreshing himself from a pint bottle of bourbon which he had discovered among Sammy's supplies. His return to the conversation might have been due to the stirring of a thought, or to the fact that the bottle was now empty.

"De Elliott Hotel?" he said. "But we just come from dere——"

"And we didn't search it," Simon said. "That was only the place where I started thinking about secret passages. So naturally I was too dumb to start there . . . Wait a minute!" He came to his feet suddenly, and his eyes were alight. "Sammy—did he say 'Elliott's' or 'the Elliott Hotel'?"

Sammy stared at him.

"He said 'Elliott's,' " he stated positively. "I never heard of an Elliott Hotel."

"Of course he did," said the Saint, with a lilt in his quiet voice like muted trumpets. "Of course he did. Anyone who meant the Elliott Hotel would say so, or call it 'the Hotel' or 'the Elliott.' They wouldn't call it 'Elliott's.' . . . Hoppy, we're on our way!"

Hoppy struggled obediently but foggily to his feet.

"Okay, boss."

"That'll be five bucks for the bourbon," Sammy said. He closed his hairy fist on the bill that Simon placed in it, and added: "Just one thing. Try to leave Fingers for me, will you? I sort of feel I ought to get him myself, for the looks of things."

"We'll try," Simon promised.

He drove back into Chicago with the speedometer needle exactly on the legal limit, for this was one time when he did not want to be stopped. His first destination was his own hotel: he was gambling that that might well be the last place where Kearney would expect him to show up again, but in any case he was riding a hunch that justified the chance.

And the piece fell into place as if it had been machined to fit, with the uncanny smoothness that so often seemed to lubricate the gears of Simon Templar's destiny.

There was a letter in his box at the desk, a product of the last delivery. It was addressed to Hoppy, but Simon opened it as soon as he saw the name of the firm of realtors it came from.

Dear Mr. Uniatz,
    We have finally been able to trace the ownership of

*the property in which you are interested at 7204 Kelly
Drive.*

*The owner is a Mr. Stephen Elliott, and we under-
stand he would consider an offer——*

Simon read no more. He stuffed the letter into his
pocket, and sapphires danced in his eyes.

"Let's go, Hoppy," he said, "and arrange an abdication."

XIV

The telephone at the clerk's elbow buzzed. He picked
it up and said : "Night clerk speaking. . . ." His eyes went
to the Saint and he said : "Yes, he just came in——"

Then his eyes bulged while they still rested on the Saint.
Simon watched them grow wider and rounder before the
man backed away from the counter and turned his head.

The Saint deliberately dawdled over lighting a cigarette,
but even his supersensitive ears could pick nothing up, for
all the rest of the conversation came from the other end of
the line, until the clerk muttered : "Okay, I'll do my best."

Simon started to move away.

"Er—Mr. Templar——"

He turned.

"Yes?"

The clerk was sweating. His face had a slightly glazed
surface from the strain of trying to look natural.

"The manager just called, Mr. Templar, and wanted to
speak to you about—about an overcharge on your bill."

"I'll be glad to speak to him in the morning," said the
Saint co-operatively. "We should have lots to talk about—
everything on my bill looks like an overcharge to me."

"He's on his way here now, sir," said the clerk from his
tonsils. "If you could wait a few minutes——"

The Saintly smile would have glowed ethereally in a
stained-glass window.

"I'm afraid I haven't time," he said. "But when
Lieutenant Kearney gets here, do congratulate him for me
on his new job. Oh, and give him this letter, will you?"

He laid the communication from the real-estate agents
on the desk, and hurried Hoppy out of the lobby before

the clerk could reassemble his wits for another attempt to delay him.

Again his car snaked through the traffic at the maximum speed that would still leave it immune from legal interference.

The Saint's hands were light and steady on the wheel, his keen tanned profile implacably calm against the passing street lights. And while he drove like a precision machine he thought about Monica. Monica drugged, her velvet voice incoherent, her enigmatic eyes blank, her proud body listless and helpless. . . . He thought of worse things than that; and a black coldness lanced through him with an aching intensity that froze his eyes as they stared ahead.

"I'm the dope, Hoppy," he said in a dead toneless level. "I should have known better than to think I could push her off the stage. . . . She put on that beggar woman's outfit again, of course. She went back to the Elliott Hotel. But on account of what Junior had spilled, she didn't last a minute. They were probably taking care of her last night while I was lying there wondering why they didn't do anything about me." His voice had a bitterness beyond emotion. "By this time they've given her a treatment and they know all the rest about me. Except where I am now. This is the showdown."

"Who'd'a t'ought it," Hoppy said amazedly. "Elliott— de old goat!"

Simon said nothing.

The house on Kelly Drive was as dark as the last time they had seen it, an unimaginative two-storey pile of brick with drawn blinds that made the windows look like sightless eyes.

Simon went to the back door, with Hoppy at his heels. Having picked the lock once before, he took a mere few seconds to open it again.

They stepped into darkness and silence broken only by the monotonous slow pulse of a dripping tap. This was the kitchen. On the other side of the room was the door at the head of the stairs that led down to the basement where initiations into the brotherhood of the beggars were performed. As Simon touched it, it gave way a fraction : it was not quite closed, but the darkness was blacker still beyond the slight opening. He stopped and listened again, and heard nothing. The darkness of the house had not seemed to indicate that there was a guard, but he was jumping to no rash conclusions.

He balanced the gun in his hand and pushed the door wider.

Then he heard it—a faint but clear rustle of movement that threw a momentary uncontrollable syncopation into his heart-beats and sent a flying column of eskimo beetles skirmishing up into his scalp. And with the rustle, a low, sleepy, inarticulate moan.

"What's dat?" breathed Mr. Uniatz hoarsely.

The Saint hardly bothered to whisper. After the first instant's shock, he understood the rustle and the moan so vividly that the needlessness of further stealth seemed to be established.

"That's Monica," he said, and went down the steps.

His pencil flashlight broke the darkness as he reached the bottom; and in the round splash where the beam struck, he saw her.

She lay on a canvas cot in one corner of the cellar. Her wrists were strapped to the side members. As he had expected, she was dressed in the grimy shapeless rags in which he had first met her; but most of the beggar-woman make-up had been roughly wiped from her face. Her eyes were closed, but as the light fell on them her eyelids lifted a little as if with an infinite effort.

"No," she mouthed huskily. "No. . . ."

"Monica," he said.

He checked the eagerness of his stride as he reached the cot, to come up to her gently.

"It's me," he said. "Simon. Simon Templar."

Her eyes sought for him as he touched her, and he could see the pin-point contraction of the pupils. He turned the flashlight on his own face, then back to her.

She knew him—the sound of his voice and the glimpse of him. Even through the mists of the drug he saw the awareness of him struggle into her mind, and saw the tiny smile that lighted her whole face for an instant. She tried to raise her head, and her lips formed his name: "Simon. . . ."

The effort was all she could make. Her head fell back and the lids closed over that shining look.

And then suddenly there was a blaze of lights that smashed away all shadows and wiped out the beam of his pencil light like a deluge would put out a match.

"Okay," said the saw-toothed voice of Frankie Weiss. "This is a tommy gun. Don't try anything, or I'll blast all three of you."

The Saint turned.

The stairs behind him had horizontal treads but no solid rises. Thus a man concealed behind them had a good vantage point. The unmistakable nozzle of a sub-machine-gun projected through one of the openings; and behind the Saint, Monica Varing lay directly in the line of fire.

"Drop your guns and reach," Frankie said.

Simon obeyed.

Hoppy said : "Boss——"

"No," said the Saint. "You haven't a chance. Do what Frankie tells you."

Hoppy's Betsy clattered ignominiously on the floor.

The gross bulk of Big Hazel Green came out from behind the stairs. She circled around them, kicked their guns out of reach, and searched them with competent hamlike hands. Then she stepped aside again, and Frankie Weiss moved out into the open.

There was a small dew of perspiration on his face, but the weapon he held was perfectly steady.

"How nice to see you, Frankie," Simon drawled. "You're looking well, too. That work-out we had together must have done you good."

"You think you're smart, don't you?" Frankie bit out of the side of his mouth. "Well, when I get through giving *you* a work-out——"

"The same old dialogue," sighed the Saint. "I wish I could remember how many times I've heard that line. Frankie, you kill me."

"Maybe you're not kidding," Frankie sneered. "Sit down on the bed and keep your hands where I can see 'em."

The Saint sat down, and Monica Varing stirred again uneasily. He felt very calm and quiet now. The inward exultation that danger could always ignite in him had steadied down and chilled. He had a cold estimate of all their chances, an equally cold watchfulness for his own first opening, an arrogant confidence that when the time came he could do more than any other human being could do.

"I just want you to know," he said, "that if you've done anything to Monica Varing——"

"Don't be ridiculous, Mr. Templar," said a new voice from the top of the stairs. "We may have to kill Miss Varing, but I would never allow *that* sort of thing."

It was Mrs. Laura Wingate.

XV

The Saint watched her come down the stairs, while his brain struggled dizzily to recover its balance. It was fantastic, preposterous. In a story, of course, he would have guessed it long ago; but he had been thinking strictly in realities. This was unreal, and yet he was seeing it with his own eyes.

She was still the same fantastic figure out of a Helen Hokinson drawing. She protruded fore and aft, a plump, apparently brainless woman whose thoughts should have dealt with nothing more dangerous than planning theatre parties or buying Renoirs she couldn't appreciate. Her lower lip protruded a little; that was the only change.

She looked at the Saint, and he felt one small flicker of chill as their eyes met. The glaring light seemed to bleach all colour out of her eyes, and the ruthless ophidian coldness of the gaze in that powdered face was shocking.

"Good evening, Your Majesty," he said.

He started to stand up.

"Siddown!" Frankie barked; and the Saint raised his eyebrows as he subsided.

"Excuse me. It was just my old-world manners. I was always taught to stand up when a lady comes into the room—especially if she's a queen."

Hoppy said incredulously: "Ya mean *dat's* de King of de Beggars? Dat old bag?"

"Shut up," Frankie snarled.

"It doesn't matter what they say now," Mrs. Wingate said. "Hazel——"

Big Hazel nodded and went to a small side table. She pulled out a drawer and took out the materials for a hypodermic injection—a syringe, ampules, cotton, alcohol. She began to fit a needle on the glass barrel of the syringe, as efficiently as a trained nurse. Simon realised that she might once have been one.

"Do we get the treatment, too?" he asked.

Mrs. Wingate gave him a pale-eyed glance.

"Of course. There are several things I need to know immediately. I want to be sure you tell the truth."

"You want to know how many people I've talked to, is that it?"

"A good deal depends on that, Mr. Templar. I have made my arrangements to disappear if necessary. But I hope it will not be necessary yet—or ever."

"I see," Simon murmured. "If you can keep your secret safe by a few more murders—very wise of you, Mrs. Wingate. I should have remembered my chess better—it's the Queen that's the most dangerous piece in the game. Not the King."

"Chees," Hoppy said blankly. "A dame—de King of de Beggars. An' I t'ought——"

"That it was Elliott. Well, we had some reason to. We were looking for a man in the first place. That's exactly the false scent Mrs. Wingate meant to leave when she coined her title. You know, Hoppy, there was an Egyptian woman a long time ago who had herself crowned Pharoah. She even insisted on appearing in public with a beard on state occasions. Mrs. Wingate never went quite that far, but the disguise was good enough, anyhow. And then she made such good use of Stephen Elliott's property. The hotel, and this. She seems to specialise in that sort of operation—like giving me Sammy the Leg's house. I don't doubt that if anyone else gets hot on the trail, Elliott is the one who's going to have the explaining to do." He gazed at Mrs. Wingate thoughtfully. "Just between ourselves, and since it won't go any farther, Laura, I wouldn't mind betting now that Elliott isn't even in the racket at all."

A chilly smile lifted the corners of the woman's mouth.

"Just between ourselves—and since it won't go any farther, Mr. Templar—you'd win that bet."

Simon nodded and watched Big Hazel break the neck of an ampule and begin to fill the syringe.

"In the same vein," he said, "would it be inquisitive to ask what happens to us after I've told you that Lieutenant Kearney knows where we are and is on his way after us?"

Laura Wingate's fat face gave no visible response.

"An old bluff like that doesn't frighten me," she said. "Especially since I shall know the truth in a few minutes. But I'm glad to answer your question. As you may remember, we have a whisky bottle which you were kind enough to open for Big Hazel. I had meant to plant that in Sammy the Leg's house, to help fix the Cleve Friend killing on you. Now, Miss Varing's interference has made me change my plans. I shall use it somewhere else to prove that you killed your man Uniatz in a quarrel over some stolen jewels —I think I shall arrange for them to be stolen from me. Shortly afterwards you and Miss Varing will be found in your car, both shot with your gun, with a suitable farewell note which you will write while you are drugged—the victims of a sensational suicide pact. . . . Go ahead, Hazel."

The room felt colder to Simon Templar when she had ceased to speak. He lost then any compunctions he might have entertained before. Those bleached, cold eyes regarded him dispassionately as Big Hazel advanced on him with the syringe in one hand and an alcohol-sodden scrap of cotton in the other.

"Roll up your sleeve, Saint," Mrs. Wingate said. "Unless, of course, you would prefer Frankie to start shooting now. But I think common sense will tell you that this will be much the most painless way—for all of you."

It was paralysing to think that this was the same woman speaking whose verbal italics and vapid girlish giggle had once made him think of her a ludicrous caricature of a stock type.

Slowly Simon began to take off his coat. His deliberate calm of a short while ago had congealed to a glacial calculation. He had left a broad enough clue for Kearney; but he had no guarantee that it would click, or click in time. He knew with great clarity what he would have to do, and what split-second timing it would demand of him.

"Hoppy," he said, "I'm afraid we've made a few

mistakes. If you'd only kept up with your marksmanship—
like a busy bee . . . bee . . ."

Hoppy blinked.

"Yuh?"

The Saint resignedly began on his sleeve.

"Forget it. You can't hit the bull's-eye every time."

He finished rolling up the sleeve, and from a corner of
his eye he saw dawning comprehension break over Hoppy's
face.

Simon said: "An underground chamber and all the
props of violent melodrama. This calls for a last-minute
rescue by the Marines, Mrs. Wingate."

The woman flickered her icy glance at him.

"Put your arm out, Mr. Templar."

Simon sighed, and offered his brown left forearm to Big
Hazel. She dabbed the cotton on it, and grasped his wrist
with a wrestler's hand.

One quick glance assured him that Frankie's tommy
gun was almost obstructed by Big Hazel's huge frame;
after that he didn't look at it. He watched the approach
of the syringe that was all but engulfed in her giant paw;
and all his whipcord muscles were relaxed and waiting.

"Now, Hoppy," he said coolly.

There came a sound he recognised—the indescribable
noise, akin to *pthoo!* that marked the expulsion of a BB
shot from between Hoppy Uniatz's teeth. . . .

For weeks Hoppy had been improving in accuracy,
force, and the principles of oral ballistics. Had the interior
of his mouth been rifled like a gun-barrel, his aim might
have been bettered, but at this close range there was no
chance of a miss. The BB, impelled with velocity and
violence, completed the last touch of outrageous gro-
tesquerie by hitting Big Hazel Green in the left eye.

"Next to a custard pie," the Saint reflected, with some
irrepressibly cynical part of his mind that sat in judgment
with an eyebrow raised, "I couldn't think of an improve-
ment. Now   "

The balance of the situation tipped with dazzling suddenness. Big Hazel's instant reaction to the introduction of
a foreign particle into her optic apparatus was to bellow
like a wounded bull, let go the Saint's wrist, and clap her

free hand to the injured organ. But simultaneously, without even waiting for that release, the Saint's free right hand was moving.

If he had merely tried to seize Big Hazel, or to hit her on the jaw, the woman would probably have got away. But Simon Templar's arm flashed down with a speed that almost blurred the vision, and his hand closed with murderous suddenness over hers. And the hand it closed on was holding a hypodermic syringe of brittle glass.

The barrel of the syringe became instantly a non-cohesive assortment of razor-sharp fragments, slicing agonisingly deeper into Big Hazel's flesh as the Saint's merciless grip ground tighter. All of her faculties were concentrated, to the exclusion of every other thought, on the immediate, vital, and hysterical necessity of opening her hand before the fingers began falling off. And being thus occupied, she was in no condition to realise that the Saint's hand had also swung her around until she completely blocked Frankie's line of fire.

At the same moment, Mr. Uniatz moved with an agility that threw a surprising sidelight on his nickname. He dived for the nearest gun on the floor, and fired almost as his paw closed on it. The only sound Frankie Weiss made was a queer sort of choking cough as he went down; and the tommy gun never spoke at all. . . .

"All right," Kearney's voice said from the top of the stairs. "Break it up, or I'll let all of you have it."

Simon pushed Big Hazel away and smiled up at him.

"Good old Alvin," he said. "Never too late to take a bow."

XVI

Monica Varing turned her head upon the pillow, and her hair moved with it in a shining skein on the bare satin of her shoulder. The robe she wore swooped downward from there in a V so deep that Simon Templar, leaning on the high footboard of her hospital bed, was aware of not wholly inexplicable vertigo whenever his eyes wandered that way.

He sighed ostentatiously.

Monica smiled. Her voice was warm temptation.

"Is anything wrong? I thought all your problems were wound up nicely."

"They are—nearly all." He grinned rather wryly. "Kearney got a promotion, Elliott cleared his good name, Laura Wingate——" The blue darkened. "Laura Wingate held out a lot longer than I expected, but she's finally made a confession. Even Fingers Schultz." The grin came back. "It seems that a gunsel named Fingers Schultz was picked up in the street last night with tyre-marks all over him, apparently the victim of a hit-run driver; but I haven't asked Sammy the Leg what his car looks like."

Monica leaned forward, clasping her knees, and smiled at him dazzlingly. The Saint enjoyed his ensuing vertigo.

"Why all the deep sighs, then?"

"Because now we'll have hardly any excuse for seeing each other. How soon do you expect to get out of this joint?"

"By evening. It was nonsense bringing me in at all, but my manager insisted on a few days' rest. To-night I play Nora as usual."

"And after the show?"

"I was waiting to be asked. What were you thinking of?" The Saint smiled.

"Exactly the same thing as you," he said.

II

THE MASKED ANGEL

At this moment Simon Templar was not quite enjoying the thrill of a lifetime.

Relaxed as much as the immediate carpentry would permit in his ringside seat between Hoppy Uniatz and Patricia Holm, he blended the smoke of his own cigarette with the cigar-and-sweat aroma of the Manhattan Arena, and contemplated the dying moments of the semi-final bout with his sapphire eyes musing under lazily drooping lids. Never addicted to obtaining his thrills vicariously, the man who was better known to the world as "the Saint" would have found small cause for excitement even if he had been addicted to such sedentary pursuits. Being there anyhow, he slouched in easy grace, the clean-cut lines of his face etched in a bronze mask of sardonic detachment as he watched the two gladiators move about the ring with all the slashing speed of ballet dancers in leg-irons performing under water, and dedicated himself uncomplainingly to whatever entertainment the soiree of sock might provide.

In the great world outside there were uncountable characters who would have considered his presence there with no equanimity. Some of them, who in one way or another had participated in much shadier promotions than prize fights, would have considered it a personal injustice that anyone like Simon Templar should still be at large when so many of their best friends were not. Others, whose standard of righteousness was vouched for by at least a badge, would have moaned just as loudly that there was nothing basically unhappy about a policeman's lot except what the Saint might plant in it.

If Inspector Fernack, for instance, had seen him there, that bulldogged minion of the law would have pondered darkly. He would have sensed from long experience in previous encounters with this amazing modern buccaneer that the Saint could have no orthodox interest in such a dreary offering of Promoter Mike Grady's salon of swat. Of course the main bout between Torpedo Smith and the celebrated Masked Angel would probably be more interesting, but Simon Templar wasn't there just for the entertainment. That was something John Henry Fernack would never have believed.

And on this occasion, for instance, he would have been right.

Jeers swept in derisive breakers over the two Ferdinands in the ring without in the least disturbing the equilibrium of their mitt minuet. The massed feet of the cash customers began to stamp in metronomic disapproval, and Simon's chair jumped as the box-car brogans on his left added their pile-driving weight to the crashing cantata. Their owner's klaxon voice lifted in a laryngismal obligato, a brassy, belly-searching ululation with overtones reminiscent of the retching bellow of a poisoned water buffalo. This, the Saint recognised, was merely Hoppy Uniatz's rendition of a disgusted groan.

"Boss," Hoppy heaved, "dis is moider!" The narrow strip of wrinkles that passed for Hoppy's forehead were deep with scorn. "I oughta go up dere and t'row 'em outta de ring."

Hoppy's impulses were beautiful in their straightforward simplicity and homicidal honesty. The small globule of protoplasm that lurked within his rock-bound skull, serving the nominal function of a brain, piloted his anthropoidal body exclusively along paths of action, primitive and direct, unencumbered by any subtleties of thought or teleological considerations. The torture of cerebration he left entirely to the man to whose lucky star he hitched his wagon. For, to Hoppy, the Saint was not of this ordinary world; he was a Merlin who brought strange wonders to pass with godlike nonchalance, whose staggering schemes were engineered with supernatural ease to inevitable success through miracles of intellect which Hoppy followed in blind but contented obedience.

The Saint smiled at him tenderly.

"Relax, chum. This isn't the fight we came to see, any-way."

The dream with the spun-gold hair on Simon's right smiled.

"Never," admonished Patricia Holm, "look gift horses in the mouth."

"To corn a phrase," the Saint observed dryly.

"Huh?" Hoppy stared at the Saint's lady in open-mouthed perplexity. "Horses?" His face, which bore a strong family resemblance to those seen on totem poles designed to frighten evil spirits, was a study in loose-lipped wonder. "What horses?"

"After all," Pat said, "we're here as guests and——"

The clanking of the bell terminated both the fight and the need for further explanation. The sound pulled the trigger on a thunderclap of boos as the unfatigued gladi-ators were waved to their respective corners to wait the decision. It came swiftly. A well-booed draw.

"What a clambake," Hoppy muttered.

"No hits, no runs, no fight," Simon murmured sar-donically.

"They had a lot of respect for each other, hadn't they?" Pat observed innocently.

"Respect!" Hoppy exploded. "Dem bums was doggin' it. I could beat bot' deir brains out togedder wit' bot' hands tied behind me." He simmered with righteous out-rage. "I only hope de Masked Angel don't knock out Tor-pedo Smith *too* quick. We oughta let him stay for at least a coupla rounds so maybe we'll see *some* fightin'."

"If there's any fighting to be seen," Simon said absently, "at least we're in a good position to see it."

The chiselled leanness of cheekbone and jaw were picked out vividly as he lighted a cigarette. Pat, glancing at the flame momentarily reflected in those mocking blue eyes, felt a familiar surge of yearning and pride. For he was a very reincarnation of those privateers who once knew the Spanish Main, a modern buccaneer consecrated to the gods of gay and perilous adventure, a cavalier as variable as a chameleon, who would always be at once the surest and the most elusive thing in her life.

"Yeah," Hoppy agreed grudgingly. "Dey ain't nut'n

wrong wit' de seats. Ya must have some drag wit' de promoter, boss."

"I've never even met him."

Simon wasn't listening really. His eyes were angled to his left, gazing through a meditative plume of smoke to where Steve Nelson was rising about a dozen seats away and climbing into the ring to be introduced as the champion who would defend his title against the winner of to-night's bout. However, it wasn't Nelson whom Simon was watching. It was the girl in the seat beside Nelson—a girl with curly raven hair, big green eyes and a nose whose snub pertness was an infinitely lovelier reproduction of her Irish sire's well-publicised proboscis.

"I suppose he just thought this would be a nice way to introduce himself," Patricia mocked. "Three little ringside tickets, that's all. Sent by special messenger, no less. Compliments of Mike Grady and the Manhattan Arena!"

The girl with the raven hair had turned and, for a brief instant, met Simon's gaze. He spoke without taking his eyes off her.

"Pat, darling, you're taking too much for granted. It wasn't Mike who sent them."

"No?"

"No. It was his daughter Connie. Third from the aisle in the front row."

She followed his gaze.

There was no hint of coquetry in the eyes of the raven-haired girl. There was something in them quite different— a swift glow of gratitude tempered by an anxiety that shadowed her clear elfin beauty. Then she turned away.

Pat smiled with feline sweetness.

"I see. How nice of her to think you might need some excitement!"

Hoppy's porcine eyes blinked.

"Boss, ain't she de Champ's girl friend?"

"So I've heard." Simon smiled and blew a large smoke-ring that rose lethargically over the seat in front of him and settled about the bald pate of its occupant like a pale blue halo.

A scattered burst of cheering greeted Torpedo Smith's entrance into the ring.

"Shouldn't you be more careful about picking your leading ladies?" Pat inquired with saccharine concern.

"I have to face the hazards of my profession," Simon explained, with a glint of scapegrace mockery in his blue eyes. "But there may be some excitement at that—although I don't mean what *you're* thinking, darling."

The memory of Connie's visit, her confused plea for him to see the fight, lingered in his mind like the memory of strange music, a siren measure awakening an old familiar chill, prescient and instinctive, warning of danger that was no less perilous because it was as yet unknown.

The crowd broke into a thunderous roar.

"It's de Angel!" Hoppy proclaimed. "He's climbin' in de ring!"

The current sensation of the leather-pushing profession was indeed mounting the punch podium. He squeezed his hogshead torso between the ropes; and as he straightened up the Saint saw that the mask was really nothing more than a black bean-bag that fitted over his small potato head with apertures for eyes, nose, and mouth, and fastened by a drawstring between chin and shoulder at the place where a normal person's neck would ordinarily be, but which in the Angel was no more than an imaginary line of demarcation. He shambled to his corner like a hairless gorilla and clasped his bandaged hands over his head in a salute to the enraptured mob.

Patricia shuddered.

"Simon, is it—is it human?"

The Saint grinned.

"He'll never win any contests for the body beautiful, but of course we haven't seen his face yet. He may be quite handsome."

"Dere ain't *nobody* seen his face," Hoppy confided. "Dese wrestlers what pull dis gag wit' de mask on de face, dey don't care who knows who dey really are, but Doc Spangler, he don't let nobody see who his boy is. May be it's for luck. De Masked Angel ain't lost a fight yet!"

"Doc Spangler?"

Hoppy's head bobbed affirmatively. He pointed to a well-dressed portly gentleman who looked more like a bank president out for an evening's entertainment than a fighter's manager, who was standing in smiling conversation with one of the Angel's seconds.

"Dat's de Doc. He's de guy who discovers de Angel from some place. Dat Doc is sure a smart cookie, boss."

The Saint smiled agreeably.

"You can say that again."

The salient features of the estimable Doc Spangler's history passed through Simon Templar's mind in swift procession—a record which, among many others, was filed with inexorable clarity in the infinite index of a memory whose indelibility had time and again proven one of the more useful tools of his profession.

"In fifteen fights," Hoppy expounded, "he brings de Angel from nowhere to a fight wit' de Champ t'ree weeks from now!"

Pat lifted an eyebrow.

"Even if Torpedo Smith beats him?"

"Aaah!" Hoppy chortled derisively. "Dat bum ain't got a chanst! De Angel'll moider him! You wait and see."

The Champ, having shaken hands with the two contenders, climbed out of the ring and resumed his seat beside Connie Grady, and the fighters rose from their corners as the referee waved them to the centre of the ring for instructions.

Pat, wide-eyed, shook her head unbelievingly.

"Simon, that man with the mask—he—he's fantastic! Those arms—his gloves are touching his knees!"

"A fascinating example of evolution in reverse," Simon remarked.

The Masked Angel was indeed a remarkable specimen. With his arms dangling alongside his enormous hairless body he was the very antithesis of the classic conception of an athlete, his sagging breasts and vast pink belly undulating in rolls, billows, and pleats of fat; and though his hips narrowed, wasp-like, to the negligible proportions of a bull gorilla's, his flabby thighs ballooned out like a pair of mammoth loose-skinned sausages, tapering to a pair of stubby tree-trunk legs.

"A freak," Pat decided. "He wears that ridiculous mask because he's a pinhead."

"But even he can do somebody some good. You've got

to admit that he makes Hoppy look like a creature of svelte and sprightly beauty."

"In dis racket, boss," Hoppy mulled with a heavy concentration of wisdom, "you don't have to be good-lookin'." Suddenly he sat up straight and strained forward. "Well, for cryin' out loud!"

"What's the matter?" The Saint followed his gaze to the ring.

Hoppy waved a finger the size of a knockwurst in the general direction of the two contestants and their handlers standing in the middle of the ring listening to the referee.

"Lookit, boss! Standin' behind Torpedo Smith—his handler! It's me old chum, Whitey Mullins!"

The fighters and their seconds were turning back to their respective corners. Whitey Mullins, a slender, rubbery-faced little man with balding flaxen hair, wearing a turtle-necked sweater and sneakers, convoyed Smith to his corner and climbed out of the ring, taking the stool with him. The Saint recognised him as one of the professional seconds connected with the Manhattan Arena.

"One of the Torpedo's propellers, I take it?"

Hoppy nodded.

"He works a lot wit' me when I am in the box-fight racket, boss." Fond memories of yesteryear's mayhem lit his gorgon countenance with reminiscent rapture. "Cyclone Uniatz, dey called me."

"That, no doubt, explains why you never get up before the stroke of ten," Simon observed.

"Huh?"

Pat giggled as the bell clanked for the first round.

The Angel shuffled forward slowly, his arms held high, peering cautiously between his gloves at the oncoming Torpedo Smith. Smith, who had crashed into the top ranks of pugilism via a string of varied victories far longer than the unbroken string of knockouts boasted by the Masked Angel, moved warily about his opponent, jabbing tentative lefts at the unmoving barrier of arms that the Angel held before him. The Angel turned slowly as Smith moved around him, the fantastic black cupola of his masked head sunk protectively between beefy pink shoulders, the little eye-slits peering watchfully. He kept turning, keeping

Smith before him without attempting a blow. The Torpedo moved about more deliberately, with a certain puzzlement, as though he couldn't understand the Angel's unwillingness to retaliate, but was himself afraid to take any chances.

There was a stillness in the crowd, a sense of waiting as for the explosion of a bomb whose fuse was burning before their very eyes.

Pat spoke at last.

"But, Simon, they're just looking at each other."

The Saint selected another cigarette and tapped it on his thumb.

"You can't blame them. It'll probably take a round for them just to get over the sight of each other."

Hoppy lifted a voice that rang with the dulcet music of a foghorn with laryngitis.

"Come on, you Angel! Massecrate de bum!"

But the Angel, without supreme indifference to encouragement, merely kept turning, shuffling around to meet the probing jabs of Torpedo Smith, peering through his sinister mask, tautly watchful.

The crowd broke into a roar as the Torpedo suddenly drove a left hook to the Angel's stomach, doubling him up, and, casting caution to the winds, followed with a swift onslaught of lefts and rights. The Angel, arms, gloves, and elbows shielding his exposed surfaces, merely backed into a corner and crouched there until the bell punctuated the round.

Pat shook her head bewilderedly.

"Simon, I don't understand. This Masked Angel doesn't look as if he can fight at all. All he did was make like a turtle while that other man tried to find some place to hit him."

"Oh, you just wait," Hoppy growled reassuringly. "Dis fight ain't over yet. De smart money is bettin' t'ree to one de Angel kayoes Smith insida six rounds. He wins *all* his fights by kayoes."

The Saint was watching the two gladiators being given the customary libations of water and between-round advice by their handlers. He smiled thoughtfully.

"The Masked Angel has a very clever manager."

The bell for the second round brought Torpedo Smith out with a rush. Gaining confidence with every blow, he drove the quivering hulk of the Angel back on his heels, bringing the crowd to its feet in a steady roar of excitement.

"Hoppy," the Saint spoke into Hoppy's ear, "has the Angel ever been cut under that black stocking he wears over his head?"

"Huh? Naw, boss! His fights never last long enough for him to get hoit." Hoppy's eyes squinted anxiously. "Chees! Why don't he do sump'n? Torpedo Smith is givin' him de woiks!"

Pat was bouncing in her seat, the soft curve of her lips parted with excitement as she watched.

"I thought the Angel was so wonderful," she gibed. "Come on, Torpedo!"

"Dey're bot' on de ropes!" Hoppy exclaimed hoarsely.

The Saint's hawk-sharp eyes suddenly narrowed. No, it was Torpedo Smith who was on the ropes now. With the Angel in control! . . . Something had happened. Something he hadn't seen. He gripped Hoppy's arm.

"Something's wrong with Smith."

Something was very definitely wrong with Torpedo Smith. He stood shaking his head desperately as if to clear it, holding on to the top strand with one hand and with the other trying to push away the black-masked monster who was now opening up with the steady, relentless power of a pile-driver.

"De Angel musta hit him!" Hoppy yelled. "I told ya, didn't I? I told ya!" His foghorn bellow rose over the mob's fierce blood cry. "Smith's down!"

Torpedo Smith, obviously helpless, had slumped beneath the repeated impact of the Angel's deliberate blows and now lay where he had fallen, face down, motionless, as the referee tolled him out.

The sea of humanity began ebbing like a tide towards the exits, the vast drone of their voices and shuffling feet covered by the reverberating recessional of a pipe-organ striking up "Anchors Aweigh" from somewhere in the bowels of the coliseum.

"Well, ya see, boss?" Hoppy jubilated as they drifted

into the aisle. "It's just like I told ya. De Angel's dynamite!"

Pat shook her golden head compassionately.

"That poor fellow—the way that horrible creature hit him when he was helpless! Why didn't the referee stop it?"

She turned, suddenly aware that Simon was no longer behind her. She looked about bewilderingly. "Simon!"

"Dere he is!" Hoppy waved a hamlike hand towards the end of the row they had just left. "Boss!"

The Saint was standing there, the occupants of the first rows of the ringside eddying past him, watching the efforts of Whitey Mullins and his assistants to revive the slumbering Smith.

Hoppy breasted the current with the irresistible surge of a battleship, and returned to Simon's side with Pat in his wake.

" 'S matter, boss?"

"What is it, Simon?"

The Saint glanced at her and back at the ring. He took a final pull at his cigarette, and dropped it to crush it carefully with one foot.

"They've just called the Boxing Commission doctor into Smith's corner," he said.

Pat stared at the ring.

"Is he still unconscious?"

"Aw, dat's nuttin'." Hoppy dismissed Smith's narcosis with a scornful lift of his anthropogenous jaw. "I slug a guy oncet who is out for twelve hours, an' when dey——"

"Wait a minute," the Saint interrupted, and moved towards Smith's corner as Whitey Mullins leaped from the ring to the floor.

"Whitey!" Hoppy bellowed joyfully. "Whassamatter, chum? Can't ya wake up dat sleeping beauty?"

Whitey glanced at him with no recognition, his wide, flexible mouth contorted curiously.

Hoppy blinked.

"Whitey! Whassamatter?"

Pat glanced at the ring with quick concern.

"Is Smith hurt badly?"

The tow-headed little man with the lean limber face stared at her a moment with twisting lips. When he spoke his high-pitched Brooklyn accent was muted with tragedy.

"He's dead," he said, and turned away.

The spectral cymbals of grim adventure clashed an eerie tocsin within the Saint, louder now than when first he heard their faint far notes in Connie Grady's flustered appeal for him to search the sinister riddle of the Angel's victories, and save her fiancé from unknown peril. They had rung in the nebulous confusion of her plea, in the tortured suspicions unvoiced within her haunted eyes. . . . Now he heard their swelling beat again, a phantom reprise that prickled his skin with ghostly chills.

He spoke softly into Pat's ear.

"Darling, I just remembered. Hoppy and I have some vitally urgent business to attend to immediately. Do you mind going home alone—at once?"

Patricia Holm looked up sharply, the startled pique on her lovely face giving way so swiftly to disquieted resignation. She knew him too well.

"What is it, Simon? What are you up to?"

"I'll explain later. I'm already late. Be a good girl." He kissed her lightly. "I'll make it up to you," he said, and left her gazing after him as he sauntered down the long concrete ramp leading to the fighters' dressing-rooms with Hoppy shambling in his wake like a happy bear.

II

The door of the number one dressing-room beneath the floor of the Manhattan Arena rattled and shook as the sportswriters milled about the corridor outside and protested their exclusion. Who, one of them shouted, did the big ham think he was, Greta Garbo?

Behind the locked door Kurt Spangler rubbed his shining bald head and listened benignly to the disgruntled din.

"Maybe I should oughta give 'em an interview, huh, Doc?" The pink mountain of flesh lying on the rubbing table lifted a head the general size and shape of a runt egg-plant. "I don't want they should think I'm a louse."

The un-Masked Angel blinked, his little brown eyes apologetic beneath the shadow of brows ridged with the compounded scar tissues of countless ancient cuts and contusions.

"Never mind what they think," Doc Spangler beamed comfortingly. "Let them disparage you—revile you—hate you." His sonorous voice sank confidingly. "It's exactly what we want."

The Angel sighed unhappily. His head dropped back on the rubbing table as the two handlers pulled off the gloves, tossed them in a corner, and proceeded to rip off the hand wrappings of gauze and tape.

"The more the newspapers hate you," Doc Spangler expounded, "the more cash they'll pay to see you get beaten." He rubbed his hands, considering the Angel with all the pride a farmer might display surveying his prize hog. "Kid McCoy, for instance," the doctor illustrated. "He made a fortune on the hatred of the mob. They paid to see him fight in the hope he would be slaughtered. Only he never was—not till after he became champion, anyway. And neither will you be, my lad. Not as long as you continue to follow my instructions."

The Angel grunted as Karl, one of his handlers, kneaded the mountainous mesa of his belly. His naked body, a pink mass of monstrous convexities, gleamed beneath the bright incandescents with a sheen of oily sweat that high-lighted the ruby splotches where Torpedo Smith's gloves had exploded. His flat button nose, the distorted rosette of flesh that were his ears, furnished further evidence that Dr. Spangler's discovery, far from being a supernova in the pugilistic firmament, was actually a battle-battered veteran, the survivor of an unnumbered multitude of beatings.

"I did like you said wit' Smith, didn't I, Doc?" the Angel mumbled.

"You did indeed! You followed my instructions to the letter to-night. Always remember to keep covered till your man seems a bit careless." Spangler patted one beefy shoulder. "You were great to-night, my boy."

The Angel lifted his undersized noggin, a grateful grimace on his pear-shaped face.

"Thanks, Doc." He sank back. "I always try to do like you say." He sighed like a deflating dirigible. "But why do the crowd gotta t'ink I'm a crum? I radder they should like me. I like *them*."

Doc Spangler sighed patiently, but was spared the need

for further exposition by an increased burst of banging on the door. He turned resignedly to the fox-faced thug who was unlacing the Angel's ring shoes.

"Maxie, perhaps you'd better go out and have a word with our journalistic friends."

Maxie nodded briefly. He went to the door, yanked it open, and stepped outside into a stream of vivid excoriation.

Doc Spangler listened a moment with admiration as the reporters' protests faded gradually down the hall.

Karl, the other henchman, had ceased his ministrations and was listening with a certain degree of envy. "Doc," he suggested, "maybe better I should go and help chase 'em away, yah?" His accent was a curious blend of Yorkville kraut and Bowery bum.

Doc Spangler smiled, glancing at the half-open door. Only Maxie's distant profanities were still audible, and that, too, finally ceased.

"I think Maxie has everything under control," Spangler said pleasantly. "Better finish taking off the Angel's shoes so he can take his shower and get dressed. We've got to have some supper."

The Angel heaved up to a sitting position.

"I'm hungry," he announced heavily. "I wanna double porterhouse and shoestring potaters."

Spangler's colourless eyes flitted tenderly over the Angel's three-storied bay window.

"You'll have a triple filet mignon with truffles à la Waldorf Astoria three times a day if we can win the title."

The Angel grinned dully.

"Leave it to me, Doc. I'll take Nelson."

"Of course you will—if you'll always remember to do exactly as I tell you. It was only by obeying my instructions that you got through that first round to-night—and don't forget it. *I* won that fight for you, my lad."

"Congratulations," said the Saint.

"Yeah," Hoppy rasped, kicking the door shut behind them. "Nice woik, Doc."

For a paralysed second, Dr. Spangler, Karl, and the massive Angel composed a tableau of staring surprise.

Then Spangler's florid wattles grew even more crimson.

"Who the devil——"

"Forgive us," the Saint interrupted. He took the cigarette from his mouth and flicked the ash reflectively, indicating Mr. Uniatz, who stood beside him with the black snout of a big automatic protruding from one hairy fist. "My friend and I couldn't resist the temptation, Doctor—especially when your man left the door to pursue those reporters down the hall." He forbore to add that Maxie was, at the moment, reposing peacefully in a corridor broom closet where Hoppy had stuffed him after an exceedingly brief encounter. "Put away the gun, Hoppy," he reproved. "This is strictly social."

Hoppy obeyed slowly. He was staring at the naked mass of the Angel as if what mental equipment he possessed failed utterly to accept the evidence of his eyes.

"Ged oudda here," Karl grated tonelessly.

His voice, like his bushy-browed eyes, was flat, dull, and deadly. The Saint appraised him with a glance—a short, squat, powerfully constructed character whose prognathous jaw matched the cubist lines of his shoulders.

"For de luvva mike!" Incredulous amazement raised Hoppy's bullfrog bass a full octave. Rapturous recognition slowly illumined his corrugated countenance like dawning sunlight on a rock pile. "Bilinski!" he shouted. "Barrel-house Bilinski!"

The Angel, who had been favouring Hoppy with the same open-mouthed concentration, slid slowly off the edge of the table to his feet. A reciprocal light dawned on the fuzzy horizon of his memory and spread over his humpty-dumpty face in a widening grin.

"For crize sake! Hoppy Uniatz!"

They practically fell into each other's arms.

"Well, well, well," the Saint drawled. "Old Home Week. Perhaps you two would like to be alone?"

"Are *you* de Masked Angel?" Hoppy burbled with hoarse delight. "*You?*"

"Yea, sure, Hoppy, dat's me!"

"Boss, dis is Barrelhouse Bilinski. Barrelhouse, meet de Saint!"

"Ged oudda here!"

Karl's voice rose half a decibel, his right hand sliding toward a pocket.

"I wouldn't if I were you, comrade." The Saint smiled deprecatingly, a glint in his eyes like summer lightning in a blue sky. His hand was thrust negligently in a pocket of his beautifully tailored sports jacket. "I'd hate having to put a hole through this coat, but your navel is such a tempting target."

Karl's hand dropped to his side.

"Doc, this is me old chum from way back when!" The Angel turned to Spangler eagerly. "Hoppy Uniatz!"

"Delighted. . . . Now, Karl," Doc Spangler said reproachfully, "don't be a boor."

"Me and Barrelhouse useta beat each udder's brains out every week!" Hoppy effervesced hoarsely. "We barnstorm all over de country oncet. One week I win, next week he wins. What a team!

"I can imagine," the Saint murmured.

Spangler smiled at Simon with revived benevolence.

"I might have known who you were, Mr. Templar, but you rather caught me by surprise, you know. I hardly expected a visit from the Saint at this particular moment."

"The pleasure," Simon bowed, "is all mine."

"Not at all, my dear fellow. I—er—I've rather expected this visit—at some time or another, knowing of your parasitic propensities."

The Saint lifted an eyebrow.

"Parasitic?"

Dr. Spangler chuckled.

"Forgive me. I was merely referring to your habit of living on other people's enterprises."

"Meaning, no doubt, that you think I've come for a cut of your take in the Masked Angel—is that it?"

Spangler shrugged deprecatingly.

"What else?"

"Doc, whassa matter, huh?" the Angel queried with a puzzled grin which exposed several broken teeth. "What's he want?"

"Take it easy, Barrelhouse," Hoppy rumbled. "Dis is strictly social."

The Saint laughed.

"You're wrong, Doctor."

"Am I?" Spangler said. "I've always known that at some unexpected point in the strange geometry of providence our paths must surely cross some day. We have much in common, Templar. We would work well together."

Mockery danced in Simon's azure eyes.

"You must be psychic, Doctor, to have recognised me so quickly. I can't recall our ever having met before."

"True," Spangler nodded graciously. "However, your face has appeared in the public prints on several occasions I can recall."

"And so has yours," said the Saint reminiscently— "generally tacked on post-office walls beneath the word 'Wanted.' "

Spangler chuckled.

"You amuse me."

The light in Simon's eyes settled into two steely points.

"Then laugh *this* off. Torpedo Smith is dead."

The startled sag of the fat man's jaw was too sincere a reflex for simulation. His stare shifted uncertainly to Karl standing beside him.

"Vot der hell!" Karl's beetling black brows matched his sneering snarl. "You tryink to scare somebody, hah?"

The Angel scratched his jaw bewilderedly, the whole unlovely mass of his gross nakedness quivering like jelly as he turned to his manager.

"Dead?" he muttered stupidly. "He's dead?"

Hoppy nodded admiringly.

"He won't never be no deader. Whereja ever get dat punch, chum? Why, when we was togedder, you stunk."

"My dear sir," Spangler said, eyeing the Saint with watchful deliberation, "if this is an attempt at humour——"

"You needn't laugh now," Simon assured him pleasantly. "Save it for later—when the police get here. They should be in at any moment."

The Angel licked his lips tremulously.

"Jeez, Doc . . . I croaked him. I croaked de Torpedo. . . ."

"He's lying!" Karl sneered. "Smith cannot be dead!"

"Listen." The Saint glanced at the door. "I think I hear them now."

They followed his gaze, listening.

And while they stood intently frozen, the Saint sauntered quite casually to the corner where Karl and Maxie had tossed the Angel's gloves, and scooped them up in one sweeping motion.

Dr. Spangler turned quickly.

"What are you doing? Put down those gloves!" Alarmed suspicion darkened his colourless eyes. "Karl! Angel!"

His voice broke shrilly.

Bilinski went into motion uncertainly, as if still wondering what he was called on to do; but with a playful push as gentle as the thrust of a locomotive piston, Hoppy shoved him back to a sitting position on the edge of the rubbing table.

"Aw, don't mind him, Barrelhouse," he grinned. "He's just noivous."

He stuck out a foot to trip Karl who, gun in hand, was diving for cover behind the table.

The Saint moved with the effortless speed of lubricated lightning, kicking the gun from the sprawling thug's hand with all the vicious grace of a *savate* champ.

"Whassamatter?" the Angel blinked bewilderedly. "Doc——"

Karl struggled to all fours. It was a strategic error; for he presented, for one irresistible moment, his rear end to Mr. Uniatz's ecstatic toe in an explosive junction that flung him end over end into the shower stall across the room.

"Help!" Spangler shouted. "Max! Max! Hel——"

His cry broke in a gasping grunt as the Saint's fist buried itself a good six inches in his paunch, collapsing him to the floor like a deflated blimp.

"Nice woik, boss," Hoppy congratulated.

"Hey's what's the big idea?" the Angel demanded, his confusion crystallising into a fuzzy awareness that the isotope of friendship had somehow exploded.

He struggled off the edge of the rubbing table.

"Aw, relax, ya fat slob!" Hoppy recommended affectionately. He clarified his suggestion with a shove that had all the delicate tact of an impatient rhinoceros slamming full tilt into a bull elephant; and the Angel, unbalanced, staggered backwards, knocking over the rubbing table and going down with it in a cosmic crash.

"All right, Hoppy," Simon called from the door as he removed the key. "Don't let's wear out our welcome."

He handed the gloves to Hoppy as they stepped out into the corridor and locked the door behind them. As they turned to leave, other gruff voices echoed faintly through the corridor leading from the end of the ramp; and the Saint's white teeth flashed in a satiric grin as he recognised the terse tonalities of the Law.

"The other way, Hoppy," he said, and turned in the opposite direction.

They sped swiftly through the underground maze toward the basement exits that opened into the street at the other end.

III

Hoppy Uniatz eased the big convertible adroitly through the midnight traffic and past the bright lights of the Times Square district; and presently gave vent to a cosmic complaint.

"Boss," he announced with the wistful appeal of an arid hippopotamus being driven past a water hole, "I gotta t'oist. Exercise always gives me a t'oist, boss."

"Keep going," the Saint commanded inexorably. His long brown fingers were carefully probing the gloves on his lap. "You can refresh yourself after we get home."

Hoppy sighed and trod on the accelerator again.

"Anyt'ing in dem gloves, boss?"

"I can't feel anything."

Simon lifted a glove and sniffed it thoughtfully. He rubbed his finger over the damp leather and tasted it.

"Barrelhouse musta loined how to speed up his punch," Hoppy ruminated. "De fat slob always can hit like a mule, but he never is able to land it much when I know him. Ho's too slow." Hoppy shook his head in perplexity. "Imagine *him* bein' de Masked Angel! Doc Spangler musta teached him plenty."

"I wonder," said the Saint.

But, whatever the secret of the Angel's success, Simon

was certain now that it didn't lie in his gloves. There was nothing wrong with them that he could determine. No weights in the padding, no chemicals impregnated in the leather. He'd seen enough of Bilinski's hand wraps to determine that there had been no illegal substance compounded therein. And yet the practically over-night transformation of a battered dull-witted hulk into an invincible gladiator with lethal lightning in his fists was too obvious a discord in the harmony of logic.

The action of that fatal second round leading up to Torpedo Smith's collapse passed through the Saint's memory again slowed down to a measured succession of mental images.

"Hoppy," the Saint reflected, "did you see that first blow which started the Torpedo on his way out?"

"Sure, boss." Hoppy nodded positively. "Barrelhouse catches him in de ropes."

"Did he hit him with a right or a left?"

"He hits him wit' both hands—lotsa times. *You* seen it."

The Saint said: "I know. But I mean that very first punch—the one that dazed Smith and laid him open for other blows. Did you see that particular punch?"

"Sure I see it, boss. We bot' see it."

Hoppy yanked the car around a final corner and slid it to a halt in front of a canopy that stretched from the Gothic doorway of a skyscraper apartment building to the kerb.

"If you remember it so well," Simon pursued patiently, "what was it—a right or a left?"

"Why, it wuz a right, a—no, it wuz a left. A hook. Or maybe——" Hoppy hesitated, his vestigial brows furrowing painfully. "Maybe it wuz an uppercut dere against the ropes. He is t'rowin' so many punches, I wouldn't know."

"That's what I thought."

The memory of Connie Grady's enigmatic anxiety and her confused half-explained fears for Steve Nelson's life rose in swelling reprise, cued in with the discord of to-night's events like the opening movement of a concerto that gave promise of more—much more—to come.

Simon got out, the gloves dangling from his hand by

their laces, entered the lobby of the building with Hoppy at his heels, and headed for the elevators.

"Maybe we oughta send out for sump'n to drink, huh, boss?" Hoppy suggested.

The Saint glanced at him. "Send *who*?"

Hoppy glanced around, becoming aware that the lobby was deserted, the desk man and lift operators off duty.

"It's after midnight, chum," the Saint pointed out as they entered the automatic elevator. He pressed the button marked *Penthouse*. The doors closed softly and the elevator purred skyward. "Besides," the Saint added as an afterthought, "I believe there's half a bottle of bourbon left."

Mr. Uniatz looked at him gloomily. "Yeah, boss, I know. Half a bottle—and me wit' a t'oist!"

"Mix it with a little water and make it go further," Simon suggested hopefully.

"Water?" Hoppy stared incredulously. "De stuff what you wash wit'?"

The Saint smiled absently, thinking of other things.

"You're definitely no child of Aquarius, Hoppy!"

Hoppy blinked with mild stupefaction, pondered a moment and gave up.

"No, I guess not," he sighed. "I wuz de child of Mr. an' Mrs. Uniatz."

The elevator stopped and they stepped out.

"I meant the sign you were born under." Simon unlocked the door and entered the apartment. "From the way you drink, you must have been born under Pisces."

Hoppy's eyes widened in wonder at this hitherto unimagined vista of biological phenomena.

"Who, me? How did dat happen?"

The Saint shrugged, tossing the gloves on the living-room divan as he turned on lights.

"I don't know," said the Saint. "It must have been shady there."

He flung himself down on the divan and stretched his long legs luxuriously, while Hoppy struggled briefly with his Delphic observation and then discarded the entire subject as the bottle on the sideboard caught his eye.

"Keerist!" he muttered. "Me tongue's hangin' out."

He made a bee-line for the half-bottle of Kentucky dew,

throttling it with an enormous hairy paw as he lifted it to his mouth, back-tilted like the maw of a baying wolf. His Adam's apple plunged in convulsive rhythm as the contents lowered an inch a second, a full four seconds elapsing before he straightened his neck again, halted in mid-swallow by the pop of a cork.

The Saint had a fresh bottle of Old Forester on his lap and was reaching for a glass from the top of a cabinet by the divan.

Hoppy's mouth pursed in hurt reproach.

"So *dat's* why it's locked," he deduced aggrievedly.

"And a good thing too," the Saint said.

He recorked the bottle, gathered the Angel's gloves on his lap, and savoured the drink with sybaritic enjoyment. Then he proceeded to re-examine the gloves; not that he expected them to yield any more secrets, but he had to be quite sure.

"Ja figure de mitts is loaded, boss?" Hoppy picked up one of the gloves. "Is dat why you want 'em?"

Simon considered him.

"Did you work that out all by yourself?"

He tossed the remaining glove aside and picked up his glass again. Hoppy took the glove he had thrown down and felt that one too.

"Ain't nut'n de matter wit' dese gloves, boss."

The telephone rang.

It was Pat, her voice a stiletto in a silken sheath.

"Simon dear, it isn't that I mind being abandoned like a sinking ship——"

"Darling," said the Saint, "I've never been called a rat more delicately. However——"

"However," she interrupted determinedly, "you could at least have phoned me as soon as you got home. I've been sitting here expecting a call every minute. What happened? Where did you go? I waited at the Arena until the cleaning people nearly swept me out."

"Good lord! I told you to go on home."

"I know, but after you disappeared down that ramp I figured you to come up again. You never did."

"Darling——"

"Don't darling me. After the police went down and

down and never came up again either, I went out to find your car, and that was gone, too."

"You poor baffled child," he commiserated tenderly. "Hoppy and I took it. There was another exit. Several, in fact——"

"I happen to have figured that out quite some time ago," she said sweetly. "What happened? What was that shouting and crashing going on down there?"

"Oh, that," the Saint murmured. "Doc Spangler lost his key, so I suppose the police had to break down the door."

"Lost his key! What key?"

"The key I have in my pocket."

"B—But——" She broke off. "Simon, if you're going to be coy——"

"Not at all. Come over for breakfast, and I'll try to give you a general idea what happened."

"And just what has your little colleen, Connie Grady, got to do with all this?"

"I haven't decided yet. We'll talk about it at breakfast."

"I'll be there," she said ominously. "And it had better be good."

"It will be. The freshest eggs, the crispest bacon, the best butter——"

"I don't mean that. Good night, Lothario."

Simon thoughtfully pulled off a shoe.

Hoppy Uniatz had disposed of the remains of his pint, and had taken advantage of the interruption to begin a strategic circling manœuvre towards the Saint's bottle. This was a more or less instinctive gravitation; his receding brow was grooved by a stream of excogitation that flowed with all the gusto of a glacier towards its terminal moraine.

"Boss," Hoppy ruminated, "I got an idea."

The Saint kicked off the other shoe.

"Be kind to it, Hoppy," he yawned; "it's in a strange place."

But Hoppy, lost in contemplation of a glorious to-morrow evolving from the stuff of his dreams, went on unheeding.

"Dis fat slob, Bilinski, who is de Masked Angel. He beats the Champ. Dat makes *him* de Champ, don't it?"

The Saint eyed him curiously. "He hasn't beaten him yet."

"But if Barrelhouse Bilinski gets de crown," Hoppy continued with growing inspiration, "dey is one guy who can take it away from him. Dey is one guy who can knock him on his can any day in de week. Dat's me, boss! If dat fat slob gets de champeenship, I'm de guy what can take it away from him. Den I'll be de champ and you'll be my manager!"

The telephone rang again.

"Excuse me," said the Saint. "My bottle seems to be moving towards your hand."

He rescued it in the nick of time, and picked up the phone.

He recognised at once the soft, husky lilt of the voice.

"I—I do hope you'll forgive my calling you at this hour," Constance Grady apologised hurriedly. "I called several times after I—I thought you might have gotten home, but there was no answer."

"I just got in," Simon explained. "I didn't have a chance to call you right after the fight as I'd promised, and I thought it was rather late to phone you now. But," he added quickly, "I'm glad you called. Thanks for the tickets."

"Thank you for using them." She hesitated, her voice dropping almost to a whisper. "You—you saw what happened. . . ."

"Yes. Very interesting."

A slight pause.

"Daddy——" she began, and stopped. "My father came home a few minutes ago. He's very upset. I—I made an excuse that I had to go on to an all-night drug store on the corner to get some aspirin. I'm talking to you from there."

"I see." The Saint's voice was speculative. "Naturally, he would be upset by to-night's accident."

"Accident? . . . Yes, I know." She hesitated again. "There was something else—something about you and that—that man you call Hoppy——"

"Oh?"

"You went into the Masked Angel's dressing-room after the fight. Daddy said there was a brawl."

"I wouldn't say that," Simon said gravely. "One of Dr. Spangler's assistants happened to trip on one of Hoppy's big feet and knock himself out. The Angel fell over a table, causing Dr. Spangler to get the wind knocked out of him."

"But . . . You—didn't go down to see this—Masked Angel because you saw something—something wrong?"

"Wrong? No, Connie, if you mean fouling or anything like that, I didn't see a thing. By the way, it seems the Masked Angel is one of Hoppy's old chums."

"Oh."

"What makes you think there was anything wrong?"

"I—I don't know. I'm—I'm just afraid." Her answer was just as vague now as it had been the first time. "I thought you might have been able to—to see something, or—or figure something out. I——"

"Why not drop in for breakfast and we'll talk it over?"

"All right." She seemed reluctant to finish, and yet unable to find an excuse to go on. "And thanks again."

The Saint poured himself another drink, and surrendered the bottle.

"Who was dat, boss?" Hoppy asked.

"A lady," Simon replied, "who is holding out on me."

"You can't trust 'em, boss," Hoppy affirmed, shaking his head. "None of 'em. I know a doll once." He sighed, shaking his head like a wistful grizzly. "She has coives like a—a——"

"A scenic railway?" Simon suggested.

Hoppy beamed.

"Dat wuz Fanny, boss! All over! I can see her now." He sighed with stentorian nostalgia. "She was de goil of my dreams!"

The Saint yawned and turned to the bedroom.

"Then let's go see her there," he said.

The doorbell rang a sudden prolonged pizzicato.

Simon halted in his tracks. Ghostly caterpillars crawled along his backbone. Instinct, sensitive and prescient, had whispered its warning of further explosions in the chain reaction he had started that night; the clamour of the bell came as if on a long-awaited cue. A faint smile flitted over his reckless mouth.

"Who da hell is dat dis time of night?" Hoppy wondered.

"Open the door and find out," Simon told him.

Mr. Uniatz slipped a meaty hand into his gun-pocket and strode out into the foyer to the doorway.

The Saint heard the door open fractionally; he grinned slowly as he recognised the impatient imperative voice that answered Hoppy's gruff inquiry. The door opened all the way. . . . The determined clomp of hard-heeled brogans entered the foyer, heading for the living-room door.

"Boss," Hoppy trumpeted in warning, "it's——"

"Don't tell me," the Saint broke in cheerfully. "Give me one guess—Inspector Fernack!"

IV

Devoted students of our hagiography who have been following these chronicles for the past several years may be a little tired of reading the exposition of Inspector John Henry Fernack's emotional state which usually punctuates the narrative at moments like this. Your favourite author, to be perfectly candid, is a little tired of writing it. Perhaps this is one occasion when he might be excused. To compress into a few sentences the long epic of failures, disappointments, and frustrations which made up the history of Inspector Fernack's endless pursuit of the Saint is a task before which the staunchest scribe might quail. And it is almost ludicrous to attempt to describe in mere words the quality of incandescent ire that seethed up in him like a roiled volcano as the Saint's welcoming smile flashed in the chiselled bronze of that piratical face.

"Of course," Simon murmured. "I knew it."

The detective glowered at him.

"How did you know?"

"My dear John Henry!" the Saint grinned. "That concerto you played on my doorbell was unmistakably a Fernack arrangement." He waved him to a chair. "Sit down, won't you? Let me pour you a drink—if Hoppy can spare it."

"Sure," said Mr. Uniatz hospitably. "Just don't take all of it."

Inspector Fernack did not sit down. In fact, he looked more as if he might easily rise into the air, from the sheer pressure of the steam that seemed to be distending his chest.

For the same routine was going to be played out again, and he knew it, without being able to do anything to check or vary its course. It was all implicit in the Saint's gay and friendly smile; and the bitterness of the premonition put a crack in his voice even while he ploughed doggedly onwards to his futile destiny.

"Never mind that!" he squawked. "What were you and this big baboon raising Cain about in the Masked Angel's dressing-room to-night?"

"You mean *last* night, don't you? It happens to be to-morrow morning at the moment."

"I'm asking you," Fernack repeated deliberately, "what were you doing——"

"It's funny," the Saint interjected, "all the places where a flying rumour will land."

"It's no rumour!" Inspector Fernack said trenchantly. "I was at the fight myself." He removed the stogie from his mouth and took a step forward, his gimlet eyes challenging. "Why did you steal those gloves?"

The Saint's brows lifted in polite surprise.

"Gloves?"

"Yes, gloves! The gloves that killed Torpedo Smith! Doc Spangler told me what happened. Why'd you take 'em?"

"My hands were cold," Simon said blandly.

An imaginative audience might have fancied that it could hear the perspiration sizzling on Inspector Fernack's face as its rosy glow deepened to purple. He thrust the stogie back into his mouth with a violence that almost choked him, and bit into it savagely.

"You be careful, Templar!" he bellowed. "If I felt like it, I could pull you in for assault, trespass, malicious mischief, *and* petty larceny!"

Simon shook his head sadly.

"You disappoint me, Inspector. A hunter of your

calibre talking about sparrows when there are tigers in them thar hills."

"You don't say!" Fernack's cigar angled upward like a naval rifle. "Meaning what?"

The Saint shrugged.

"Well, almost anything is more interesting than——" Amusement flickering in the lazy-lidded, hawksharp blueness of his eyes as he enumerated on his fingers: "Assault, trespass, malicious mischief, *and* petty larceny."

The cigar made another trip from Inspector Fernack's face to his fist, and suffered further damage in transit.

"All right, Saint," Fernack ground out, "what are you up to? And don't give me that look of injured innocence. You didn't crash that dressing-room just for the exercise."

"We wanted de Angel's autograph," Hoppy contributed helpfully.

The Inspector whirled on him.

"I didn't ask *you*!" he blared, with such ferocity that even Hoppy recoiled.

"John Henry," the Saint mused wistfully, "our association through the years has been a beautiful thing—in a futile sort of way—but there are moments when you really embarrass me."

"I'll bet!"

"Why should you take Spangler's word that *I* stole those gloves? You know what *he* is. Besides, what makes you think there's anything wrong with them? What was the doctor's opinion as to the cause of death?"

Inspector Fernack placed the cigar in his mouth, his eyes fixed on the Saint.

"Concussion," he said. "We'll get the medical examiner's report in the morning."

The Saint nodded.

"Concussion. Undoubtedly caused by the psychic dynamite that Doc Spangler has put in the Angel's punch."

"Or by a hunk of lead in one of those gloves!" the Inspector growled.

His eyes wandered searchingly about the room.

The Saint said: "You spoke to the Masked Angel, of course?"

"I spoke to him, of course. Why?"

"What was *his* theory, if any?"

"*His* theory!" Inspector Fernack snorted scornfully. "Why, that moron Bilinski doesn't know he's alive! But he's staying in jail till we find those gloves, understand?" His eyes narrowed. "How long have you known Bilinski? How did you recognise him as the Masked Angel? Is he a friend of yours?"

The Saint smiled wryly.

"Please, Inspector," he protested. "My social standing is not indestructible." He turned to Hoppy. "Well," he sighed, "if it's a matter of getting your little playmate out of the cooler, you'd better bring the Inspector his souvenirs."

"Okay, boss."

"I thought so!" Inspector Fernack bared his teeth in uneasy triumph.

Hoppy shuffled to the divan, bent over, and reached under it.

"Here dey are!" he announced, hauling them out. He thrust the damp leather mitts at Fernack with all the graciousness of a dyspeptic mastodon. "Take 'em!"

The Saint selected a cigarette from the silver box on the table.

"I borrowed them for the same reason you want them," he said. "I was afraid there'd be a substitution before you thought of it."

He held a lighter to his cigarette, smiling at the Inspector over its little golden spear-point of flame.

Fernack scowled, staring at the Saint for a longish moment.

"So that's your story!" he began with an imminent crescendo. "Now let me tell you——"

And there, in a hopeless anti-climax, he stopped. Galling memories of past pitfalls into which his headlong suspicions had tripped him in previous encounters with the Saint seemed for once to take all the conviction out of his attack. What, after all, was he going to tell the Saint? That he was under arrest for stealing a pair of boxing gloves?

The Saint was engagingly frank.

"I examined them quite carefully, John Henry," he said, "and they're really quite in order, believe me. None of the stitches has been tampered with, or the lining torn, or any chemical such as oil of mustard soaked into the leather. I also had a look at Bilinski's hand wraps. No plaster of Paris, pads on tinfoil, or calking compound. No hunks of lead——"

"All right, wise guy!" Fernack exploded. "If these *are* the gloves, the police lab. will tell me all I want to know!"

The Saint spread his hands with mock resignation, laughter sparkling in his cobalt eyes like sunlight on an Alpine lake.

"Of course, John Henry, if you don't believe *me*. However, if you should ever feel the need of any further enlightenment, always remember that our motto is service. Sure you won't change your mind about that drink?"

"All right!" Fernack grated, repeating himself. "Be a wise guy. Play the lone wolf. But remember this, Templar. Sooner or later you're going to make a false move, a mistake you can't get out of. And when that happens, brother, I'll be right there waiting to tag you for it!"

"You an' who else?" Hoppy inquired brilliantly.

Inspector Fernack ignored him. He thrust a finger at the Saint.

"One of these days you're going to reach out just a little too far—and you're going to draw back a bloody stump!"

The Saint's face crinkled in a shrugging smile as he put his cigarette to his mouth with a careless gesture. And as if by accident its glowing tip touched the finger Inspector Fernack held under his nose.

The detective jerked his hand back with a yelp.

"Oh, sorry, John!" Simon exclaimed contritely. "That should teach me a lesson, shouldn't it?"

Fernack glared at him speechlessly. Then, thrusting the gloves under his arm, he turned and stalked out of the living-room. Simon followed him politely to the apartment's threshold.

"Good night," said the Saint, as Fernack yanked open the door. "If you should ever need me, you know where to find me."

"If I ever want you," Inspector Fernack growled, "I'll find you, don't worry."

He strode out; and with a cheerful grin at the two

harness bulls waiting outside by the elevators, Simon quietly closed the door.

"Well," he sighed. "now maybe we can get some sleep at last!"

Hoppy yawned in soporific sympathy, but had enough presence of mind to reach for the Old Forester, which still contained an appreciable amount of fluid.

"I better have a nightcap," he explained. "I don't wanna stay awake t'inkin' about Torpedo."

"A nightcap that size," Simon observed, watching the level of the bottle descending, "could double as a sleeping-bag."

He retrieved what was left and poured it into a glass, for a private relaxer of his own.

He tried to tot up what scores there were on hand, to determine exactly where he stood at the moment. He had to confess to himself that so far he'd been working with mists, trying to assemble a concrete pattern, a design out of the stuff that emanated almost entirely from his intuitive processes. The promise of hovering danger had dissolved in two unsatisfactory climaxes : the dressing-room brawl and Fernack's visit. Unsatisfactory because they resolved nothing, answered no questions, gave no reason for the ghostly centipedes he still felt parading up his spine. . . . The mystery of Connie Grady's disproportionate agitation, the Masked Angel's incredible victory, still stood as prime question-marks.

But perhaps, he told himself, they weren't real question-marks. Perhaps he'd been overdramatising his perceptions. Connie was young and in love. Her fear for Steve's safety could well have inspired her strangely distraught plea. And the Masked Angel might have initially stunned Smith with such a short, swift jab that his eye had missed it entirely.

He told himself this and knew he was kidding himself. He knew he had missed nothing in the fight. Therefore there must have been something else—something that he still had to search for.

He stood up and stretched himself.

And once again the telephone rang.

"This is getting monotonous," said the Saint.

He lifted the instrument from its cradle.

"Templar's Telephone Chums, Incorporated," he said. Silence.

It was a kind of receptive cylindrical silence, open at both ends.

"We're having a breakfast meeting at 9 a.m.," Simon confided into the receiver. "Would you like to come, too?"

He heard a faint click—a sudden blank deadness.

The Saint hung up thoughtfully, and an airless draught prickled along his nerves like a spectral breeze. It was a well-remembered sensation, a wave-length registered on the sensitive antenna of a sixth sense which selected and amplified it throughout his being into an unmistakable alarum. It had warned him before more times than he could remember of impending danger and sudden death— just as it whispered to him now.

Someone had hung up as soon as he'd recognised the Saint's voice. Someone who wanted to make sure whether he was there.

"Hoppy," he said, "something tells me we're going to have more visitors to-night."

Mr. Uniatz's cogitative machinery ground to an ex-cruciating halt.

"What for, boss?"

"It's the price we pay for being so irresistibly attractive."

He was taking a rapid mental inventory of the room, until his eyes settled on a table lamp with a fairly long cord. He pulled the plug out of the baseboard outlet and broke the lamp cord off close to the lamp, while Hoppy stared at him.

"What gives, boss? What's dat for?"

The Saint nodded at the empty whisky bottle still clutched in Hoppy's hand.

"Take that dead soldier, go to the bathroom, fill it with water, and bring it over there."

Hoppy opened his mouth to speak, closed it, and lum-bered off obediently, confident that on whatever path the Saint pointed for him to follow, devious though it might be, a goal would unfold somehow at the end.

From the chest of drawers in his bedroom the Saint took a slim leather case which, on being unzipped, revealed a highly specialised collection of peculiar articles. Skipping the more obviously illegal tools, he selected a small spool of copper wire, a roll of adhesive tape, and a razor-blade knife. Armed with these, he returned to the entrance hall, where Mr. Uniatz extended the whisky bottle to him as though it contained an unclean substance.

"Here's de water, boss. Whatcha gonna do wit' it?"

"Just hold it for me a minute," said the Saint. He began to cut several inches of insulation from the broken end of the lamp cord. "We are preparing a phylactery against zombies," he explained.

Hoppy's jaw sagged.

"We're preparin' a what against who?"

"An apotropaion, so to speak," the Saint elucidated.

Hoppy moved nervously aside as the Saint went to the front door and taped one of the two strands of the lamp cord against the metal door-knob. He watched in silent wonder as the Saint unrolled a length of copper wire, wound the spool end a couple of times around the radiator pipe, and slipped the other end under the door until it projected a foot into the hall outside.

"All right, Hoppy, give me the bottle."

Simon stepped outside and carefully poured the water on the tile floor in front of his door so that the protruding wire lay in a shallow puddle. He went a couple of paces down the corridor, turned and studied the approach to the living-room door, then came back.

"Boss," Hoppy sighed, voicing his perennial complaint. "I don't get it."

"You will," said the Saint.

He fastened the other bared end of the drop cord to the radiator with another strip of adhesive and carefully closed the door. Finally he pushed the plug into a nearby baseboard outlet, and turned to Hoppy. "Well," he said, "there it is."

Hoppy stared at the closed door; and his lucubratory processes, oozing like a glutinous stream between narrow banks, at last achieved a spreading delta of cognition. A slow enchanted grin dissolved his facial fog like sunlight on a jungle swamp.

"Chees, boss," he said in awesome incredulity, "I do get it!"

"Congratulations."

"In case de zombies you're expectin' should touch de door-knob," Hoppy deduced triumphantly. His eyes were worshipful. "Ya even got de water puddle grounded, huh?"

The Saint laid his hand on Hoppy's shoulder in an accolade.

"Nothing escapes your eagle eye, does it?"

"Oh, I got experience in dis line, boss," Mr. Uniatz acknowledged deprecatingly. "Once I do a job on a mug's car wit' a stick of dynamite wired to de starter. De whole mob says it's one of de biggest laughs I ever give dem."

The Saint surveyed his work with an artist's satisfaction.

"That water grounded to the radiator should lend some authority even to 110 volts—especially if he's in his stockinged feet." He turned, picking up the wire, knife, and tape, and headed back toward his bedroom. "Let's grab some shut-eye while we can. It'll be daybreak in a few hours."

v

It was two hours later when he opened his eyes, instantly and completely awake, with every nerve alive and singing. He lay motionless save for the silent closing of his fingers on the gun at his side, every sense toned to razor keenness, straining to receive consciously whatever it was that had alerted him. From the next bed Hoppy's snoring rose and fell in majestic rhythm, its pipe-organ vibrato accompanied by a piccolo phrase with every exhalation. . . .

Then he heard it—a faint scratching of metal—and recognised it instantly.

A skeleton key was probing the front door lock.

He was out of bed and on his feet in one smooth soundless motion, and laying a hand on Hoppy's mouth. The snoring ceased abruptly; Simon swiftly spoke in his ear, and Hoppy's groggy eruption died aborning. He relaxed, and the Saint removed his hand.

"Listen."

The faint scratching of metal was barely audible.

Hoppy nodded, one hand scratching for the gun under his pillow, his anticipatory grin almost as luminous as the moonlight that poured into the window.

"De zombies!" he hissed in a resounding whisper that brought Simon's hand back upon his mouth again.

"Quiet!" the Saint breathed savagely.

There was a brief silence, and it seemed for a moment as if the man working on the door had indeed heard him. Then it came again—a scrape of metal—and suddenly the metallic click of tumblers falling into alignment, and the snick of an opening bolt.

"He's coming in," Simon whispered in Hoppy's ear. "Don't make a sound or I'll brain you with this gun butt."

He took his hand off Hoppy's mouth and moved with the effortless ease of a cat through the living-room. He could hear the creak of the bed as Hoppy got out and padded after him. They paused by the archway to the entrance hall, staring into the almost darkness, intent on the pale rectangle of the front door.

As they waited there, the Saint couldn't help feeling that somehow, despite his conviction that this visit rose from his recent conflict with Spangler, it didn't quite add up. For he thought he knew Spangler's character pretty thoroughly; and so primitive a motive as simple revenge simply didn't agree with his knowledge of the man. Revenge for revenge's sake was a luxury too expensive—and dangerous—to be compatible with Doc Spangler's conservative nature. The worthy doctor might have better reason later on, but so far the Saint couldn't imagine him going to so much trouble merely to assuage a sore belly.

There was another moment of silence. . . . Then, without hearing it, but almost as if he sensed a momentary and fractional change in the air pressure, the Saint knew that the front door was starting to open.

Hoppy edged past Simon, as though straining on a leash.

Simultaneously, several things happened in such swift succession that they had the effect of happening almost all at once : a sizzling shower of golden sparks flamed from the door-knob, a wild howl split the silence, there was a mad scramble of slipping feet, the thud of a falling body, the blast of a gunshot, and the rattle of plaster cascading to the floor.

The Saint and Hoppy leaped forward almost on top of

the gunman's yell, with Hoppy ahead of Simon by virtue of his head start.

Simon's warning cry came too late.

Hoppy's joyous battle bellow leaped to a yell of consternation as he grabbed the door-knob amid another constellation of sparks bursting about his hand. He leaped backwards, skidding on a rug, and sat down with a cosmic crash in front of the doorway.

The Saint ripped the cord from the electric outlet with one hand, reached over with the other and tried to pull open the door against Hoppy's obstructing weight.

"Okay, boss, okay!" Hoppy grunted protestingly as Simon rolled him over with a yank at the door.

He scrambled to his feet as the Saint disappeared into the hallway. But even as he snatched open the front door, Simon knew that the quarry had escaped. The "In Use" signal light of the automatic elevator gleamed at him in yellow derision.

Hoppy charged past him and skidded to a halt.

"Where'd he go, huh? Where'd he go?" he demanded feverishly.

Then he caught the glow of the elevator signal light and whirled for the stairs.

The Saint grabbed his arm and stopped him.

"Come back, Pluto," he said disgustedly. "That elevator will be at the bottom before you've gone down three flights."

He dragged Hoppy back into the apartment as a murmur of alarmed voices, with a few doors opening and closing, drifted faintly up the stair well. Muttering to himself, Hoppy joined the Saint in the darkness before the living-room window and stared down at the moon-silvered street before the building entrance far below. Suddenly, as the realisation that the would-be raider would probably be leaving by that exit dawned upon him, a vast feral grin spread over his face. He raised his gun.

The Saint noted the car parked before the building, a little distance behind his—a dark sedan that hadn't been there when he'd arrived there that night. He caught a glimpse of hands in the moonlight—hands that carried an odd sparkle—resting on the visible portion of the steering-wheel.

Hoppy crouched beside him, his big black automatic clutched in a hairy fist resting on the window-still, and stared lynx-eyed at the canopied building entrance eighteen floors below. Presently he rasped in an awful tide of anxiety : "Boss, maybe he goes out de back——"

He broke off as a man darted out from under the canopy a figure reduced to miniature, scurrying towards the parked sedan.

Mr. Uniatz raised his gun and was aiming carefully when Simon's hand clamped on his wrist in a grip of iron.

"No!" he ordered. "We'll only have Fernack back—and next time he won't be so easy to get rid of."

"Chees, boss !" Hoppy complained mournfully, staring at the sedan roaring down the street. "I had a bead on him."

"In the dark? Shooting downward at that distance?" Simon snapped. He turned away, crossing the living-room. "Don't be a goddam fool. Besides"—he stepped out of the darkness of the living-room into the hallway—"there's been enough noise for one night."

Hoppy shuffled after him, muttering indignantly : "Nobody can gimme de business an' get away wit' it."

The Saint looked at him resignedly.

"Don't blame *him* ! Grabbing that door-knob after I'd wired it was your own damn fault."

"I wouldn'a done it if it wasn't for him," Hoppy insisted sullenly. "Besides, how do I know he can run like dat? All de zombies I ever see in pitchers move slower dan Bilinski. Dis musta bin a new kind, boss. Maybe somebody gives him a hypo."

"Maybe somebody does," Simon agreed. "And the doc's name could be Spangler."

He switched the lights on at the entrance and looked around. The loose rug that had been involved in Hoppy's downfall was a touselled heap in the middle of the floor; and as he lifted one corner to straighten it he saw the gun underneath it.

He picked it up gingerly—a heavy "banker's" model revolver with a two-inch barrel.

"Chees," Hoppy said. "De lug forgets his equaliser. Now all we gotta do is find out who it belongs to, an' we know who he is."

"That piece of logic," said the Saint, "has more holes in it than Swiss cheese. However——"

He broke off as he became aware that the elevator doors were opening in front of him. For one instant he was tense, with his forefinger curling instinctively on the trigger of the weapon in his hand. Then he saw the passenger clearly.

He was a rabbity little man draped in a flowered bathrobe, with pince-nez supporting a long black ribbon.

"I," he enunciated pompously, "am your neighbour downstairs, Mr. Swafford. Has there been any trouble?"

He stepped back suddenly, with his eyes popping, as Hoppy moved into full view from behind the Saint.

"Trouble?" Simon inquired politely. "What sort of trouble?"

Mr. Swafford seemed hypnotised by the baleful apparition glaring at him over the Saint's shoulder.

"I," he swallowed. "I—— Please forgive me," he said hastily, "but there was some rumour—about a shot, I think it was. Some people in the building seem to think it came from up here."

Simon turned to Hoppy.

"Did you hear a shot?"

Mr. Uniatz fixed Mr. Swafford with a basilisk glare. He growled : "Boss, dis guy must be nuts !"

Mr. Swafford gulped and amended hastily : "Of course I don't say it came from your apartment. It was just what some of the tenants thought. They seem to have jumped to the conclusion that someone was being shot, but I assure you——"

"I'm sure," the Saint broke in pleasantly, "that there must be a more productive form of exercise than jumping to conclusions, don't you think, comrade?"

Mr. Swafford retreated another step, his eyes bulging wider as they confirmed their impression of the gun in the Saint's hand and the fallen shower of plaster from the ceiling.

"Oh, yes, of course," he said weakly. "I never——"

c.s. – 6

"I'm sorry you were disturbed," said the Saint benevolently. "My friend here is just in from Montana, where men are men and have notches in their guns to prove it. When they're having fun, they just blaze away at the ceiling. I've just taken his six-shooter away and tried to explain to him——"

"Scram before I step on ya like a roach!" Hoppy bellowed, squeezing past the Saint.

Mr. Swafford stumbled backwards, his pince-nez dropping from his long nose and dangling by their ribbon; he turned and scurried precipitately back into the elevator.

"Good night, Mr. Swafford," Simon called breezily, as the closing elevator doors blotted out the little man's pallid stare.

He turned back into the apartment, shutting the door behind him.

"Boss," Hoppy said, following him, "Dis is gettin' monogamous. Just one t'ing after anudder."

"That sounds almost bovine to me," said the Saint. "But it'll probably get worse before it gets better."

He was sure that he had recognised the squat silhouette of Spangler's henchman, Max, fleeing from the building toward the waiting sedan. But he was still wondering, as he fell asleep, just why Doc Spangler had sent him.

VI

Hoppy was in the penthouse kitchen frying bacon with concentrated absorption late the next morning when the door-bell rang. The Saint, seated in the adjoining breakfast alcove, put down the morning paper and stood up.

"I'll get it, boss," Hoppy offered, laying down the fork in one hand and the comic section clutched in the other.

"Never mind." Simon strode across the kitchen. "I don't want to take your mind off Dick Tracy."

The opening door revealed a vision in daffodil yellow with hair to match and a quizzical smile.

"Pat!" Simon drew her in and held her at arm's length, boldly admiring. "You're a sight to be held!"

He suited the action to the word.

She laughed breathlessly, pulling away.

"Darling, you have one of the most elemental lines since Casanova."

His eyes caressed her figure. "The most elemental lines," he said, "are never spoken. They're looked at."

"Do I look as good as Connie?" she inquired with arched eyebrows.

"Much better." He took her hand and led her toward the kitchen. "Hoppy!" he called, "bring on the vitamins."

"Comin' up, boss!" Hoppy sang out, and came around to deposit a glass of pale amber liquid in front of her as she sat down. "Vitamins," he grinned, and retreated back to his stove.

"Thank you." Pat smiled and lifted the glass.

"Wait." Simon reached over and took the glass from her. He sniffed it. "I thought so!"

"What's the matter?" Pat asked. "Isn't it all right?"

He pushed the glass back.

"Smell it."

She sniffed the glass and sat up, laughing. "Brandy!"

Hoppy's head appeared over the top of the alcove partition.

"Whassamatter, boss?"

"Thanks for the compliment," said Patricia, "but I'm not quite up to your kind of fruit juice."

Mr. Uniatz's brow furrowed in hurt bewilderment.

"It's from grapes, ain't it? Grapes is fruit, ain't it?" He reached behind him and raised up the bottle for all to behold. "It says so, right here on de bottle."

The Saint waved him away in despair.

"Never mind," he said. "Bring on the solid food."

"Okay, boss." Hoppy removed the offending liquor and drained it at a gulp. He went back into the kitchen and looked over the partition on to the top of Pat's blonde head. "Dijja read about de fight in de paper dis morning?" he asked.

"They arrested the Masked Angel, didn't they?"

"But not for long," Hoppy said complacently. "We fix dat, don't we, boss?"

Pat's clear eyes studied the Saint.

"What does he mean—you fixed it up?"

"We informed the law that the Masked Angel is an old

chum of Hoppy's," Simon explained glibly. "Naturally, with that kind of a character reference, they're bound to let Bilinski go."

"I don't trust you," Patricia said coldly. "Not for a minute. What goes on?"

"Goes on?" The Saint's eyebrows lifted.

"I know you too well. You wouldn't have left me last night the way you did unless something had——"

She broke off as the door-bell sounded briefly.

"I'll let her in, boss," Hoppy said cheerfully, and paddled out of the kitchen.

"'Her'?" Patricia quoted acidly. "Miss Grady, I presume?"

"A purely professional visit," he said calmly. "After all, she *is* engaged to Steve Nelson."

Pat's cool red mouth curved cynically.

"A passing fiancé, no doubt."

Simon's eyes closed in pain.

"My dear girl," he protested.

He got to his feet as Hoppy trumpeted from the hallway. "It's Connie Grady, boss!"

She hesitated in the kitchen door, slim and dewy-fresh, her short auburn curls making her look very young and almost boyish, with Hoppy looming up behind her like a grinning Cerberus.

"Come in, darling," said the Saint. He took her hand and led her to the breakfast alcove. "Miss Grady, this is my colleague, Miss Holm."

"Hullo, Connie," said Patricia sympathetically. "Welcome to the harem."

Connie Grady glanced uncertainly from Pat to Simon. "I—I didn't know you were having company," she said. "I didn't want to——"

"It's perfectly all right," Simon assured her. "Pat really is my colleague in—er—many of my enterprises. Anything you say to me you can say to her with equal freedom." He waved to Hoppy. "That's another of my colleagues— Hoppy Uniatz."

"Likewise, I'm sure," Hoppy beamed. "I seen ya lotsa times when your pop was runnin' de old Queensbury Gym, remember? Ya useta bring him his lunch."

Her elfin features crinkled in a smile.

"Yes . . . I remember."

"Sit down," said the Saint. "We're just starting."

He saw her settled in the booth and pulled up another chair for himself, while Mr. Uniatz doled out plates of bacon and eggs and cups of coffee with hash-house dexterity.

Connie picked up her fork and tried to start, but the effort of restraint was too much. She looked full at the Saint, with the emotion unashamed on her face.

"You saw what happened," she said, her voice small and tense. "The Angel killed a man last night. . . . *Now,* do you wonder that I don't want Steve to fight that—that gorilla?"

"I can see your point."

"When I was talking to you last night," she began, "I— I——" She fumbled as if groping for the right words.

Simon passed Patricia the sugar with harlequin courtesy. She didn't seem to see it.

She said sweetly : "Last night?"

"On the phone, after you called," Simon elucidated smoothly. "She wanted to know what went on, too. Her father was rather upset by our little visit to the Masked Angel's dressing-room after the fight."

Patricia's red mouth pursed in a sceptical "Oh !"

Connie found the words at last : "I was hoping and praying they'd keep that—that man in jail—that the fight would be called off . . ." Her voice broke. "But they're releasing him."

"Are they?" Simon asked with interest. "I didn't see anything about it in my paper."

"Daddy was over at police headquarters first thing this morning with Spangler—he's the Masked Angel's manager."

The Saint nodded.

"I see. So they got the Angel out of the jug in spite of Hoppy's recommendation."

"Steve is going through with this fight—if you don't do something about it." Connie Grady's voice strained against her self-control. "He'll be killed !"

Hoppy gulped on a mouthful that would have choked a horse.

"Killed? De Champ? Why, he'll moider de bum!"
Connie turned on him sharply.

"You think so? After what the Masked Angel did to
Torpedo Smith last night? That—that so-called bum has
beaten every man he's fought."

"Under Doc Spangler's ministry, at least," the Saint
amended.

"Aah, dey was fakes," Hoppy derided. "Dey musta
bin!"

"When Torpedo Smith was killed last night," she said
tensely, "do you think *he* was faking?"

"You know, of course," Simon said to Connie, "who
the Masked Angel really is, don't you?"

She nodded wearily.

"Yes, of course. Daddy owns part of him."

She looked up quickly, as if suddenly realising what she
had said. "I mean," she stumbled confusedly, "he doesn't
have any interest in him directly—that is, not really. It's
just that Spangler owes Daddy money, and—and——"

"Of course," Simon soothed gently, "I understand. It's
just that Doc Spangler is paying off your father from his
earnings on the Masked Angel."

She seemed grateful for the lead.

"Yes. Yes, that's it."

"After all," the Saint observed casually, "it's not considered ethical for a matchmaker to hold a financial interest
in any of his contestants—or at least a major share—so
naturally Mr. Grady would avoid that sort of thing.
Especially where a championship bout was concerned."

Connie Grady looked up suddenly.

"I don't want Steve to be one of those contestants!" she
burst out, her emerald eyes misting. She turned away. "I
sound—ridiculous, don't I? I—I wouldn't dream of asking
this of anyone else in the world. You—you're the only
person I could possibly imagine being capable of—
somehow arranging it so that the fight would never
happen,"

"Exactly what are you suggesting?" Pat asked curiously.
"Do you think the Saint could persuade Nelson not to
fight?"

Connie flashed her a startled glance.

"Oh, no!" she said. "If he knew I'd come here to ask Mr. Templar—he'd never forgive me." She turned to Simon pleadingly. "There must be some—other way I can't say how. I only know that you've done things—in the past —that were like miracles. . . . Daddy has told me about— some of your adventures."

"Well, well," said Patricia admiringly. "Simon Templar, the Paul Bunyan of modern crime. Have you another miracle up your sleeve?"

Then she caught the stricken look on Connie's face and her laughter softened. She put an arm about the girl's shoulders and looked up at the Saint questioningly.

"Simon, what do you think?"

"I think," said the Saint, "that we ought to go on with breakfast before it all gets cold, or Hoppy eats it."

He deliberately devoted himself to his own plate, and insisted on that matter-of-fact diversion until even Connie Grady had to follow with the others. He knew that the let-down was what she needed if she could be eased into it, and for his own part a healthy appetite was mixed with the need for an interlude of constructive thinking in approximately equal proportions. If it was obvious that Connie's concern for Steve Nelson was absolutely real, it was no less plain to the Saint that she still hadn't come out with everything that was on her mind.

He waited until the commonplace mechanics of eating had achieved an inevitable slackening of the tension, and then he said almost casually: "Of course, one thing we might do is shoot Barrelhouse Bilinski——"

"No, no!" Connie gasped; but her tone was now more impatient than fearful. "I didn't mean anything like that. I don't want—anybody hurt." She shook her head. "There must be something—something else you could do. You're clever . . ."

Simon considered the tip of his cigarette a moment, the smoke trickling from his mouth.

"Does your father know you're here?" he asked.

"Of course not!" The idea seemed to startle her. "I couldn't tell him I'm trying to have the fight stopped— any more than I could tell Steve!"

"Steve is pretty good at his profession," Simon remarked.

"Does he know how you feel about his chances against the Angel?"

"How could I tell him? I've tried to make him quit now —with the championship. It hasn't done any good. He's so sure, so confident! If he only had sense enough to be afraid, to realise!"

"Realise what?" Simon queried mildly.

"That it's not—not worth risking his life——"

"He's retiring after this next fight, according to the papers," Patricia said.

"Yes, I know. He promised me. . . . But it may be too late by then."

Hoppy was shaking his head uncomprehendingly.

"You talk like he's a cream puff," he said. "He's de Champ, ain't he?"

"Connie," said the Saint gently, holding her eyes, "is there any other reason why you think Steve won't win? Something you haven't told me yet?"

She drew back.

"No." She turned away. "I've told you everything. I—— Spangler used to be a doctor once," she said quickly. "I mean a real doctor, I—— Suppose he uses his hypnotism? I know how crazy that sounds, but something will happen to Steve! I know it will!"

None of this was particularly fresh grist for Simon's cogitative mill. He sighed.

"If Steve gives his usual performance," he reasoned, "I don't see that Bilinski stands a prayer. As for Doc Spangler's hypnotic powers—I wouldn't worry too much about them if I were you, Connie."

Her mouth trembled.

"I'm sorry. I might have known that you'd talk just like Steve does. . . . You and that—trainer of his."

Simon's brows lifted.

"Trainer?"

"Whitey Mullins."

Hoppy, reaching for the coffee-pot, turned eagerly.

"Ya mean Whitey's trainin' de Champ? Say!" Ho beamed with the fanged grimace of a delighted dinosaur. "Whitey's a great guy."

The green eyes flashed at him.

"Is he? What does Mullins care what happens to Steve? All *he* cares about is getting even with Spangler. He's just using Steve for a cat's-paw!"

Hoppy blinked, his mouth open.

"I didn't know de Champ's a southpaw, but everybody knows Whitey has it in for de Doc ever since Spangler finagles Bilinski's contract away from him. Dat's an old story." He shook his head dazedly. "And all de time I t'ink Nelson is a right-hander! He fights like one."

Pat suppressed a smile.

"There doesn't seem to be much wrong with having a handler who's so interested in seeing the Angel beaten."

"But the Angel won't be beaten," Connie said hopelessly. "Steve'll be killed! He hasn't a chance!"

Simon studied her broodingly.

"You're very sure of that," he said, and reached into his pocket to bring something out. He went on without a change of tone : "Did you ever see this before?"

On the table between them he laid the revolver which last night's visitor had left behind.

By no perceptible sign, the Saint sensed a sudden change in her, an inner freezing, her eyes coming in focus on the gun, her whole being gripped by that thanatoid stillness that stands on the threshold of panic.

"Where," she said in a small, tight voice, "did you get —that?"

"It was left here last night as a sort of—calling card."

Patricia was staring at him.

"Last night?"

"Some hopped-up heister crashes de joint," Hoppy snorted. "He gets away before we can even see who it is. But we give him such a scare he forgets de rod."

"You didn't tell me!" Pat accused. "You finished that brawl at the Arena over here, didn't you?" She searched Simon's face narrowly, and sensed the truth with the swift certainty of an intuition ground to psychic fineness by the countless abrasions of past experience. "Someone followed you here and tried to kill you!"

The Saint bowed.

"Darling, you know our kind of friends too well."

Connie Grady stood up. She gathered up her purse and

gloves with unsteady hands. Her face was pale, the magnolia skin drawn and haggard. She tried to ignore the revolver on the table, but her eyes kept flitting back to it, under the spell of some kind of frightening fascination.

"I'm sorry I bothered you like this," she said with nervous breathlessness. "It was silly, really. I——" She broke off, walking quickly to the door. "Good-bye."

"No, wait!"

"Please."

She almost ran out of the apartment, and the front door slammed behind her.

Patricia and Hoppy returned their blank stares to the Saint—Patricia's tinged with irony.

"Too bad," she said. "And you were just starting to make such an impression."

"Chees," Hoppy said between mouthfuls, resuming his assault on the food, "de Torpedo gettin' killed last night kinda made her blow her top, huh, boss?"

"It was that gun," Pat stated, "that upset her. Why?"

Simon picked up the revolver and turned it idly in his hands.

"My crystal ball doesn't work like yours," he said, and he smiled at her. "Rather an attractive little thing, isn't she?"

"Oh, rather," Pat agreed, her smile sweetly corrosive; "if you like them on the slightly hysterical side."

Simon laughed, his fingernail tracing the small intertwined letters engraved on the metal just above the stocks of the gun.

"Poor Melusina," he sighed whimsically. "I'm afraid her dear old daddy is making her cry."

"Melusina? What are you talking about? I thought her name was Connie."

"So it is. The term was merely analogous. Melusina was a fairy. A French fairy." Simon grinned provocatively. "If you ever delved into such matters in your youth, dear, you'll remember the story."

"I never was as good at fairy tales as you," Pat said demurely.

"Melusina," Simon continued imperturbably, "was no end attractive and quite easy to take—even if she was on the slightly hysterical side. However, she happened to suffer an injury from her father, for which, if memory serves, she had him imprisoned inside a mountain. She, in turn, was punished by being turned into a snake from the waist down every Saturday night."

"She ought to have been able to wriggle out of that one," Patricia said dryly. "But what has it got to do with Miss Grady, if anything?"

"Boss, don't she t'ink Smith got killed by accident?" Hoppy demanded.

"Inasmuch as you raise the question," Simon said, "I'll give you an answer. No."

"Obviously," said Patricia. "But what do *you* think?"

"She's quite right. It wasn't an accident."

Mr. Uniatz absorbed half a cup of coffee at a gulp, scowling interestedly.

"Ya mean de Torpedo ain't knocked off fair and square?"

The Saint nodded thoughtfully.

"Indubitably not—if instinct serves, and I think it does. At any rate, we're going to look into the matter."

"What are you going to do, Simon?"

The Saint smiled at her, and then at the gun lying on the palm of his hand.

"We're going to call on the man who owns this," he said. "Wish we could take you along, but unfortunately . . ."

"But you said you didn't even see who it was who left that gun here!" she exclaimed. "How do you know who——"

"I know who owns these initials," said the Saint patiently, lifting the gun for her inspection. He showed her the monogram in fancy script on the metal. "They're rather difficult to untangle, but I think you can make them out."

Hoppy leaned over.

"Initials?" he queried, peering at the gun. "Where?"

"M . . . G.," Pat read. "M.-G.? But who is M. G.?"

"Off-hand, I'd say it was Connie's father, Michael Grady, wouldn't you?" Simon kissed her and stood up. "Let's get started, Hoppy. We may be able to dig her old man out of the mountain."

VII

The Saint entered by one of the side entrances of the Manhattan Arena and found himself, as he expected, in the office wing of the building. The corridors and reception-rooms were alive with voices and sporting gentry of varied interests and importance; for this was a cross-roads of the indoor sporting world, and through these catacombs paraded its foremost and hindmost representatives.

Simon moved silently and inconspicuously along the shadowed wall of the main hall and stepped into the main reception-room.

It was a bare and unkempt ante-chamber, its hard chairs and bare benches occupied by a garrulous covey of promoters, managers, sports-writers, ticket speculators, and professional athletes of varied talents and notoriety, all obviously waiting to see the great Mike Grady. A fog of tobacco smoke hung over the room like stale incense burnt to strange and violent gods; the voices of the votaries droned a ragged litany punctuated by coarse yaks of laughter. There was something about them that marked them as a distinct species of metropolitan life; each was subtly akin to the other, no matter how different their outer hides might be. It lay, perhaps, in the mutual bold-ness of their eyes, the uninhibited expression of primitive emotion, the corner-of-the-mouth asides and the sudden loudly profane rodomontades in lower-bracket dialects. Their eyes appraised him pitilessly as he threaded his way through them, like circus animals taking the measure of a new trainer; but in the same moment their inquisitorial glances flipped away again, as if even under his easy elegance they recognised instinctively a fellow member of their own predatory species.

The girl at the switchboard near Grady's office door, who doubled as receptionist, surveyed the Saint in the same way as he approached her. But even her deadpan appraisal softened responsively to the intimate flattery of his smile, the irrepressible proposition of his blue eyes, and the devil-may-care lines of chin and mouth. . . . He was opening the door of Grady's private office before she sud-denly remembered her duties as sentry of the sanctum.

"Hey, come back here!" she cried. "You can't go in there!"

Like other women who had tried to tell the Saint what he couldn't do, she thought of her objections a little late. The Saint was already in.

Michael Grady was sitting tilted back in his swivel chair, his feet resting on the edge of his huge desk, his broad, snub-nosed face turned upward at the ceiling as he cuddled a telephone in the crook of his jaw and shoulder. His gaze swung downward as he heard the door close, and his eyes, which matched the Saint's for blueness, bulged with embryonic eruption.

The Saint waved a debonair greeting and sank into a worn leather club chair facing him.

The promoter grunted a couple of times into the telephone, his eyes fixed on Simon Templar's, and hung up, his feet returning to the floor with a crash.

"And who the hell might you be?" he blasted.

A rich brogue was still ingrained in his gravelly tenor, although as the Saint well knew it had been thirty years since he had left his native Ireland. The ups and downs of Mike Grady's turbulent career to his present eminence as promoter of the Manhattan Arena was a familiar story to the city's sporting gentry; it was a career which on the whole, Simon knew, had won Grady more friends than enemies—and those enemies the kind an honest but headstrong man easily makes on his way to the top.

"The name," Simon announced, "is Simon Templar."

Grady stared at him, digesting the name, seeking a familiar niche for it, his brows drawn in a guarded frown. He opened his mouth as if to speak, then closed it again as recognition dawned in his eyes and wiped away the frown. He leaned forward on his desk.

"The Saint?" he asked unbelievingly, and sprang to his feet without waiting for a reply. "Of course! I should've known!" He came from behind the desk, extending an eager hand. "Glad to meet you, Saint!"

Simon rose to his feet and allowed his arm to be used like a pump-handle.

"And it's a shame you've not visited me before," Grady enthused. "Why, only yesterday one of the boys brings up your name as a possibility for master of ceremonies for the Summer Ice Follies we're puttin' on soon. The Saint and Sonja Henie! Can't you just see that billin'! It'd be sensational! You'd pack 'em in! We'd have it all in the papers —on billboards—on the radio——"

"And in skywriting," said the Saint. "Well, I suppose the world will always beat a path to the door of the man who builds a better claptrap, but I didn't come as a performer in that line. I—er—already have a—sort of profession, you know."

"A profession? You?" Grady smiled jestingly. "And what would that be?"

"I'm what you might call a haunter," said the Saint.

Grady's brows knitted.

"A haunter?"

"Of guilty consciences."

"That," said Mr. Grady after a pause, "I don't get."

Simon helped himself to a cigarette from the dispenser on the desk.

"Well," he said engagingly, "take your conscience, for example."

Grady grinned at him.

"And why would you be hauntin' *my* conscience? It's crystal clear."

Simon struck a match.

"Is it?"

"Indeed it is."

"Even about your secret partnership with Doc Spangler?"

Grady's grin faded. He turned abruptly, went back behind his desk, and sat down. His finger-tips tapped a nervous tattoo on the top of his desk for a moment.

"Even if that were true," he said finally, "would it be a crime?"

The Saint also sat down again, lowering himself through a leisured breath of smoke.

"I always heard you were an honest man, Mike," he said quietly. "Spangler's a crook, and you know it."

Grady flushed.

"I don't know anything of the sort!" he snapped. "So

he served time once. What of it? A man can make a mistake."

"I know," Simon nodded "And you put him back on his feet; gave him a job at the Queensbury Gym."

"The best damn' masseur I ever had!"

"Very likely. He was an M.D. before they took away his licence for peddling dope." Simon consulted his cigarette ash. "Mike, you even advanced him money to go into business as a fight manager, didn't you?"

Grady stirred impatiently.

"Well, what of it?" he demanded. "When I got this job here at the Arena I gave up the gym. Doc didn't want to work there without me, so I loaned him a couple of grand."

"For which he gave you a share in Barrelhouse Bilinski as collateral."

"Well——" Grady chuckled, but his humour was laciniated with unease. "It didn't seem like much collateral at the time. He wasn't the Masked Angel then, you know."

"I know."

"Well, then," Grady said, spreading his square freckled hands expressively, "you know how good Spangler is. A great fighter he's made out of a broken-down stumble bum."

The Saint shook his head sadly.

"Mike," he protested, "anyone, a child—even Connie, your own daughter—might be sceptical of that. In fact, if she knew about your partnership with Spangler, she might even be afraid that you're mixed up in something not quite——"

Grady stiffened, his face reddening.

"And what the hell has my daughter to do with this?"

The Saint's disclaimer was as bland as cold cream.

"Why, nothing at all, Mike. I merely mentioned her as a possibility."

"Well, you just leave her out of this!" Grady glared at him and then looked away restlessly. "Maybe it isn't according to Hoyle for me to have a financial interest in Bilinski," he grumbled, "but it doesn't matter a damn to me if he wins or loses, just so I get my two grand back."

"By the way," said the Saint, "how does Spangler get away with Bilinski wearing that old sock over his head?"

"He has special permission from the Boxin' Commission,"

Grady replied curtly. "It's a legitimate publicity stunt."

"If there is such a thing," Simon admitted. "But it certainly improves his appearance."

"He'll have to take it off for the championship fight," Grady informed him sourly, "when he gives Steve Nelson the beatin' he deserves!"

The Saint's probing eyes drooped with offensive restraint.

"You seem to lack a certain enthusiasm for your future son-in-law," he observed.

"Not *my* son-in-law!" roared the promoter. "No common knuckle-head box fighter is going to marry the daughter of Mike Grady, I can tell you. I don't know what tales you been hearing, but she's not marrying that punk, you can depend on it!"

"What are you going to do—forbid the banns?"

"I'll not see her tied to a lowser with no more future than a cake of ice," Grady said belligerently. "I've seen what happens to the most of 'em after their fightin' days are done, with their brains addled and the eyes knocked out of 'em, no money saved and their wives drudges!"

The Saint built an "O" with a smoke-ring.

"So that's why you quarrelled."

"I wouldn't call it a quarrel." The promoter's eyes glittered. "I told him just what I've told you, and I told him to let Connie alone."

"But if Steve is retiring after his fight with the Angel, as he says——"

"Sure! That's what he says," Grady snorted. "How many times have I heard *that* one before! So he's retiring. On what?"

Simon shrugged.

"On the purse, I suppose. Unless, of course, he gets killed before he can collect it. The way Smith was."

Mike Grady put his elbows on the desk and cupped his forehead in his hands, staring down at his desk.

"That was a terrible thing to happen," he said sombrely. "But it was an accident." He looked up defiantly. "It wouldn't happen once in a million fights."

The Saint gazed at him thoughtfully. A pattern seemed to be unfolding. So Grady wanted no part of Connie's fiancé. He was in semi-partnership with Doc Spangler. But

did he disapprove of Nelson enough to arrange his death?
Was he of the same stripe as Spangler? . . . Somehow the
Saint couldn't quite accept that. Grady was not wanting in
the essential elements of humanity. A hotheaded, obstinate
old blowhard, perhaps—but not a wicked man. Shrewd,
conniving, scheming maybe—but not a crook. Somewhere
the thorn of conscience pricked. Somewhere beneath the
flinty carapace was the naïvely sentimental heart. An
expert in such things, the Saint felt certain of his diagnosis.
And yet . . .

"Perhaps," said the Saint. "But I collect those one-in-a-
million chances." He slipped the snub-barrelled revolver
out of his pocket and laid it almost casually on Grady's
desk. "No doubt it was also one chance in a million that
I found this in my apartment last night."

Grady stared at the gun in open-mouthed amazement.

"Where the hell did you get that?" he demanded
stupidly.

"It's yours, of course?"

"Sure it's mine. My initials are on it! Where'd you
get it?"

"I told you. In my apartment last night. After my little
interview with Spangler last night, some character broke
into our little ivory tower with the apparent idea of air-
conditioning us with your heater. Unfortunately we had
just booby-trapped the door in preparation for a visit from
the tax collector. This other character didn't have a sense
of humour, so he went away in a sort of huff."

Grady thrust himself from his chair and walked to the
window. He stared out blindly, his hands folded across his
chest, his face a thundercloud.

"I don't understand," he muttered. "Unless he sold it,
or——" He turned to Simon abruptly. "That gun was
stolen from me," he said flatly, "by Steve Nelson!"

The Saint tapped the ash from his cigarette dispassionately.

"Stolen?" he murmured.

"Yes, stolen!" Grady returned to his chair. "Last week.
Right in this office. He took the gun and I've never seen
it since—that is, until this moment."

"How do you know he took it?" the Saint asked.

"How do I know he took it!" Grady bawled. "The lowser nearly broke my arm!"

"Oh," Simon deduced innocently. "This, I take it, was during the quarrel you didn't have."

Grady glowered at the gun on the desk.

"If it wasn't a matter of business and money out of my pocket, I'd have had him thrown in jail for so long——"

"That Connie wouldn't even know him when he did come out?"

"Skip it."

"You pulled that gun on him, didn't you? And he took it away from you. Was that it?"

Grady's high blood pressure became painfully evident.

"I said skip it!" he shouted. "I was defending myself—not that I couldn't handle the lowser with me bare hands if I had to!"

Simon rose to his feet and retrieved the gun.

"You won't mind if I borrow this until I trace the character who tried to use it on me last night?"

"Help yourself," Grady grunted darkly. "Did you have any idea who it was?"

"Do you think Steve Nelson could answer that question?"

Grady scowled and shook his head.

"It doesn't sound like him—sneakin' into a man's house. . . . No, it couldn't have been! The lowser must have sold it or—lost it. Whoever got it from Nelson is the man you'll be wantin'."

The Saint stood up.

"That's who I'm going to find," he said. "I'll see you again, Mike."

Before the promoter realised that the interview was over, he had opened the door and sauntered out.

There was a sudden dampening of volume in the conversation about him as he emerged from Grady's office. Whereas he had attracted little attention on entering the reception-room, his effrontery in crashing Grady's office ahead of everyone else now made him a marked man, the target of a concentrated battery of indignant eyes. But the Saint seemed wholly unaware of the hushed hostility as he paused by the girl at the switchboard and watched her plug in a connection.

"Yes, Mr. Grady," she said. And after a moment : "Dr. Who? . . . Yes, sir, I'll get him for you right away."

She reached for the telephone directory on a shelf beside her.

"Crescent 3-1465," the Saint prompted helpfully.

She looked up like a startled gopher; and Simon Templar gave her the same friendly smile with which he had short-circuited her before.

"It was Dr. Kurt Spangler you wanted, wasn't it?" he said, and strolled on out before she could find her voice.

Hoppy Uniatz had the engine of the convertible racing as Simon opened the door, and he scarcely gave the Saint time to sit down before he banged in the clutch and sent the car roaring up the street and lurching around the first corner against the lights.

"What are you trying to do?" Simon asked. "Pick up a ticket?"

"Don't worry, boss," Hoppy said. "De getaway is a cinch. I drove lotsa dese jobs before. Dijja blast him good?"

Simon considered him.

"What on earth are you talking about?"

"Dat bum, Grady! Ya just give him de business, don'tcha?"

The Saint shook his head patiently.

"No, Hoppy, no. I never said that our visitor last night was Mike Grady. Let's head for Riverside Drive—I mean to talk to Steve Nelson in person."

VIII

The blue convertible swept up Riverside Drive through the sixties, past seventies, with the sun-drenched wind whispering through Simon Templar's crisp black hair; it was a clean brisk wind cooled by the majestic mile-wide ribbon of the Hudson which ran parallel on their left, its shining waters stippled by the wind in a million breaking facets that caught the bright sunlight in broad mosaics of burnished gold. All in all, the Saint thought, it was much too gay and lovely a day for exploring spiritual sewers, or delving into the fetid labyrinths of murder.

They were in the eighties before the Saint signalled Hoppy to slow down.

"It's that house at the end of the block," he said.

The big car swooped to the kerb and drew to a halt before one of the three-storied brown stone buildings which stand along Riverside Drive like autumnal spinsters, their old-fashioned elegance reminiscent of a more sedate and happier era.

"De champ live here?" Hoppy asked with some wonder.

"It says so in the directory."

"Wit' his dough, I'd be livin' on Park Avenue."

"That's why you wouldn't have his dough for long." Simon got out of the car. "Wait for me, Hoppy. I won't be long."

A glance at the letter-boxes revealed that Steve Nelson had an apartment on the second floor. Simon opened the door and went to the foot of the thickly-carpeted stairway. The gloom inside was stygian by contrast with the brightness of the street, but he was able to make out the doorway of Steve Nelson's apartment at the head of the stairs. From the same direction came the sound of male voices raised in argument.

Simon gripped the ornately carved banister and bounded upwards lightly and with absolute silence; before he reached the top, however, the voices suddenly rose to shouting violence. There was a girl's scream, and the door flew open with a crash. A bull-necked citizen staggered backwards out of the door, followed by a taller, quick-moving younger man who gripped him by the shoulder, spun him around with a jerk, and sent him crashing down the stairs with a savage kick.

If the Saint hadn't been in the way, it is probable he would have continued to the bottom without more than two bounces. But, as it happened, Simon caught the impact of his weight on one arm and shoulder, lifted him to his feet, and had a good look at his face.

"Why, Karl!" Simon greeted him affably, keeping a firm grip on the dazed thug's lapel. "How you do get around."

Recognition and fear flared simultaneously in the gunman's eyes. With a sudden turn he jerked away and leaped the rest of the way down the stairs and disappeared out the door, leaving his coat in the Saint's hands.

"The Saint!" Connie Grady gasped.

There was a pale thread of repressed panic in her startled voice. She was standing in the doorway of Steve Nelson's apartment, staring down at Simon over one of Steve Nelson's broad shoulders.

The Saint went on up the stairs, with Karl's coat over his arm.

"Your playmate must have been in a hurry," he murmured, "Doesn't he know there's a clothing shortage?"

Nelson, blond and slim-waisted, gazed at the Saint puzzledly. He turned to Connie.

"It's the Saint," she said. "Simon Templar. I told you I met him yesterday. . . . My fiancé, Steve Nelson," she introduced them.

As Nelson turned to take Simon's hand, the Saint caught a glimpse of Connie's eyes over his shoulder, strained and pleading. So she was afraid he'd spill the beans about her visit to his apartment that morning.

"I'm afraid you came at rather a difficult moment," she was saying with a nervous laugh.

"If that character ever comes back again," Steve Nelson said deliberately, "he'll lose more than just a coat." He grinned. "Glad to know you, Saint. I've sure heard a lot about you. Won't you come in?"

Steve Nelson's apartment inside was considerably more attractive than the conservative exterior of the landing seemed to indicate. Simon looked about him approvingly.

"Do sit down, won't you?" Connie invited, and he could feel her nervousness like a secret between them.

The Saint sat down, stretching his long legs luxuriously as he fished for his cigarettes.

Nelson dropped into a chair across the table and pushed a little wooden donkey towards him. He pumped its tail and a cigarette flopped out of its mouth into the Saint's lap.

Simon retrieved it admiringly.

"Quite a gadget," he remarked easily. "Too bad you haven't got one that tosses out undesirable guests with equal facility."

"That's one thing I'd rather do by hand," Nelson said. "You know him, eh?"

The Saint's shoulders lifted slightly. "Karl? We've met." He glanced at Connie. She was still standing, watching him tensely. "One of Doc Spangler's favourite thugs." He struck a light and lit his cigarette, aware of Nelson's silent curiosity about his visit. "Unfortunately," he commented, "his mind has too much specific gravity—which is only natural, perhaps, when you consider that there's more solid ivory on top of it than even my friend Hoppy Uniatz can boast."

"Who?" Nelson asked wonderingly.

They all turned to the door as a sudden story of giant footfalls came pounding up the stairs.

"That would be him now," Simon announced calmly.

"Boss!" Hoppy's laryngismal bellow shook the panels of the door almost as forcefully as the crash of his fist. "Boss, you all right? Boss!"

The Saint sprang to his feet, but Connie was already opening the door.

Hoppy surged in, looking around alertly. He spotted Simon with a gusty sigh of relief.

"Hoppy," Connie cried in alarm. "What's the matter?"

"Chees!" wheezed Mr. Uniatz. "I see dat monkey Karl comin' out after you go in, an' when you don't come out after him——"

"You really thought that brainless ape had taken me? You didn't stop him to find out?"

Mr. Uniatz floundered with embarrassment.

"Well, I chase him, boss, but he dives into somebody's basement on West End Avenoo, an' I'm kinda worried about what goes wit' youse, so I come back to find out."

The Saint handed him Karl's coat.

"He was just streamlining his wardrobe. You can have it—it's about your size and certainly your style."

He turned to Nelson. "This is Hoppy Uniatz. Hoppy—meet the Champ, Steve Nelson."

Hoppy thrust out a hamlike paw as he grabbed the coat with the other.

"Likewise, I'm sure," he beamed.

"This your sparring partner?" Nelson asked, looking Hoppy up and down with respect.

"Not Hoppy," said the Saint regretfully. "He never learned the Queensberry rules in his life. When Hoppy fights, he uses everything he has—including his head, elbows, knees, and feet. That is, when he can't use brass knuckles, a beer bottle, or a blackjack."

"Well, yeah," Hoppy admitted, "a sap makes t'ings easier, but ya can't handle it wit' dem gloves on."

"I guess not," Nelson said politely.

"But I'll sure be glad to spar wit' youse, just de same," Hoppy said. "I myself can knock dis Masked Angel kickin' and so can you."

"That's what the Angel's manager seems to be afraid of," Nelson said. He turned to Simon. "He sent that bum I threw out to proposition me."

The Saint regarded him steadily.

"Tell me more."

"Spangler's offering him the Angel's share of the purse!" Connie broke in, a note of hysteria in her voice. "Steve'll get the whole purse if he—if——"

She was trembling.

"Take it easy, baby," Nelson soothed, putting an arm around her shoulders. He looked at Simon. "I get the Angel's cut of the purse if I throw the fight. That's the proposition." He showed his teeth humourlessly. "The Boxing Commission will get a kick out of it when I tell them."

Simon shook his head.

"I'm afraid Spangler will only deny it."

"But Connie's witness!"

"Of course. But Karl was drunk. He didn't know what he was doing or saying. And he was kidding anyway. Karl's a great little kidder. At least that's what Spangler will say, and Karl will agree with him absolutely. Spangler may even fire him—in public anyway—for being a bad boy." The Saint shrugged. "I wouldn't bother about reporting it to the Commission if I were you, Steve. Just go ahead and flatten the Angel. Tell the Commission afterwards."

"No!" Connie cried. "Steve ought to report it first. Spangler shouldn't be allowed to get away with it. He's a crooked mánager and it's going to be a crooked fight!"

"I can take care of myself," Nelson said irritably. "The fight's going on, baby, come hell or high water. And I'm not going to get hurt. After all the good men I've fought, you have to worry about a stumble bum like the Angel!"

"Lookit, Champ," Hoppy said proudly. "I got a idea."

"What?"

"Whyncha tell de Doc you'll take his proposition—cash in advance? Get de dough an' den knock de fat slob for a homer. What's wrong wit' dat?"

"I'm afraid it would offer undesirable complications," Simon vetoed amiably. "There are enough complications to straighten out as it is." He pulled Mike Grady's gun from his pocket. "This, for instance," he said, and handed it, butt first, to Steve Nelson.

For the space of two seconds a startled stillness froze the room.

Then Nelson put out his hand slowly and took the weapon. He glanced at it, looked at the Saint a moment, then turned to meet Connie's wide stare. Her eyes were dark with apprehension.

The narrow margin of Mr. Uniatz's brow knotted in puzzlement.

"Boss," he said hoarsely, "ya don't mean it was *him*?"

The champion's eyes flashed to the Saint.

"What's this about?" he clipped. "Where'd you get this?"

"From some character who paid us a call last night. We've been trying to find out who he was and return it to him, in case he feels undressed without it. Mike Grady admits the gun is his, but he claims you stole it from him."

"That's ridiculous!" Connie jumped up, her eyes flashing. "Daddy was—he wasn't himself!" Sudden tears spilled down the curve of her cheeks. She continued with difficulty: "He—he'd been drinking too much. Steve had to take the gun away from him."

She flung herself on the sofa and buried her face in her hands. Steve Nelson put his arm about her shoulders.

"That's okay, baby," he comforted, "that's okay."

Hoppy stirred uncomfortably; but the Saint accepted the emotional demonstration and Nelson's uncertain glare with Indian equanimity. He was completely impersonal, completely unconfused.

He lighted another cigarette, and exhaled with judicious patience.

"All I'm interested in," he said, "is how that gun happened to find its way into my apartment last night."

Nelson seemed uncertain whether to explain or fight.

"Sure, I—I took the gun away from Grady, but how it got into the hands of a burglar I don't know. I gave it back to Connie to give back to her father." He turned to her. "You did return it to him, didn't you, honey?"

She sat up, drying the teary dampness from her nose, and shook her head in silent negation.

Nelson stared at her.

"You didn't?"

She stuffed her handkerchief away.

"I didn't want him to have it!" she said vehemently. "He wasn't safe with it. After what he did to you——"

"But——"

"I gave it to Whitey to get rid of," she said. "I told him to drop it in the river!"

"I know Whitey," said Mr. Uniatz. "He's a good trainer, Champ."

"He's my manager too, now," Nelson said.

Simon stroked the ash-tray with the end of his cigarette, clearing the glowing end.

"Since when?" he inquired.

"We signed the papers yesterday." Nelson turned back to Connie. "Whitey never said anything about you giving him the gun."

"Why should he? I just told him to get rid of it and not say anything to anybody."

"Whitey's okay," Mr. Uniatz insisted, to make his point absolutely clear. "He can do ya a lotta good."

"Sure," Nelson asserted moodily, "and he's honest—which is a damn sight more than you say for most of 'em—not that your dad isn't honest, honey," he amended quickly. "We never quarrelled over that."

The Saint drew his trimmed cigarette end to a fresh glow.

"It sounds cosy as hell," he murmured. "But I'd still like

very much to find out what brother Mullins did with that gun after he got it."

The girl said : "I don't know. . . . I don't know."

Footfalls sounded on the stairway outside and the door-bell rang.

"That's probably him now," Nelson said. "He's going to the gym with me."

He opened the door and Whitey Mullins stepped in, as advertised.

"Hiya, Champ," he greeted, and stopped short as he caught sight of Hoppy heaving to his feet.

"Whitey!" Mr. Uniatz welcomed, surging forward and flinging a cranelike arm about Whitey's shoulders in leviathan camaraderie.

Mullins staggered beneath the shock of its weight; his derby slipped over his forehead and he pushed it back crossly.

"Easy, you big ape!" he snarled.

"We just hear you are de Champ's new manager," Hoppy bellowed happily.

"This is the Saint," Steve Nelson introduced. "You've heard of him."

Whitey Mullins's pale eyes widened a trifle; his mouth formed a nominal smile.

"You bet I have."

He thrust out a narrow monkey-like hand. "I seen you at the fights last night, didn't I?"

The Saint nodded, shaking the hand.

"I was there."

"Sure you seen us," Hoppy said. "You're de foist one tells us de Torpedo is crocked, remember?"

"I never wanna have nuttin' like that happen to me again," Mullins said grimly. "It's awful. I still can't figure how it coulda happened. The Torpedo was in great con-dition. The poor guy musta had a weak ticker—or sump'n." He turned to Simon, a faint gleam coming alive in his pale eyes. "I heard you raised a stink with that louse Spangler after the fight."

The Saint launched a smoke-ring in the direction of the gun lying on the table and smiled dreamily.

"The stench you mention," he said, "was already there.

Hoppy and I merely went to investigate its source."

"Yeah," Hoppy corroborated. "De Angel stinks out loud! Why, dat bum can't fight."

"How can you say that," Connie objected tensely, "when he's just killed a man in the ring?"

"That was an accident." Mullins waved away her fears with an impatient gesture of one thin hairy hand. "That crook Spangler will be eatin' off'n his social security when we get through with him, huh, Champ? You'll murder that big beef he stole from me!"

His hatchet face was venomous, as though distorted by an inward vision of vengeance.

"Whitey," Connie said, "what did you do with that gun?"

Whitey's rapt stare came back to earth and jerked in her direction.

"Gun?" he said blankly, and followed her glance at the table. "Oh, *that*."

He looked quickly at Steve, at Simon and Hoppy, and back to Connie again.

"Yes, that," she said. "I told you to get rid of it."

"I did," Whitey said. "How did it get here?"

Hoppy grunted: "Some heister crashes de Saint's flat last night. He leaves de rod."

"Yeah? Who was it?"

"That," said the Saint amiably, "is what I'd like to know. If you got rid of this gun, what did you do with it?"

Mullins snapped his fingers as if smitten by recollection.

"Oh, I almost forgot!" He reached into his coat, extracted a wallet, and selected a ten and a five. He offered the two bills to Connie. "Here. It's your dough."

"Mine?" She didn't touch the money. "Why?"

"It's the dough I got for it at th' hock shop," he explained. "Ten bucks on the rod—five bucks for the pawn ducat I sell for chips in a poker session the other night."

"She shook her head quickly.

"No. You keep it. For your trouble."

Whitey unhesitatingly replaced the money in his wallet. "Okay, if you say so."

"Who did you sell the ticket to?" Simon inquired casually.

"Mushky Thompson," Whitey said. "But it goes through his kick like a dose of salts. Pretty soon it's movin' from one pot to another like cash."

"Yes, but who got it in the end?" Nelson asked.

"I quit at three in th' morning. Who it winds up with, I couldn't say." Whitey glanced at his wrist watch. " 'Bout time we was headin' for the gym, Stevie."

"Was Karl sitting in on the game?" Simon persisted.

Whitey blinked.

"I don't think so."

"That's an expensive gun, Whitey," Simon pursued mildly. "Is ten all you could get on it?"

Mullins spread his hands, expressively.

"No papers, no licence. Ten bucks and no questions asked is pretty good these days."

"I haven't been following the market lately," Simon confessed. "Where did you hock it?"

The trainer lifted his derby and thoughtfully massaged the bald spot in his straw-coloured hair with two fingers of the same hand.

"It's a place off Sixth Avenue, as I recall," he said finally, dropping his chapeau back on its accustomed perch. " 'Neath Forty-fourth. The Polar Bear Trading and Loan Company."

The Saint picked up the gun again.

"Thanks. I may need this a bit longer—if nobody minds." He slipped it into his pocket and glanced at Nelson. He said inconsequentially: "I wouldn't do any boxing until that hand heals, Steve."

Whitey's eyes flashed to the hand Steve Nelson had been carrying palm upwards to conceal the raw gash along its back. He swore softly as he examined it.

"It's just a scratch," Nelson scoffed. "I was going to take care of it before we left."

"The next time our friend Karl visits you," Simon advised him, "don't give him a chance to touch you. That finger jewellery he wears is more dangerous than brass knuckles."

"Karl!" Whitey turned with outraged incredulity. "He was here."

"He had a little proposition," Nelson said. "Wanted me

to throw the fight for both ends of the gate."

"The louse!" Mullins exploded. "The dirty no-good louse. I mighta known Spangler'd try sump'n like that. He knows that ham of his ain't got a chance."

Simon crushed out his cigarette in the ash-tray.

"I'd feel even more sure of that if I could drop in and watch you train, Steve," he said. "In fact, I'd rather like to work out with you myself."

"Any time," Nelson said.

"To-morrow morning," said the Saint. "Come on, Hoppy—let's keep on the trail of the roving roscoe."

IX

The only connection that the Polar Bear Trading and Loan Company might possibly have had with the animal for which it was named, Simon decided as he entered the premises, was the arctic quality of its proprietor's stare. This personality, however, was a far cry from the conventional bearded skull-capped shylock that was once practically a cliché in the public mind. He was, in fact, a pale, smooth-shaven young man with curly black hair, elegantly attired in a sports jacket and striped flannels, who scanned the Saint as he entered with eyes of a peculiar ebony hardness. He barely lifted a brow in recognition as he caught sight of Hoppy on Simon's heels.

"Hi, Ruby," Hoppy said. "I have a idea I remember dis jernt from 'way back. Long time no see, huh?"

To the Saint's unsentimental blue eyes, Ruby slipped into a familiar niche like a nickel into a slot. Just as a jungle dweller knows at a glance the vulture from the eagle, the ruminant from the carnivore, so the Saint knew that in the stone jungles of the city this specimen was of a scavenger breed—with a touch of reptile, perhaps. And the fact that Mr. Uniatz knew the place of old was almost enough to confirm the discredit of its agate-eyed proprietor.

Ruby flinched instinctively as Mike Grady's revolver appeared in the Saint's fist, held for an instant with its muzzle pointed at the pawnbroker's midriff, before Simon laid it on the counter.

"This gun," said the Saint, "was pawned here a few days ago. Remember?"

The pawnbroker studied it a moment. His delicately curved brows lifted slightly, the tailored shoulders accompanying them upwards in the mere soupçon of a shrug.

"I see lots of guns," he said tonelessly. "Every day."

He looked at Simon with eyes that had the blank unfocused quality of the blind.

"Whitey Mullins hocks it," Hoppy amplified. "Ya know Whitey."

"However, he didn't claim it himself," Simon went on. "Someone else did—a few days ago. I want to know who."

"Who are you?" Ruby asked in his flat monotone. "What gives?"

Hoppy grabbed his shoulder in a bone-crushing clutch and, with his other hand, pointed a calloused digit directly under Simon's nose.

"Dis," he explained unmistakably, "is de Saint. When de boss asks ya a question, ya don't talk back."

Ruby shook off Hoppy's paw and flicked imaginary contamination from where it had been. He looked back to the Saint.

"So?" he said.

"This gun," Simon continued pleasantly, "was redeemed. Who turned in the ticket? I promise there's no trouble in it for you."

The young man across the counter sighed and stared moodily at the gun.

"Okay, so you give me a promise. Can my wife cash it at the bank if I get knocked off for talkin' too much?"

"No," Simon conceded. "But your chances of living to a ripe and fruitless old age are far better, believe me, if you do give me the information I want."

The pawnbroker's eyes slid over him with stony opacity.

It began to be borne in upon Mr. Uniatz that his old pal was being very slow to co-operate. His reaction to that realisation was a darkening scowl of disapproval. Backgrounded by the peculiar advantages of Hoppy's normal face, this expression conveyed a warning about as subtle as the first smoke rising from an active volcano. . . . Ruby caught a glimpse of it; and whatever cogitation was going on behind the curtain of his face reached an immediate conclusion.

"Why ask me?" he complained wearily. "I don't ask his monicker. I ain't interested. He's a tall skinny jerk with a face like a horse. He bought a set of throwing knives from me once. That's all I know."

The Saint's perspective roamed through a corridor of memory that Ruby's description had faintly illuminated. A nebulous image formed somewhere in the vista, and tried to coalesce within recognisable outlines; but for the moment the shape still eluded him.

"Give you ten on the rod," Ruby offered disinterestedly. Simon picked up the revolver and slipped it back into his pocket.

"I'm afraid it isn't mine," he said truthfully; and a sardonic glimmer flickered in the young pawnbroker's eyes for an instant.

"You don't say."

"As a matter of fact, it belongs to George Murphy, whose initials are M.G., spelled backwards," Simon informed him solemnly, and sauntered from the shop with Hoppy in his wake.

It was perhaps the way the black sedan roared away from the kerb at the end of the block that pressed an alarm button in the Saint's reflexes. It forced itself into the stream of traffic with a suddenness that compelled the drivers behind to give way with screaming brakes. For one vivid instant, as if by the split-second illumination of a flash of lightning, Simon saw the driver, alone in the front seat, hunched over the wheel, his hat pulled low over his eyes, his face hidden in the shadow of the brim, a glimpse of stubbled jowl barely visible. He had an impression of two others crouched in the deeper shadow of the back seat, their faces obscured by handkerchiefs, the vague angle of their upraised arms pointing towards him. . . . All this the Saint saw, absorbed, analysed, and acted upon in the microscopic fragment of time before he kicked Hoppy's feet from under him so that they both dropped to the sidewalk together as the black sedan raced by, sending a fusillade of bullets cracking over them into the pawnshop window beyond.

Hoppy Uniatz, prone on his stomach, fumbled out his gun and fired a single shot just as the gunmen's car cut in ahead of a truck and beat a red light.

"Hold it!" Simon ordered. "You're more likely to hurt the wrong people."

They scrambled up and dusted off their clothes.

"You okay, boss?" Hoppy asked anxiously.

"Just a bit chilled from the draught of those bullets going by."

Hoppy glared up the street at the corner where their assailants had vanished.

"De doity lowsers," he rumbled. "Who wuz it, boss?"

The Saint had no answer; but if he had, it would have been interrupted by the yelp of the curly-haired young man peering pallidly from behind the edge of the pawn-shop doorframe.

"Get the hell away from here!" he bawled, with a shrill vibrato in his voice. "Get yourselves knocked off some other place."

Hoppy turned on him redly, like a buffalo preparing to charge; but Simon grabbed one beefy bicep and yanked him back on his heels.

"Stop it, you damn fool!" he snapped. "Don't take it out on *him*!"

He stepped to the doorway, drawing the knife strapped to his forearm.

From within the pawnshop Ruby's voice, strident with fear, screeched: "Come in here and so help me God, I'll blast ya!"

Simon spotted him crouching behind a counter, goggling over the sights of a sawed-off shotgun. He thrust out a knee as a barrier to Hoppy's impulsive acceptance of the challenge, and began working quickly.

He was aware of the scared faces starting to peer out of windows, of people moving out of doorways and peeping around corners. A crowd seemed to be converging from every direction, drawn by the shots and the wildfire smell of excitement.

In a few seconds he cut out one of the bullets imbedded in the doorframe. He dropped the scarred slug in his pocket and moved away.

"Let's get out of here," said the Saint, taking Hoppy's arm. "I still think it would be a social error to be arrested on Sixth Avenue, even if they have tried to change the name to 'Avenue of the Americas'."

X

"Who done it?" Mr. Uniatz asked once more, his neanderthaloid countenance still furrowed with the remnants of rage. "He makes me get mud on dis new suit."

The Saint grinned as he swung the convertible around a corner.

"Never mind, Hoppy," he said. "It helps to tone down the pattern. . . . Anyway, all I saw was two gentlemen with handkerchiefs over their faces in a black sedan with no rear licence plate."

Hoppy scowled.

"I seen dat too," he grumbled. "What I wanna know is, who wuz dey?"

"Did you notice the outside hand of the fellow driving the car? It flashed in the sun."

Mr. Uniatz blinked.

"Huh?"

"He was wearing a lot of finger jewellery."

"Finger jewellery?"

"Rings—large flashy rings."

For a long moment Hoppy strove painfully to determine the relation of the driver's digital ornamentation to his identity.

"Ya can't never tell about pansies," he concluded despondently.

The car swung east to Fifth Avenue and then south, moving leisurely with the traffic.

The Saint was in no hurry. He wanted a breathing spell to summarise the situation.

So far, two attempts had been made to murder him since the affair in the dressing-room the previous night. An emotional thug might have found the Saint's insolence sufficiently provocative to inspire an urgent desire for his death; and certainly a blow in the solar plexus would be regarded in some circles as an act of war, and worthy of an act of reprisal. But somehow the Saint could not conceive of Dr. Spangler, even with that kind of provocation, taking the risk of a murder charge. For Spangler was neither emotional nor reckless. He was an operator who had learned from experience to be thrifty of risks, to allow as much a margin of safety as possible to every enterprise. An attempt to bribe Nelson was in line with that; but the only motive Spangler was likely to consider strong enough to justify an attempt at murder would be the fear that the Saint's interference might affect the Angel's chance of taking the title.

Would Spangler, even with a guilty conscience, have taken alarm so precipitately? Would he be afraid, on such scanty evidence, that the Saint had discovered the secret of the Angel's victories? . . . For that matter, was there any secret more sinister than common chicanery and corruption? So far, he could only conjecture.

"And that," said the Saint, "leaves us just one more call to make."

"Who we gonna see now, boss?" asked Mr. Uniatz, settling philosophically into the social whirl.

"That depends on who's home."

Simon swung the car towards Gramercy Park, and presently slowed down as he turned into a secluded side street lined with grey stone houses as conservatively old-fashioned in their way as the Riverside Drive brown stones were in theirs, but with a polished elegance that bespoke substantially higher rents.

"What home, boss?" Hoppy insisted practically.

The Saint peered at the numbers of the houses slipping by.

"Doc Spangler's."

Hoppy's eyes became almost as wide as shoe buttons.

"Ya mean it's de Doc what tries to gun us?"

"It was more likely one of the bad boys he chums around with," said the Saint. "But he probably knew about it. Bad companions, Hoppy, are apt to get a man into trouble. Of course you wouldn't know about that."

"No, boss," said Mr. Uniatz seriously.

The Saint was starting to pull in towards one of the grey stone houses when he saw the other car. The rear licence plate was on now, but there was no doubt about the genesis of the neat hole with its radiation of tiny cracks that perforated the rear window. Simon pointed it out to Hoppy, as he kept the convertible rolling and parked it some twenty yards farther down the block.

"Chees," Hoppy said in admiration, "I hit it right in de middle. Dey musta felt de breeze when it goes by."

"I hope it gave them as bad a chill as theirs gave us," said the Saint.

They walked back to the house and went up the broad stone steps and rang the bell. After a while the door opened a few inches. Simon leaned on it and opened it the rest of the way. It pushed back a long lean beanpole of a man with a sad horse face and dangling arms whose wrists stuck out nakedly from the cuffs of his sweater. And as he saw him, a gleam of recognition shot through the Saint's memory.

The tall man's recognition was a shade slower, perhaps because his faculties were slightly dulled by the surprise of feeling the door move into his chest. He exhaled abruptly, and staggered back, his long arms flying loosely as though dangling on strings. As he recovered his balance he took in Hoppy's monstrous bulk, and then the slim supple figure of the Saint closing the door after him and leaning on it with the poised relaxation of a watchful cat, the gun in his hand held almost negligently. . . . Slowly, the long bony wrists lifted in surrender.

The young pawnbroker's description repeated itself in the Saint's memory. Also he recalled Mike Grady's office and a tall thin character among the loiterers in the reception. This was the same individual. The odyssey of the gun was beginning to show connections.

"Who are you, chum?" Simon asked, moving slightly towards him.

"I know him, boss," Hoppy put in. "De name is Slim Mancini. He useta be a hot car hustler."

"I work here," the beanpole said in a whining nasal tenor that had a distinct equine quality about it. He sounded, the Saint thought, just like a horse. A sick horse. "I'm the butler," Mancini added. He glanced back at a door down the hall and opened his mouth a fraction of a second before the Saint stepped behind him and clamped a hand over it.

"No announcements, please," the Saint said, his other arm curving about Mancini's neck like a band of flexible steel. "This is strictly formal. You understand, don't you?"

The man nodded and gasped a lungful of air as the Saint removed the pressure on his throat.

"Slim Mancini—buttlin'!" Hoppy sneered hoarsely. "Dat's a laugh." He grunted suddenly as Simon jabbed a warning elbow into his stomach.

The muffled voices in the room down the hall had gone silent.

"Walk ahead of us to that door," the Saint whispered to Spangler's cadaverous lackey, "and open it and go in. Don't say anything. We'll be right behind you. Go on."

Mancini's sad eyes suddenly widened as he stared over the Saint's shoulder, apparently at something behind him.

Simon rather resented that. It implied a lack of respect for his experience, reading background, and common intelligence that was slightly insulting. However, he was accommodating enough to start to turn and look in the indicated direction. It was only a token start, and he reversed it so quickly that Mancini's hand was still inches from his shoulder holster when the Saint's left exploded against his lantern jaw.

Simon caught the toppling body before it folded and lowered it noiselessly to the carpet.

Mr. Uniatz kicked it carefully in the stomach for additional security.

"De noive of de guy," he said. "Tryin' a corny trick like dat. Whaddas he t'ink we are?"

"He'll know better next time," said the Saint. "But now I suppose we'll have to open our own doors——"

Blam!

The stunning crash of a heavy-calibre pistol smashed against their eardrums and sent them diving to either side of the hallway.

The Saint lay there, gun at the ready, waiting. The shot had come from the room ahead, where they'd heard the voices; but he noticed that the door was still shut. . . .

Seconds passed. . . . A weak moan, muffled by the closed door, punctuated the silence.

Simon signalled Hoppy with a lift of his chin, and they stood up again and advanced noiselessly. He motioned Hoppy back into the shadows as they reached the door. Then he turned the knob, kicked the door open, and stayed to one side, out of reach of possible fire.

There was silence for a moment. All he could see in the sunlit portion of the room visible to him was a huge fireplace and a corner of a desk. . . . Then from within came a challenge in an accent that was unmistakable.

"Well?" Dr. Spangler barked impatiently. "Come in!"

The Saint stood there a moment, looking into the triangle of the interior visible to him, estimating his chances of meeting a blast of gunfire if he showed himself. In the two seconds that he stood there, weighing the odds, he also realised that an unexpected diversion had taken place. What it was he didn't know. But it did lend some excuse for hoping his presence might yet be miraculously undiscovered. . . . It was a flimsy enough hope, but he decided to gamble on it. He signalled Hoppy to stay back and cover him as best he could, and stepped into the room.

Doc Spangler was seated at the desk, leaning forward, his arms on the desk, staring at him. Beyond him in a corner of the big room was Karl, down on one knee beside the prostrate body of a man whose head was concealed by the squat body of Spangler's ursine lieutenant. There was a gun in his hand, pointed at the Saint from his hip, as if he had been interrupted in his examination of the man he had apparently just shot.

For one second it was quite a skin-prickling tableau; and then Simon took a quick step to one side which placed Spangler's body between him and Karl's gun muzzle.

"Better tell your baboon to lay his gun on the floor, Doc," he suggested, and his smile was wired for sudden destruction. "You might get hurt."

Spangler half turned in his swivel chair toward Karl.

"You imbecile!" he spat, his usual fat complacency temporarily disconnected. "I told you to put up that gun! It's gotten me into enough trouble for one day. Put it on the floor as he says."

Karl laid the gun down slowly, grudgingly, glooming balefully past Spangler at the Saint.

"Thank you," said the Saint. "Now get up and stand away."

Karl rose to his feet slowly and shuffled aside as the Saint stepped around the desk and came to a startled halt.

He was looking down incredulously at the face of the man lying on the floor. One side of it was caked with blood and the hair was red with it, but that presented no obstacle to recognising the owner. It was Whitey Mullins.

XI

Mr. Uniatz's heavy breathing reverberated in Simon's ear.

"Dey got Whitey!" His head jerked up suddenly at Karl and Spangler, his gun lifting. "Whitey was me pal!" he snarled. "Why you——"

Simon stopped him.

"Don't shoot the Doc—yet. Whitey may need him." The Saint's eyes were cold blue chips. "Let's have the score, Spangler, and make it fast."

"He isn't dead," wheezed the fat man damply. "It's only a graze. He brought it on himself, coming here to my home to assault me. Karl had to stop him, but he didn't hurt him much. You can see that for yourself. The bullet just grazed his scalp and went into the wall there—see?"

He pointed a plump finger to a hole in the wall above Mr. Mullins's prostrate form.

Whitey moaned and opened his eyes.

"Saint!" he mumbled feverishly.

Simon pocketed his automatic and bent over him.

"Take it easy, Whitey. It's okay." He went on without turning his head : "Doc, I'll bet you a case of Old Forester that Karl doesn't live to draw that gun he's trying to sneak out of his pocket."

"Eh?" Spangler grunted blankly.

Hoppy's attention flashed back to the danger on hand, swivelling his gun to the thug's belly. One of Karl's hairy paws had already dipped halfway into a coat pocket.

"Reach!" Mr. Uniatz rasped.

"Hands empty, please," Simon smiled pleasantly over his shoulder.

The squat gunman slowly dragged his hand out of his pocket and raised both arms over his head.

Simon stepped over to him and extracted a Colt automatic from his pocket. Then he proceeded to run his hands with expert deftness down Karl's sides, under his arms, inside his thighs, and along his back. He patted his sleeves, paused, and plucked another gun from inside one of the gunman's cuffs. It looked like a toy, no larger than a magnified watch charm, but it held a ·22-calibre shell in its chamber.

"Forgive me for underestimating you, comrade," he said. "You're a walking arsenal, aren't you?"

He pulled what seemed to be a fountain-pen from Karl's breast pocket and examined it briefly. He chuckled, pushing Karl so that he stumbled backwards. Simultaneously, Simon exploded a capsule of tear gas from one end of the "fountain-pen" squarely into the gangster's nose. Karl clutched his face with both hands and reeled half-way across the room, tripping over a chair and crashing to the floor.

"That stuff spreads!" Spangler gasped. "We'll all get it——"

"Take it easy," said the Saint. "The windows are open, and there isn't enough in one of those pills to do much harm unless it's shot straight at you."

"What do you want?" Spangler demanded, a glister of panic in his eyes. "Why did you come here?" He looked down at Whitey as the trainer gripped the edge of the desk for support and pulled himself to his feet with Hoppy's quick aid. Spangler pointed at him, his eyes narrowing. "I understand. You're working for *him* now!"

Simon lighted a cigarette.

"Don't confuse yourself, Doc. Hoppy and I represent our own business only—the Happy Dreams Shroud and Casket Company. I'm sorry we weren't able to accommodate your boy Karl last night. We'd have liked to give him a fitting, but he was in such a hurry. . . ."

He glanced at Karl who, on all fours, was crawling blindly toward the door.

A leer of gargoyle delight transfigured Hoppy's features as he observed the proffered target. He took three steps across the room and, with somewhat better form than the previous night, launched a thunderous drop kick that caught the unfortunate thug squarely, lifting his entire body off the floor in a soaring ballotade, and dropped him sprawling in a corner.

Spangler stared fascinated at his limp cohort, and then again at Hoppy. His gaze swung uncertainly back to the Saint. He cleared his throat.

"I fail to comprehend," he began, with an attempt to regain his habitual pomposity, "why you should——"

"I'm quite sure you do comprehend," the Saint broke in suavely, "why I should resent your sending that goon over to my apartment last night to kill me."

Spangler opened and shut his mouth like a frog.

"*I* sent him to your apartment?" he said in shocked tones.

"You hoid him!" Hoppy growled.

"But my dear boy, I did no such thing!" Doc Spangler plucked a handkerchief from his breast pocket and mopped his shining pink brow. He frowned at Karl, who was beginning to stir again in the corner. "If he took it upon himself to—uh—visit you last night, it must have been a matter of personal inspiration. I had nothing to do with it, believe me."

"Strangely enough," said the Saint surprisingly, "I do."

"He's lyin'," Whitey grated fiercely. "He was gonna knock me off if you hadn't come when ya did."

"That's entirely untrue," Spangler said. "Mullins forced his way in here; he was abusive and threatening, and when he tried to attack me physically Karl had to fire a shot in my defence."

"However," the Saint continued, "a repeat performance was staged less than an hour ago near Sixth Avenue, with three characters and a black sedan taking the chief rôles in another attempt to reunite Hoppy and me with our illustrious ancestors."

"I assure you, sir, that I——"

"Excuse me," the Saint interrupted. "I'm willing to believe that Karl might attempt a solo mission on account of the kicking around we gave him in the dressing-room, but there were three men in the second try. I'm rather certain the driver was Karl. He might have done that to grind a private axe, but the other two must have had other inducements, Doc, old boy. Inducements supplied by you, perhaps."

Spangler shook his head bewilderedly.

"But—you're entirely off the track, dear boy. Karl has been here in the house for the past three hours."

"Then he must have a twin running around loose gunning for me. . . . As for the other two—I'd lay some odds that one of them was your new butler, Jeeves Mancini, the demon major-domo, who seemed to be sort of lying down on the job when I saw him. The third man," said the Saint dispassionately, "may very well have been you."

Spangler's expression of outraged innocence would have done credit to a cardinal accused of committing bigamy.

"But that's simply preposterous. I haven't left the house yet to-day. As a matter of fact, Karl and Slim and I were about to leave for the gym to meet the Angel when you arrived." He spread his hands. "Surely you're not serious when you say you actually expected to find three anonymous snipers—men who tried to shoot you from a car like movie gangsters—here in my house?"

"I don't say I had that idea all along," Simon admitted. "It just kind of grew on me when I found their car parked in front of this house. *Your* Stanley Steamer, I presume, Dr. Livingstone?"

"What!" Spangler's eyes were round with appalled amazement. "My dear boy, are you sure you're not feeling the heat? My car has been parked there all day."

"I did feel the heat," said the Saint gently, "of your car's engine. For a jalopy that hadn't been moved all day, it was awful feverish."

"Standing out there in the sun——"

"It might get the chill off. But I hardly think the sun was quite hot enough to burn those holes through the rear window and the windshield."

Spangler sank back into his chair, shaking his head helplessly.

"I don't know what you're trying to prove," he protested earnestly. "But if you mean those bullet holes, they've been there for nearly a month now. One of the boys became a little exuberant one night and——"

"Skip it," said the Saint amiably. "I didn't come here to torment you by putting the stretch on your imaginative powers. Any time a good story is needed, I'm sure you can come up with me. I just wanted to make one point for the record. The next time any uncomfortable passes are made at me or any of my friends—among whom I am going to include Steve Nelson—I am just automatically going to drop by and beat the guts out of you and any of your team mates who happen to be around. It may seem rather arbitrary of me, Doc, but an expert like you should be able to allow for my psychopathic fixations. . . . Let's go, Whitey."

Whitey let go the desk unsteadily.

"Okay. I can make it," he said, and waved away Hoppy's helpfully offered hand. He followed Simon, spitting contemptuously on the floor as he passed Karl's cowed figure huddled in the corner.

As they sped northward up Fifth Avenue, Mullins explained the predicament in which the Saint had found him.

"I guess I was nuts," he said, "goin' into that den of thieves alone, but I went off my chump just thinkin' of that lousy fink sendin' his stooge to proposition my boy."

"You shoulda gone heeled, pal," Hoppy said.

"I did." Whitey slapped his right hip. "But I just figured on bawling Spangler out, not killin' him; and then I get blasted from behind."

"How long were you there?" Simon asked.

" 'Bout half an hour. Say!" Whitey's voice lifted as though remembering. "It couldn'a been Karl who was with those mugs what you said tried to gun you. He was in that room with Spangler most of the time I was cussin' the Doc." His pale eyes brightened with thought. "Y'know, there's a coupla hot guys with the Scarponi mob who Spangler hires sometimes for jobs. They look a lot like Karl."

The Saint shrugged.

"He still might have made it. I figure that Karl got some

of his pals together in a hurry after he left Steve's place, and followed Hoppy and me when we left. I wouldn't give him an alibi unless he punched a time clock. You certainly weren't in shape to time everything to the minute." He glanced at Whitey. "We'd better drop you off at a doctor's so you can get that fixed up. How do you feel?"

"Oh, I'm okay, Saint," Whitey minimised. He felt his blood-clotted head gingerly. "The slug took a li'l hair off, that's all. Just drop me off at Kayo Jackson's gym. I'll wash up there."

"It's your noodle." Simon swung the wheel to his left and cut westward towards Sixth Avenue.

"Did you mean it," Whitey asked after a moment, "when you said you'd work with the Champ?"

The Saint fished a cigarette from his breast pocket and punched the dashboard lighter.

"You're the trainer, Whitey."

Whitey found a match in his pocket and struck it with his thumb, cupping the flame as he held it to the Saint's cigarette.

"Kayo'll go nuts when I tell him," he grinned. "Wit' you and the Champ workin' out here together, we'll pack 'em in."

"At two bits a head," Mr. Uniatz mentioned, rather quickly for him. "So whaddas de boss get out of it?"

"I'll see that Kayo shells out with the Saint's cut of the gymnasium gate, don't worry."

"Hoppy is my agent," said the Saint.

He was thinking more about the slug he carried in his pocket—the slug he had dug out of the pawnshop door-frame. He had to ponder the fact that neither Karl's guns nor Slim Mancini's were of the same calibre—and in spite of what he had said, he couldn't really visualise Doc Spangler doing his own torpedo work. There was at least negative support for Whitey's evidence that Karl had been in the house during the time the Saint thought he'd seen him at the wheel of the gunmen's car. Yet Simon found it impossible to reconcile his indelibly photographic impression of the man who had driven that car with the possibility that it had been someone other than Karl. . . . If it hadn't been Karl, then it had certainly been his identical twin.

XII

The dawning sun arched a causeway of golden light through the Saint's bedroom window, glinting on his crisp dark hair as he laced on the heavy rubber-soled shoes in which he did his road work with Steve every morning. Hoppy, bleary-eyed, leaned against the door-frame, watching him unhappily.

"Chees," he complained hoarsely, "will I be glad when de fight is over to-morrow night! I'm goddam sick of gettin' up wit' de boids every mornin' to do road-work wit' Nelson." He yawned cavernously. "Dis at'letic life is moider."

"*What* athletic life?" the Saint inquired with mild irony. "The only road-work *you* do is follow behind in the car with Whitey."

Hoppy sighed lugubriously.

"Dat ain't de pernt, boss. It's just I don't get de sleep a guy needs at my age."

"Well, I must say you wear the burden of your years with lavender and old dignity," Simon complimented him. He stood up and headed for the door. "Come on, Steve and Whitey will be waiting for us."

Hoppy groaned and followed like an exhausted elephant.

They found Nelson near the Fifty-ninth Street entrance of Central Park, alone.

"Whitey's got another of those headaches," he explained. "I think maybe that bullet Karl grazed him with last month must have shaken his brains up worse than he admitted."

The Saint nodded, breaking into an easy, jogging trot beside Nelson as they struck out northward along the side of a winding park road.

"Could be," he agreed.

Mr. Uniatz climbed into the car again, and waited disconsolately for several minutes in order to give them a good head start. Then he started the car up and followed slowly behind.

Some thirty minutes later the Saint and Steve Nelson were jogging eastward along the inner northern boundary of Central Park, following the edge of the park road. The

Saint's long legs pumped in smooth, tireless rhythm as he breathed the dew-washed fragrance of blooming shrubs that covered the green slopes. At that early hour there was practically no traffic through Central Park, and he filled his lungs with air untainted by the fumes of carbon monoxide and tetraethyl lead. . . . During the past weeks the regimen of training in which he had joined Steve Nelson had tempered his lithe strength to the whiplash resilience of Toledo steel and surcharged his reflexes with jungle lightning; and as he ran his blood seemed to tingle with the sheer exultation of just living. He drank deeply of the perfume of the morning, smiling at a sky of the same clear blue as his eyes, his every nerve singing, feeling his youth renewed indestructibly.

He glanced back once at the brooding shadow of Hoppy's face behind the wheel of the car far behind, and chuckled softly. Nelson, trotting beside him, asked : "What's funny?"

The Saint nodded over his shoulder.

"Hoppy. He's miserable. Nobody to talk to. Nothing to drink."

Nelson looked back and grinned.

Ahead to his left over the park wall some distance away Simon could see the broad terminus of Lenox Avenue coming into view. Directly in front of them, through the trees, he caught the gleam of the lake that lies at the northern end of the park. The park road swoops sharply to the right at this point, paralleling the lake for a distance as it winds southward again.

The easy purr of an approaching car blended against and quickly drowned out the sound of the Saint's car hugging the edge of the road. The overtaking car accelerated as it came up to them and whooshed past, disappearing round the curve some distance ahead.

The Saint looked after it thoughtfully. Only two private cars had passed them since they'd started running—and both of them had been this same big limousine with the curtained windows.

"I hope you won't be too busy the day after the fight," Nelson said, glancing at him.

The Saint pondered his remark for a moment.

"That all depends. Why?"

"Connie and I have set the date for our wedding. Will you be my best man?"

The Saint's quick, warm smile sparkled at him. "It'll be a pleasure, Steve."

Nelson slapped him on the back as they jogged along. "Thanks."

"Will you be staying on at your place on Riverside Drive?"

"Yeah. Having it redecorated. As a matter of fact they started work to-day. It was the only date I could make that would have it finished when we get back from our honeymoon, but the place is a mess right now."

"Why don't you move in with me until the day after to-morrow?" Simon suggested. "We've got a spare bed that you're welcome to."

"That's swell of you, Saint."

"No trouble at all. Besides, it'll be easier to keep an eye on you."

They padded on with tireless ease, tucking another mile behind them. The city was beginning to take on life. In the distance Simon could see the subway entrance cupolas at the head of Lenox Avenue with early morning workers hurrying towards each of them. But the park as yet seemed quite deserted. The lake was like a sheet of silvered glass with a covey of green rowboats huddled along the near shore about their mother boathouse. . . . As they approached the curve in the road the path along the road narrowed and the Saint crossed over to the opposite side to run parallel with Steve.

He had just reached the curve when he heard, with startling suddenness, the roar of a car approaching behind him. He glanced over his shoulder. The black limousine that had already passed them twice was crossing over to his side of the road with swiftly increasing acceleration, rushing straight at him. In that split second he perceived with crystal clarity the tall, bony, high-shouldered figure hunched over the wheel, eyes crinkled with murderous intent, and knew instantly that the driver had stalked them in the hope of catching him apart from Nelson.

He flung himself down the gentle embankment that sloped to the sidewalk before he even heard Nelson's warn-

ing yell. The big limousine screamed around on two wheels
as it tried to stick to the curve, but its mile-a-minute
momentum was too great. It bounded sideways over the
slope, entirely clearing the iron railing that bordered the
sidewalk, struck the concrete pavement with a sickening
crash, and took a fifteen-foot bounce into the lake, landing on its top, its wheels just visible above the water and
still spinning.

The Saint leaped to his feet and ran to the water's edge
with Nelson sprinting down the embankment after him. A
screech of brakes knifed the morning stillness as Hoppy
leaped out of his car to join them.

"He ran at you deliberately!" Nelson blurted as he
came up.

"That's my trouble—I can't keep my fans away," said
the Saint, and plunged into the water.

"Let him croak!" Hoppy bellowed breathlessly as he
came running up. "De bum was trying to get ya!"

The Saint needed only one dive to tell him what he
wanted to know. Nelson read the truth on his face as he
came to the surface and rejoined him on the sidewalk.

"You know him?" he asked.

"Doc Spangler," the Saint said laconically, "is going to
need a new butler."

He glanced up at the park's Lenox Avenue entrance.
Several people, appearing magically, were running down
to the scene of the "accident."

"Let's get out of here," he said, and bounded back over
the iron fence and up the embankment.

Hoppy and Nelson followed him. They got into the car
and sped away as an approaching police car siren lifted
its high, clear alarum on the morning air.

"Spangler again," Nelson muttered grimly, staring
straight ahead.

A stream of earnest profanity issued from Mr. Uniatz's
practised lips.

"You shoulda stuck a knife in de rat when you was
under wit' him," he concluded. "Dose dumb jackasses back
dere are liable to pull him out before he drowns."

"They'll have to pull him off that steering column first,"
Simon said callously. "He's stuck on it like a bug on a pin."

"But why," Steve Nelson puzzled, "did he try to do it? What has he got against *you*?"

"Maybe he thinks I'm bringing you luck. If I'm out of the way, he's backing the Angel to take care of you."

Nelson said nothing for a moment. Then he shook his head.

"It doesn't make good sense," he said. "I don't get it."

The Saint shrugged.

"Forget it. Spangler and his outfit are a bunch of psychopaths, anyway." He unhooked a key from his ring and handed it to Nelson. "Here—to the apartment. I'll use Hoppy's key."

Nelson took it with troubled gratitude. "Thanks—thanks a lot, Saint. I expect I'll take my stuff over some time this afternoon. I've got some things to do before I move."

"I've a few things to attend to myself," said the Saint. "Move in whenever you're ready."

They let Steve Nelson out at the Fifty-ninth Street end of the park where he'd parked his car. He put a hand on the Saint's arm, leaning over the door of the convertible.

"Tell me," he asked worriedly, "what goes on between you and Spangler? Why does he hate you so?"

A bantering smile touched the Saint's lean, cynical face.

"We're allergic, I guess," he said. "Don't worry about it."

Steve sighed and shook his head perplexedly. He turned and walked to his car.

"Where to now, boss?" Hoppy inquired as the Saint drove the car out into the tide of Fifth Avenue.

"Mike Grady's," Simon Templar said flatly.

XIII

Mr. Michael Grady was incredulous. He leaned forward in his swivel chair, his mouth open and his eyebrows lifted in soaring arches.

"Two attempts on your life!" he repeated. "By Spangler?"

The Saint, relaxed in one of Grady's worn leather chairs, studied him through drifting cirrus clouds of cigarette smoke.

"Not by Spangler in person, perhaps. He's too smart—and too fat for that." He sent a playful smoke-ring soaring over Mike's carroty dome like a pale blue halo. "He merely pays people to try to kill me. Of course," he added thoughtfully, "when I say two attempts, I'm not counting the first try by brother Karl. Let's say he did that on his own and give the good Doc the benefit of any doubt I may have on that particular score. . . . The other attempts were more up Doc Spangler's alley. One showed organised effort. The other—well, it could have been an accident, you know, giving Mancini an out if he got caught. Both those last tries had brains behind them."

A confused scowl furrowed Grady's brow.

"Any why," he asked, "should you be so quick to make a case against Doc Spangler? He told me all about your crashin' his house and roughin' up his hired help and then accusin' him of those same things you've come to me about."

"Really?" Simon flicked ash into a nearby tray. "The Doc is burning his candour at both ends these days."

"There are men," Grady said sententiously, "who make more than a man's proper share of enemies for no proper reason." He pointed a stubby finger at the Saint. "And you, Mr. Templar, are one of them."

The Saint bowed graciously.

"I've always been rather proud of my enemies, Mike. They're usually the sort that every man ought to make." His mouth curved in a crooked smile. "Did your friend Spangler tell you that Karl also shot Whitey Mullins? We found him bleeding on the carpet when we got there."

"I know all about that! If Whitey or anybody else goes to another man's house to threaten and raise a shindy, he should be prepared to take the consequences." Grady's lip curled scornfully. "And that's the manager Nelson picks for himself, is it? Ivory from the neck up! It's two of a kind they are, and no mistake." He leaned forward again. "Why, I ask you, why in God's name should Spangler want to put you away? Why? Give me one reason I can believe."

The Saint smiled sympathetically.

"I know—mysterious, isn't it? Or have I already told you that he's afraid I might be able to show Steve how to beat the Angel?"

Grady snorted impatiently.

"Nuts to that! There's no man livin' who can beat the Angel! Neither you nor anyone else can make a winner out of a second-rater like Steve Nelson!"

The Saint's brows lifted politely.

"Second-rater? He only happens to be the champion. If you're betting your shirt on the Angel, I hope you have a good laundry. You might have to wait a long time for——"

He stopped short as he saw Grady tense, staring past him. The Saint looked back.

Connie Grady and Steve Nelson stood in the open doorway. They came in, hand in hand, Nelson shutting the door behind them as they entered, his youthful face set and determined.

The Saint rose lazily to his feet as Grady's eyes flashed with angry suspicion from Nelson to his daughter.

"What's the meaning of this?" bellowed the promoter, kicking his chair away and coming out from behind his desk.

Connie's lips parted to speak, but Nelson stepped forward before she could say a word.

"You'd better ask *me* that, Mr. Grady," he said, and glanced at the Saint. "Sorry, I didn't know you were here, or we'd have waited."

"All right!" Grady roared. "Then I'm askin' *you*! What the hell do you mean bustin' into my office? And how many times have I got to be tellin' you to keep away from my daughter, you penny-ante palooka!"

"Don't you dare talk to him like that!" Connie cried, her green eyes flashing angrily. "I'm going to marry him right after the fight, with or without your permission!"

Grady's mouth dropped open. He swallowed.

"The hell you say," he finally choked out.

"Perhaps," Simon murmured, "you family people would like to be alone."

He edged toward the door, but Nelson grabbed his arm.

"No, stick around. You're my best man, aren't you?"

Grady wheeled on the Saint.

"Best man, is it?" he yelled. "So it's a plot!"

"Not so far as I'm concerned," the Saint said hastily.

"You listen to me, Mike." The fighter seized Grady by the lapel. "Seeing that you're going to be my father-in-law, you might as well——"

"In a pig's eye!" Grady sputtered. "Let go me coat, you punch-drunk jerk, or I'll—I'll——"

He turned wildly and grabbed a boxing trophy that stood on his desk. Nelson ducked nimbly and clutched his wrist, shaking the heavy metal statuette from his grasp.

"You might as well get used to the idea, Mike," said the Saint. "It seems to be settled that Steve loves Connie and Connie loves Steve, and they're going to be married, and since they're both of age I don't see what you can do about it."

"Oh, Daddy!" Connie pleaded, coming round to face him. "You're acting like a spoiled brat. You've got nothing against Steve——"

"Let go me arm!" Grady snapped at Nelson. "Or are you trying to break it, you foul-fightin' blackguard?"

Nelson released him and stepped back.

"I came here to tell you because I don't want you to say I ever did anything behind your back, Mike," he said palely.

Connie threw her arms around her father, looking up into his face.

"Darling, you know darn well you haven't any real reason for not liking Steve."

"I know it's all on account of your wanting Connie to have the best, Mike," Nelson said. "I know I'm not a millionaire, maybe, but——"

"We'll have enough," Connie put in. "Even"—she looked at Steve nervously, the shadow of her fear passing over her face—"even if he didn't fight to-morrow night."

"I'll be in plenty good shape to take care of a wife," Nelson grinned. "Especially *after* to-morrow night."

Grady gazed at him a moment with lacklustre eyes. Then he pushed Connie away, grabbed his hat from a corner of his desk, jammed it on his head, and stalked to the door.

"Dad, wait!" she cried.

The door slammed behind him.

"Congratulations," the Saint smiled from the depths of the club chair into which he had retired, one leg slung ver a leather upholstered arm. "He'll dance at your wedding yet."

"Oh, I do hope so," said the girl. The rosy flush of effort that had tinted her smooth elfin features was fading to an unhappy pallor. "Oh, Steve . . ."

"Cheer up," said the Saint. "He really likes him. He just guessed wrong about Steve at first and he's too bull-headed to admit it."

He climbed to his feet once more.

"Have lunch with us," Steve invited eagerly. "Will you? We have a table at the Brevoort. We're going over to your place first so I can leave my stuff, and then we——"

"Bless you, my children," the Saint interrupted, "but I have a prior engagement, unfortunately. Some other time, perhaps."

He lifted a hand in a debonair gesture of farewell, opened the door, and sauntered out rather abruptly before the argument could continue.

He did not mean to be rude, but he had a sudden pellucid intuition where Michael Grady had gone, and he did not want to be too far behind.

XIV

Mike Grady sat slumped in a corner of the sofa in Doc Spangler's study, moodily chewing an unlit cigar. Spangler, his elbows on the desk, pressed his fingertips together with injured reproach pointedly visible behind a film of charlatan good humour.

"My dear Mike," he argued, "every successful man in this game is the natural target of vile rumour and malicious gossip. I'm hurt that you, with all your experience with that sort of thing, should give even hesitant credence to this thing you've mentioned."

"I didn't say I believed it," Grady said heavily. "I just want to get your side of it, that's all."

"If Karl attacked Templar, it was entirely on his own volition, Mike, I assure you. After all, the Saint gave him sufficient reason, don't you think?"

"Okay," Grady said. "Maybe so. But what about the thing that happened this morning? I picked up this paper on my way down here. It's on the front page—look." He

picked up the early afternoon edition from his lap
tossed it on to Spangler's desk. "According to that, it w
an accident. But was it? Did Templar tell me the truth.
Did Mancini try to run him down?"

Spangler shrugged, spreading his hands helplessly.

"Now how would I know? Certainly Slim had as much
reason as Karl had to attempt a, shall we say, retributive
act? That is, if it *wasn't* an accident, which it may well
have been." He sighed. "After all, the manhandling that
both of them have suffered from Templar and that gorilla
of his would be enough to tax the forbearance of far less—
uh—angelic creatures than Karl and Slim, poor fellow.
After all, Mike, I'm no nursemaid. Nor do I keep any of
my employees on a leash."

"Yeah, yeah," Mike agreed restlessly, removing the cigar
from his mouth. "But that isn't all. There's talk. About that
last fight. Torpedo Smith's death is still being—well, talked
about. There are rumours——"

"Rumours, rumours . . ." The fat man shook his head
ruefully. "And you listen? Where do you suppose they
originate? From Steve Nelson's camp, of course. Trying to
discredit me, to smear the Angel. Nelson knows very well
he hasn't a chance against my man, so he's preparing his
alibi in advance. Can't you see that? You know and I
know that the real reason the Angel wins is because of the
psycho-hypnotic technique I use in my training methods.
It gives that great hulk of a fellow power and speed many
times greater than any man is normally capable of."

"Maybe so." Grady stuck his cigar back between his
teeth and wagged a warning forefinger at Spangler. "But I
tell you right here and now, Doc, if that man Smith was
killed because of anything—shady——"

The good humour vanished completely from Spangler's
meaty face.

"My dear Mike!" he protested aggrievedly. "Trust my
intelligence if nothing else!" He spread his hands widely.
"What possible reason could *I* have to wish him harm?"

"A very good reason indeed, Doctor," drawled the Saint.

Both men's eyes jerked to the open doorway.

Simon Templar stood there, the automatic in his hand
held with deceptive negligence.

he Saint!" Spangler got out.

n unhealthy flush suffused his florid face, and his
nds dropped to his lap behind the desk.

"Yes, gentlemen," Simon Templar smiled. "However,
you'll notice this little gadget I'm holding is not a harp.
Hands on the desk, please, Doc."

Spangler obeyed slowly, the habitual good humour on
his face distorted into a parody of itself.

Grady found his voice.

"What's this?" he rasped cholerically. "Are you following me around?"

"Rather fortunately for you, I am," said the Saint. "I
overheard just enough of your conversation to settle a lot
of early doubts about your honesty. Which only leaves your
intelligence more in doubt than ever."

Spangler suddenly yelled: "Karl! Help!"

Simon shook his head regretfully.

"Don't strain your larynx, Doctor. It won't do you any
good. We met Brother Mancini's successor at the door. My
friend Mr. Uniatz is watching over him in the hall to see
that no one disturbs his slumber." The Saint glanced at the
knuckles of his left hand affectionately. "If this happens
much more often I'm afraid the Butler's Union will put
you on the black list."

Grady climbed to his feet, an angry glint in his eye.

"Now look here——" he began.

There was a sudden scurry of footfalls in the hall, and
the outer door slammed open just ahead of a wrathful howl
from Hoppy.

The Saint sighed: "I guess Karl is on his way to
report to you now. I was hoping he'd sleep longer than
that."

"What's the meaning of this?" Grady spluttered.

"Yes," Spangler said, all pretence at good humour
blotted out by the venomous hatred that simmered behind
the onyx sheen of his eyes, "what do you want?"

"Your signature," said the Saint easily. He walked up
to Spangler's desk, fishing two cheques from his pocket.
He laid them before Spangler. "You'll notice that both of
these are for the same amount. The amount, you can
verify, is the total of the winner's shares of all the purses

that your masked moron has won through practices that are extremely illegal."

Spangler looked up at him sharply, his hands slipping off the desk.

"You're stark raving crazy!" he blared.

"Do keep your hands on top of the desk, Doctor," Simon reminded him pleasantly. "That's better. . . . Both of these cheques, you'll observe, are payable to the Simon Templar Foundation for the Relief of Distressed Pugilists."

"What?" Spangler squealed incredulously.

"What kind of racket is this?" Grady demanded.

A ghost of a smile touched the Saint's face. He stepped to one side and glanced at the door as Hoppy's heavy footsteps pounded back through the outer door, into the hall-way, and clomped to a halt in the doorway of the room.

Mr. Uniatz stood there a moment, catching his breath.

"He got away," he announced with dark disgust. "When I wasn't lookin'."

"Don't worry about it," Simon said. "We'll put an ad. in the paper." He turned to Spangler, who had risen to his feet behind the desk as the massive frame of Mr. Uniatz filled the doorway. "As you see, Doc, I've already signed one of those cheques. Now you are going to sign the other."

Spangler turned sharply to Grady.

"You're a witness, Mike. It's blackmail, extortion!"

"Hardly that," Simon corrected him. "Those are simply the stakes in our bet, Doctor. I'm betting that Barrel-house Bilinski is knocked out to-morrow night."

For a long narrow-lidded moment Doc Spangler gaped at the Saint. And then a slow glistening grin began to spread over his face.

"And that," he queried softly, "is what you want me to sign?"

The Saint nodded amiably.

"Exactly. If you don't I'm afraid our friend Inspector Fernack will have to drop in and ask you some awkward questions. . . ."

A deep chuckle seemed to boil up deeply from within the fat man's rotund belly. The chuckle broke into a laugh that shook his chins.

"My dear Mr. Templar!" he said deprecatingly, waving a pudgy hand. "Put away that gun." He wiped his eyes with his cuff as though overcome by some secret joke, and looked down at his desk, still chuckling. "Where's my pen?" He found it and pulled the cheque toward him, leaning over the desk. He looked up. "Mike Grady will hold these cheques, of course?"

"That's okay with me."

"Now wait." Grady frowned, plagued by a vague troubled puzzlement. "I don't want no part——"

"Of course you do," the Saint insisted persuasively. "I assure you this is on the up-and-up, Mike."

"At least," Spangler agreed genially, "I know I can trust *you*." He bent over and signed the other cheque with a flourish and held them both out to Grady. "If you please, Mike."

Grady took them reluctantly.

"Nothing would please me more," Spangler gurgled, "than to have your cheque bounce, Mr. Templar. I should enjoy sending you to jail for something like that. It would certainly look well in the newspapers." He licked his lips as if already tasting the Saint's ignominy. "Famous Adventurer Sentenced to a Year and a Day in County Hoosegow!"

"That wouldn't be nearly so embarrassing," the Saint said imperturbably, "as twenty years in Sing Sing for second-degree murder. I don't think you really wanted to kill Torpedo Smith. But nevertheless he died on account of you."

Spangler's jaw fell open. He started to speak.

"Now look here," Grady tried again. "I don't like this a bit, Saint. I don't want to be mixed up in any——"

"Just the same, you're going to hold those bets," said the Saint. "And you want me to drive you back to your office—now. Come along."

"I warn you," Spangler said bleakly, "that I shall hold both of you to the exact terms of that bet. If you try to welsh on it, the Betting Commissioner——"

"Your fadder's moustache!" Mr. Uniatz quoted delicately.

He spread a large horny hand over Spangler's beefy

face, and pushed with the force of a locomotive piston. Doc Spangler crashed backwards against his chair and toppled thunderously to the floor, chair and all. He was still lying there as Simon and Hoppy conducted Grady firmly out of the room and out of the house.

"I can't tell you how glad I am," the Saint said as they drove northward up Fifth Avenue, "to know that you're not in cahoots with Spangler, Mike. That was the thing that bothered me most of all."

"Thanks for the bill of health," Grady responded caustically. "It's that relieved I am." He scowled. "But I can't say I go for the high-handed way you have of order-in' me about at the point of a gun!"

"Forgive me," the Saint apologised, "but I couldn't take any chances of being deprived of your company for lunch."

"I got too many things to do, Saint. No time for lunch. Just get me back to the Arena as quick as you can."

"It won't take much time," Simon smiled dreamily. "I've got a table at the Brevoort. . . ."

Grady frowned : "Well—I'll see if I can make it."

They parked in front of the Arena and Simon accompanied Grady inside to his office.

The girl at the switchboard called out as they entered Mike's office : "There's been several calls from your daughter, Mr. Grady, and from Mr. Mullins. . . ."

"Okay," Grady grunted, and picked up the stack of letters and messages piled upon his desk. "Wonder what Whitey Mullins wants," he muttered, thumbing through the sheaf. "According to this pile of call notes, he's phoned about six times."

The telephone rang. Grady lifted the receiver.

"Who? . . . Okay, put him on. . . . Hello, Whitey? . . ." Mike Grady suddenly stiffened as he listened. He paled visibly and for a few seconds listened in silence. Presently he asked : "In the Saint's apartment? What was he doing there? . . . Yes, of course, I'll be down as soon as I possibly can."

He hung up and turned to the Saint.

"Steve Nelson has been shot," he said. "In your apartment."

The Saint's whole being seemed to stand still in the same

timeless stasis that affected the expansion of his ribs.

"Karl," he said slowly and bitterly. "Waiting for me in my apartment. . . ."

Grady looked stupidly at him.

"No. . . . At least Whitey says the police don't think it was anyone layin' for you at your place. Whoever did it they think was waitin' for you on the roof of the apartment house across the street. There's a bullet hole in the window of the room where Connie found him."

"Connie?" the Saint repeated, knowing even as he said it how it must have happened.

"She was waiting for him in the car while he went up to your place to leave his things. He was going to stay with you, wasn't he?"

Simon nodded.

"Where is he?"

"Bellevue. They got the bullet out of him. Whitey says they think he's got a fifty-fifty chance." Grady's face furrowed with pain. "The poor kid. . . . He's a helluva fine boy, Saint. I've been just a damn fool, and that's a fact!"

He glared at Simon defensively.

"Listen, Mike." The Saint gripped his arm. "Whoever did it must've thought it was me. It could only have been one of Spangler's men. It was my fault that this happened."

"But why should Spangler want to do *you* in?"

"He's afraid that I'll find out what he's been up to. I started the whole thing by butting in after the Torpedo Smith fight. Now I've got to finish it. Listen—I've to take Steve's place to-morrow night!"

Grady's eyes bulged.

"What?"

"You heard me! You've got to put me in against the Angel!" The Saint's steely fingers tightened about Grady's arm. "You've got to, Mike!"

"Bu—but——"

Grady stopped short and looked at him for a long moment. He stepped backwards and eyed him up and down critically. He said finally: "Well, you look big enough. And hard enough, I guess. I've heard how you can hit. . . ."

"I've been working with Steve," said the Saint. "I'm in as good condition as a man ever was, Mike. And I can take Bilinski, believe me!"

"But it's ridiculous!" Grady exploded. "There's never been such a fight——"

Simon said swiftly: "Make an announcement in the ring. Tell them about my bet with Spangler. If they want their money back, they can have it. If they just want to see a fight—even if it's only the Saint ——"

"*Only* the Saint!" Grady's eyes took fire. A luminous inspired glow spread over his round, freckled face. "Holy mackerel! Maybe it won't be a championship fight as advertised, but with *you* in it——"

"Come on, then." Simon pulled him towards the door. "Let's go—I've got to get hold of Whitey right away!"

xv

The opening preliminary was already under way when the Saint, with Hoppy and Patricia Holm, strode through the tag-end of the crowd of street urchins who eddied about the "artists'" entrance of the Manhattan Arena.

Whitey met them in the doorway.

"I was gettin' worried," he said anxiously. "What happened to ya? The show's started."

He started them down the corridor that turned off to the dressing-room section. The Saint stopped him.

"Whitey, will you show Miss Holm to her seat? I don't think she can find her way up front from this part of the Arena."

The tempting curve of Miss Holm's red mouth drew to a pout.

"You mean I've got to spend the next hour or so in solitary refinement?"

"Well, you certainly can't spend it in my dressing-room," said the Saint. "It's not exactly a ladies' boudoir."

Whitey nodded to Patricia, in visible awe of her golden-blonde beauty.

"Sure, just follow me," he said. He turned to Simon. "I'll check on the Angel's hand-wraps on my way back."

They disappeared round a turn from where the roar of

the crowd was flowing like the muted roar of distant surf.

The Saint went on with Hoppy to his dressing-room, feeling the ghostly fingers of peril once more playing their familiar cadenza along his vertebræ and up through the roots of his hair. . . . He knew, his every instinct told him, that to-night he was fighting for greater stakes than glory or dollars. To-night would be more than a mere encounter with padded gloves. To-night he would be fighting for his life.

A swarthy snaggle-toothed character in a dirty polo shirt was seated on a broken-down chair as they entered the dressing-room. Hoppy recognised him at once.

"Mushky," he growled. "I t'ought you was in de Angel's corner."

"So I am, chum, so I am," Mr. Mushky Thompson agreed affably. "I gotta take a gander when you bandage de Saint's hands."

"That's what I admire about this business," Simon remarked cheerfully. "Everyone trusts everyone else."

Hoppy fixed Mr. Thompson with a baleful glare.

"Out, ya bum," he ordered.

"Now wait," Mushky protested. "It's de rules. I——"

"Oh, let him alone," said the Saint. "Whitey is watching the Angel, isn't he? It isn't exactly a unilateral proposition."

"Sure," Mr. Thompson agreed with hasty anxiety. "No cause for gettin' mad, Hoppy. I'm just one of de hired hands."

Hoppy grunted and proceeded about the business of laying out the hand bandages, adhesive tape, rubber mouthpiece, collodion, ammonia, and other paraphernalia of the modern gladiator.

"You working with Karl, Mushky?" the Saint asked casually as he slipped out of his street clothes.

Thompson shook his head.

"Naw. . . . He—uh—got kicked in the face by a beer-wagon horse. Broke his jaw in two places, I hear."

Hoppy looked up at him a moment, and broke into a deep guffaw.

"Ya don't say," he yakked.

Simon slipped into his dark purple sateen trunks and

began to lace his boxing shoes swiftly as Hoppy tore strips of adhesive tape into suitable knuckle strips. Mushky Thompson lounged in his chair with a cigarette dangling from a corner of his mouth until Hoppy had finished taping the Saint's hands with practised precision, reinforcing the bones without impairing their freedom. Then Mushky got to his feet.

"Good luck," he threw over his shoulder. "You'll need it."

"T'anks," Hoppy said—and did a take after the gibe sank in.

"Come back here!" the Saint snapped as Mr. Uniatz started after the Angel's second. "Don't start anything *now*, you idiot!"

Hoppy made unintelligible gravelly noises through his bared teeth, his nuclear mind infected as much by the vibrant blood cry of the mob as by the taunt. Impending battle—his own or anyone else's—was apt to make Mr. Uniatz emotionally unstable.

Three preliminaries and a semi-final later, the Saint lay on the rubbing table, completely relaxed, listening to ten thousand throats vibrating the walls in a massive chorus of excitement. The semi-final bout had ended in a knock-out, he guessed, from the uproar. He stretched his length peacefully, his eyes closed, everything in him settled into an immeasurable stillness amid the swirling rumble of vociferation. Dimly and indistinguishably he heard the orotund bellow of the announcer introducing somebody after the roar of the crowd had died down a bit : and shortly afterwards the man who had been introduced began speaking over the audience public-address system, and he recognised Grady's unmistakable accents even though he could not make out the words.

Hoppy stumbled into the dressing-room, breathless from battling the crowd *en route*.

"What a mob!" he wheezed, his eyes gleaming. "Grady's up dere makin' dat announcement!"

A swellin' ululation rose in a gathering tidal wave of sound and broke thunderously upon their ears.

"Say," Hoppy exulted, "sounds like dey like what he told 'em, huh?" He came over to the Saint. "Boss, what does Spangler say when Grady tells him ya goin' in for Nelson?"

The Saint yawned.

"Oh, he raised a little stench about it at first, but Mike reminded him that my bet stated that Bilinski would be knocked out—it didn't say by whom. So he changed his mind. . . . By the way, did Pat get a good seat?"

"Yeah," Hoppy chuckled hoarsely. "An' guess who's she sittin' next to!"

"Are you training for a quiz programme, or would you just like to tell me?"

"Inspector Foinack!"

The Saint considered him reverently for a moment, while the forthcoming possibilities of that supernal juxtaposition developed the gorgeous gamut of their emotional potential.

"Oh, my God!" Simon breathed. "I'd rather watch that than my own fight."

There was a patter of footsteps and Whitey Mullins darted into the dressing-room. His face was contorted with savage glee.

"Okay," he croaked. "You're on, Saint. They're waitin' for you!" He snatched up the water bucket. "Grab the water-bottle and sponge," he yelped at Hoppy, and went to the door.

The Saint swung his long legs off the table to the floor and stood up. He followed Whitey out of the door into the corridor, with Hoppy bringing up the rear.

"Brother, I only wisht it was that lousy crook Spangler you was smackin' around to-night," Mullins grated with vitriolic bitterness as they mounted the ramp into the Arena, "and not just that dumb ox he stole from me."

Simon sensed an excitement, a temper in the crowd that was different from the usual mass tension of the ordinary fight attendance at Grady's weekly shows. It was electric with anticipation of the unexpected, a breathless waiting watchfulness that he felt as he mounted to the apron of the ring and slipped between the ropes amid a thunderclap of acclaim. There was a slight note of hysteria in it, he thought as he seated himself on the stool in his corner and looked about the ocean of faces that spread on every side.

The Masked Angel hadn't appeared yet, but the Saint

rather expected that Spangler would try every trick in the bag, including the petty one of wearing down the opposition's nerves by making him wait.

He failed to spot Pat among the buzzing tide of faces at the ringside, but everything beyond the glare of light centring on the ring was little more than a smoke-dimmed blur. The faces, void of all individuality, were such as one encounters sometimes in nightmare sequences, a phantasmagoria of eyes and noise—hard, critical, and skin-prickingly theriomorphic. . . . He wondered momentarily if Steve was in good enough shape to listen to the fight from his bedside. . . . Connie had been with him nearly all day at the hospital. . . .

A roar like an approaching forest fire filled the packed coliseum with surging clamour as the Masked Angel appeared up the ramp, preceded by Doc Spangler and followed by a cohort of handlers bearing the various accessories of refreshment and revival. The incredible bulk of the Angel loomed up over the apron of the ring and squeezed between the ropes in his corner, his plates of sagging fat quivering like chartreuse jelly. Unmasked now, his ridiculous little nubbin of a head bobbed from side to side in acknowledgment of the roars of the mob, his round little cheeks and button nose more an inspiration for laughter than the fearsome horror his black mask had aroused.

Behind him, Doc Spangler leaned over his shoulder and spoke softly into an ear that was the approximate size and shape of a brussels sprout.

As the Saint watched them from beneath lowered lids, he felt once again the spectral footfalls of ghostly centipedes parading his spine, knowing that his real danger was as yet undetermined, the point of attack unknown. How it would come, in what shape or form, he wasn't quite sure. He'd covered all the possibilities, or so he thought; but whether the threat, the unknown secret weapon that the Angel must surely possess, would come from an act of the Angel himself, or from some outside agent, he wasn't quite sure. All he had was an idea. . . . He felt its shadow upon him like a ghostly mist, ambient and all-pervading. . . .

The bell clanged sharply a few times; the throbbing hum

of the crowd subsided somewhat. The main-bout referee, dapper and fresh in white tennis shoes and flannels, stepped to the centre of the ring and gestured the Saint and the Angel to come to him.

Simon rose, followed by Whitey and Hoppy, and came forward to face the Angel, who shambled up to the referee flanked by Spangler and Mushky Thompson. The Angel towered over them all, an utterly gross, unlovely specimen of so-called homo sapiens.

The referee droned the familiar formula: ". . . break when I say break . . . no hitting in breaks, no rabbit or kidney punches . . . protect yourself at all times . . . shake hands, come out fighting . . ."

They touched gloves, and the Saint walked nonchalantly back to his corner. He rubbed his feet a couple of times on the resin sprinkled there while Hoppy pulled the stool out of the ring. . . . The sound of the bell seemed unreal and far away when, after what seemed an extraordinarily long time, it finally rang.

XVI

The Saint turned and moved almost casually out of his corner to meet the slowly approaching Angel. Bilinski shuffled forward, peering between forearms lifted before him, his body almost doubled over so that his elbows guarded his belly while his gloves shielded his face. No legally vulnerable square inch of his body was unprotected. He came forward steadily, inch by inch, making no attempt to lead or feint, merely coming forward with the massive low-gear irresistibility of a large tank, peering intently, cautiously—almost fearfully, Simon thought—between the bulging barriers of his ham-sized arms.

The Saint moved around him in a leisurely half-circle, every muscle, every nerve completely at ease, relaxed, and co-ordinated. He was oblivious of the crowd now, studying his problem with almost academic detachment, the latent lightning in his fists perfectly controlled. He couldn't help feeling the same guarded wonder that he knew Torpedo Smith, and for that matter all of the Angel's opponents, must have felt at the apparent impotence of the

Angel's attack right up to the moment of the blow that
sent them on the way to oblivion. He thought to himself :
*Nothing happens the first round . . . nothing ever happens
the first round. . . .* The crux of his problem, he felt sure
was what the Angel did to open his victims for the inevitable knockout later on. . . .

Bilinski, apparently growing tired of following Simon
round the ring, stopped in the centre and remained there,
crouched, merely revolving to follow the Saint's lacka-
daisical circumvolutions about him.

The cash customers began to shake the stadium with the
drumming of their stamping feet in the familiar demand
for action. A demand, Simon thought, which was no more
than fair. . . . He stepped in, threw a left that cracked like
a whiplash against the Angel's fleshy forearms, and crossed
with a downward-driving right that strove to crash past
into the massive belly beyond. But the Angel instinctively
brought his arms closer together so that the Saint's gloved
fist thudded into their bone-centred barrier.

Bilinski, visibly startled by the numbing shock of the
blow, even though he did catch it on his guard, flung his
arms about the Saint in an octopus-like clutch, sagging
slightly in order to let his overwhelming weight smother
his opponent's efforts to strike again; but Simon, familiar
with the old strength-sapping trick, merely relaxed with
him and waited for the referee to come between them.

From her seat at the ringside Patricia Holm, her blonde
hair wild with excitement, her hands gripping the arms of
her chair, pleaded with tense anxiety : "Watch him, Simon,
watch him ! Be careful !"

"He'd better watch while he can," Inspector Fernack
gibed sardonically. He leaned back in his seat beside her
and yelled : "All right, you Angel, shake him loose and
let him have it ! Give him one for me !"

The referee was still battling to break the Angel's
drowning-man grip when the bell ended the round.

As he walked to his corner the Saint noticed that there
were no boos from the crowd over the inaction of that
opening round. There was merely a more intense current
of anticipatory excitement, as though everyone felt that
they were about to witness a phenomenon of nature which,

while it might be delayed somewhat, would take place as ineluctably as a predicted eclipse of the sun. . . .

The betting, Simon knew, was not on whether or not he'd be knocked out, but rather precisely when and how that cataclysmic event would occur.

Hoppy wiped non-existent perspiration from the Saint's brow.

"Dat foist round wuz slow-motion, boss," he rasped encouragingly. "Howja feel?"

The Saint smiled coolly.

"Fine. Where's Whitey?"

"He forgot de towels." Hoppy thrust the mouth of the water-bottle at Simon's lips. "Take a drink?"

The Saint leaned back and turned his face away slightly as the water poured out of the uplifted bottle and slopped over his neck and chest.

"Chees, boss!" Hoppy peered at the Saint's face. "Dijja get any?"

"All I need. Wipe my face."

Hoppy reached about vaguely for a non-existent towel, seized the Saint's dressing-gown draped over the edge of the ring apron, and used it instead to mop the moisture from Simon's face and body.

"Hoppy," said the Saint in a low voice, as his faithful disciple started to fan him with the robe. "Hoppy, listen."

"Yeah, boss?"

"This is important," Simon said quickly. "Keep the cork in that water-bottle—understand? Don't let anyone try to spill the water that's left in it. Do you get that, Hoppy?"

Hoppy nodded foggily.

"Yeah, but—but——"

"Hold on to that bottle!" Simon said urgently, obsessed with the nightmare problem of impressing a course of action on Mr. Uniatz's reflexes beyond any possibility of confusion. "Don't let it get away from you. I want it after the fight. Put it in your pocket or in that robe—and keep it under your arm. Don't drink out of it whatever you do. If anyone tries to spill it or break it, grab him and hold on to him! Is that clear?"

"Sure, but I don't get it, boss. Why——"

The warning whistle blew its shrill alarm, and Simon

sprang to his feet as Hoppy ducked out of the ring, taking the stool with him.

The bell clanged and the Saint moved out. . . . He could only hope that his hunch was right, that he had really penetrated the mundane secret of Doc Spangler's psycho-hypnotic technique. If he guessed wrong, there might still be catastrophic surprises in store. He was answering a gambit of whose ultimate denouement he was not at all certain.

Now the Saint opened up. He darted in with the effort-less speed and cold-eyed ferocity of a jungle cat, his lithe body moving in a fierce harmony of scientific destruction, his shoulders flinging a shower of straight javelin-like blows, striving to penetrate the fortress wall of wrists, arms, and gloves that guarded the Angel's head. . . .

Bilinski began to give ground, crouching lower and lower beneath the onslaught. Suddenly the Saint changed his mode of attack, his fists winging up from beneath in a series of whiplash uppercuts. One of them managed to catch the Angel on his nominal forehead, jarring his head back momentarily. Almost simultaneously with the first blow, another crashed through the Angel's guard and left the little bulb of nose a bloody splotch.

Bilinski began to give ground faster, the first glimmer of real fear in his dull little eyes. But still he refused to retaliate; he went on catching the Saint's blows on his arms, gloves, shoulders, elbows, rolling instinctively with every one that he caught, like the battle-conditioned veteran he indisputably was. And as he felt the ropes touch his back he leaned against them and bounded forward again, taking advantage of their spring, hurling his gross tonnage against the Saint and flinging his arms about him once again, shuffling around so that the Saint's back was to the ropes instead. Inexorably he pushed Simon backwards against the rubberised strands.

Pat was on her feet, jumping up and down.

"Get away from him, Simon!" she screamed. "Get away from him!"

"Aw, sit down!" Fernack blasted at her. He cupped his hands about his mouth and yelled: "Knock him kicking, Angel! Hit him one for me! For Fernack!"

Pat turned on him furiously.

"Yes," she shouted, "for poor feeble Fernack!" and brought a flailing hand down on the top of the detective's derby, jamming it down over his eyes.

A localised area of laughter was swallowed in a sudden earthquake as the crowd surged to its feet *en masse*.

The Saint was obviously in trouble. He was still against the ropes, even as Torpedo Smith had been, shaking his head as though trying to clear it, as the Angel, close up to him, pumped short deliberate blows into his body. They lacked concussive snap, but were nevertheless sickening with the monstrous weight that lay behind them. The Angel seemed to be trying to shake the Saint loose to give himself room for a conclusive blow. That he would succeed seemed a matter of a very brief time. The Saint was already staggering and apparently holding on blindly.

In the Saint's corner, Hoppy Uniatz, his face tortured into a mask of pleading horror, leaned over the bottom strand of the ropes, his clenched fists pounding the canvas desperately.

"Boss!" he begged, his raucous voice screeching with the intensity of his emotion. "Boss, get away from dem ropes. Don't let him crowd ya! Boss!"

Patricia's eyes filled with frightened tears.

"Simon!" she sobbed. "Get away, get away!"

And strange things were happening to Inspector John Henry Fernack—things which, in abstract theory, he would have hooted at as fantastically impossible. Faced with the reality of his old adversary's imminent downfall, a thing which in his heart of hearts he had long ceased to believe possible, he found himself inexplicably on his feet, howling: "What's the matter, Saint? You gonna let that dumb lug do that to you? Move around, Templar, move around!"

But the Saint seemed finished. He let the referee come between him and the Angel, and staggered along the ropes, apparently helpless and ripe for the knockout blow. . . . He wondered, as he peered at the Angel with eyes that he hoped had a glazed appearance, how many more of those sickening body blows he could have taken if the referee hadn't parted them when he did. . . .

This, the Saint knew, was the final move in his play, the all-deciding feint. It would, he hoped, open the Angel's guard sufficiently to permit a blow to the jaw. It would prove something else as well. For he knew that Bilinski's experience would have warned him against such a trick— *unless he had reason to believe that the Saint's sudden torpor was not faked, but real!* For the Angel must know perfectly well that he had struck no blow that could have dazed his opponent to that extent. Nevertheless, he was opening up more and more, as if he expected the Saint to give ground—as if, indeed, he was ready for Simon to collapse about this point. The Saint doubted that the Angel actually knew how this was being achieved. He was taking Spangler's word for it, and going on past corroborative experience. . . .

The Saint slumped against the ropes, and not one person in the entire mob could have suspected the grim triumph that coursed through his every nerve as the Angel charged in for the slaughter, wide open, a bone-shattering right hurtling at the Saint's jaw.

But the blow never reached its destination.

For even as the Angel started it, Simon Templar's right hand came up from where it had been sagging near the floor, and landed, with the approximate velocity of an ack-ack shell and the same general concussive effect, flush on the Angel's froglike chin. Barrelhouse Bilinski's feet were jolted up a good three inches off the floor; and when he came down again, his eyes glassy, his arms flailing loosely, he continued all the way down—down to the canvas like a mountainous mass of boneless gelatine.

He lay there twitching slightly; and it was evident to the blindest of the now completely hysterical audience that he would continue to lie there until someone carried him away.

The Saint strolled to his neutral corner as the referee began the formality of counting out the sleeping Angel. He failed to see either Hoppy or Whitey as he leaned against the ropes, and for a moment he was puzzled. Then, through the deafening hullabaloo, he thought he heard Hoppy's bronchitic foghorn somewhere below. As the referee completed his toll and Mushky leaped into the ring

to retrieve the Angel's carcass, Simon slipped through the
ropes and into the midst of the raving, eddying ringside
mob, looking about anxiously.

"Hoppy!" he called.

Through the unbroken pandemonium and the pleas of
the newspaper reporters and cameramen converging upon
him, he heard Hoppy again, this time more distinctly:
"Boss, I got him! I got him!"

"Where are you?" Simon shouted.

"Under de ring! This way!"

The great pipe organ burst into "Hail the Conquering
Hero Comes" as Simon peered beneath the apron and
saw, silhouetted against the supporting joists, Mr. Uniatz
holding down a set of kicking arms and legs by the simple
expedient of sitting on the body that sprouted them.

"He gives me an argument when I don't let him spill
out de bottle," Hoppy explained in stentorian confidence.
"So I do like ya tell me."

"Bring him out," said the Saint.

Several score spectators crowded around, seething with
excitement, while the photographers, frustrated in their
efforts to get the Saint back in the ring, aimed their
cameras at him crouched under the apron. Their flash-
bulbs went off in broadsides as Hoppy wrestled with his
quarry.

The blue uniforms of policemen were converging on the
spot; and over the hubbub and the pealing of the organ
Simon heard the brassy tones of another familiar voice
approaching.

"One side, get outta the way! One side! What's going
on here?" Inspector Fernack trumpeted as he fought his
way through the crowd.

Hoppy finally dragged out his kicking clawing captive
by the collar of its turtle-neck sweater.

"He tries to pull dis rod on me!" he said, and handed
the gun to Simon. He yanked the man to his feet, as
Fernack broke through the final barrier of humanity.
"Stand up, youse!"

As the Saint had expected, it was Whitey Mullins.

"What the hell goes on here?" Fernack demanded; and
Simon handed him the gun.

"Take this, John Henry. I've got a slug I dug out of a pawnshop door-frame that I think'll fit it. And I'll give you odds that the bullet that laid out Steve Nelson will also fit Whitey's gun."

XVII

Simon and Patricia were in Steve Nelson's hospital room next morning when Inspector Fernack arrived. Connie Grady was also there, accompanied by a subdued and sympathetic Michael. Mr. Uniatz was also present, accompanied by a breakfast bottle of bourbon. It was like Old Home Week.

"I hear you're doing fine, Champ," Fernack said. "How soon is Grady going to match you with the Saint?"

"From what I heard on the radio," Nelson answered, "maybe it's a good thing I'm retiring."

Connie squeezed his hand.

"If you'd like to tell me more about this," Fernack said, with as close to a tone of respect as he had ever used in speaking to the Saint, "I'd be willing to listen. We picked up Spangler last night, by the way—he was just packing for a trip."

"Congratulations, John Henry," Simon grinned. "Never let it be said that the Police Department lets lawns grow on its feet."

Fernack grimaced.

"What I want to know," he said, "is how you figured Whitey was working with Spangler."

"Well——" the Saint began thoughtfully, "it was the way Whitey kept plugging his hatred for Spangler that first made me suspicious. Then later, when we were at Spangler's place and found Whitey apparently wounded by Karl's bullet, I noticed that the blood on his scalp had already begun to mat. He couldn't have been shot by the bullet we'd just heard fired, which he claimed. It takes a little longer than that for blood to clot. I realised then and there that he'd actually been grazed by the bullet Hoppy sent through the rear window of the car he and Karl and Slim had used when they shot up the pawnshop. Probably, when they realised I was in the house, Spangler had Karl fire into the wall to make it appear that he was the one who'd shot Whitey—thus concealing the fact that Whitey had been one of the gunmen, and prolonging his usefulness as Steve's manager."

"If he was Spangler's inside man," pondered Fernack, "Whitey must've seconded *all* of the Angel's opponents. We'll check on that."

"I've already done that. Quite a while ago. And Whitey *did* second the Angel's opponents. Every one of them. That's how the barrel always rolled them out inside of two rounds. . . . I felt pretty sure that Whitey must've been doping the Angel's opponents, of course, if he was tied up with Spangler as I suspected. It would be easy for him to fix up his fighters' water with a few drops of something, and Spangler would know what to prescribe that wouldn't show up in case of accidents."

"Okay," Fernack agreed, "but if it was only knockout drops, what killed Torpedo Smith?"

"Why, you saw it yourself. The Angel hit him when Smith was already half asleep—and believe me, Brother Bilinski can really hit when he has lots of time. I know!"

"Darling," Patricia said, "you won't be permanently injured, will you?"

"I hope not," said the Saint.

WATCH FOR THE SIGN
OF THE SAINT

HE WILL BE BACK